"*The Inferno* is simply superb. I could not put it do[wn] ... *Inferno*, the narrator travels through the various re[gions of hell] ... to some of the most famous persons who ever live[d] ... gained the whole world but lost their souls. The book, however, ends on a note of grace and hope. I gladly commend it to you. It may even change your life and your eternal destiny."

—Daniel L. Akin, president, professor of preaching
and theology, Ed Young Sr. Chair of Preaching
Southeastern Baptist Theology Seminary,
Wake Forest, North Carolina

"If you are familiar with *The Divine Comedy*, you will love *The Inferno*. A retelling of Dante's famous work, Winston Brady uses a modern context and famous figures of the past, as well as inspiration from great authors, to take us on a journey that begins with the worst parts of humanity and ends with redemption."

—Robert Luddy, president CaptiveAire Systems,
founder, Thales Academy

"One of the many virtues of this brave and imaginative work is that it shows us how the greatest literary classics, far from imprisoning us, provide us with a ladder up to insights we might never have been able to articulate on our own. Winston Brady has not only made Dante an inheritance; he has made Dante his own."

—Wilfred McClay, Victor Davis Hanson
Chair of Classical History and Western Civilization,
professor of history, Hillsdale College

"What an important and powerful message for our time! *The Inferno* is the compelling story of one man who wakes up in hell after attempting suicide, convinced life holds no meaning. As the narrator travels through hell, he meets well-known historical and literary figures who based their lives on Satan's glittering lies—that we can be like God, that God doesn't want the best for us, and that happiness can be found apart from Him. But as the narrator discovers in the dramatic conclusion, it's never too late to find true and lasting joy."

—Vaneetha Risner, author, *Walking through Fire:*
A Memoir of Loss and Redemption and
The Scars That Have Shaped Me:
How God Meets Us in Suffering,
regular contributor, *Desiring God*

"In this loving and deeply perceptive tribute to Dante, Winston Brady, while ushering us through the levels of hell, takes us on an eye-opening, well-researched journey through the virtues and vices of American history, literature, and politics. Borrowing further insights from Bunyan, Milton, Tolkien, and Lewis, Brady explores the nature of temptation, sin, and repentance, building up to a marvelous court room climax that puts not only the protagonist but God himself on trial."

—Louis Markos, professor in English and scholar in residence, Houston Baptist University, author of *Heaven and Hell: Vision of the Afterlife in the Western Poetic Tradition*

"Winston Brady demonstrates a rare ability to pair heart-achingly honest autobiography with poetic drama in this tribute to the literary geniuses of Dante Alighieri and Ernest Hemmingway. In this telling of *Inferno*, Brady allows his reader to walk alongside him on Brady's own journey through hell to redemption. That journey includes encounters with some of the most colorful historical characters who help elucidate Brady's own intellectual journey, giving the reader a glimpse of both the head and heart of the author as his soul winds and wends its way through a deeply Christian faith in divine forgiveness evoking not only Dante's original *Inferno* but also John Bunyan's *The Pilgrim's Progress*. Brady's tale of misery and mercy is sure to stir the heart, challenge the mind, and uplift the soul of any reader who takes the journey with him through the *Inferno*."

—Clifford Humphrey, executive vice chancellor of the College System of Florida

"A deeply personal and moving adaptation of Dante's masterwork, Winston Brady's new novel takes readers on an unforgettable journey across the highs and lows of human existence to the promised land of redemption."

—John Hood, president, John William Pope Foundation

"Mr. Brady has written an outstanding and very timely novel! All too often, classic books like the *Divine Comedy* or *The Pilgrim's Progress* are surrounded with false reverence: either readers are too intimidated by their reputations to pick them up at all or fail to see their relevance to the here and now. In *The Inferno*, we get a story that's as accessible today as its predecessors were centuries ago. Brady peoples Hell with characters familiar to a twenty-first-century American audience (like exchanging Virgil for Hemingway) and tweaks its design to serve a Reformed story. *The Inferno* is thus both a bridge to the classics for students of today, and a story for those students in its own right."

—Jeremy Tate, founder and CEO of the Classic Learning Test

"Dante's *Comedy* is a beautiful allegory that reveals the spiritual journey of man and through the centuries it has inspired many who found themselves lost from God's hand. Winston Brady has taken this allegory and translated it into modern times where our current cultural climate breeds despair and hopelessness about the future of humanity. As the journey of Evan Esco progresses through the darkest places, he is able to see there is hope and redemption through Christ and that the writers of the past can be a guide to lead him even closer to finding Christ in the darkness, because of each author's writing expressing a journey to answering some of the greatest human questions. As Evan explores these perspectives, he is drawn closer and closer to THE Answer and ultimately stands face-to-face with the One who is the healing balm for his wounds. Winston Brady's inspiration from the *Inferno* has given us a modern-day allegorical tale that will fill each reader with the light of hope to help them navigate these dark times."

—Dr. Anika T. Prather, director,
High Quality Curriculum & Instruction at
The Johns Hopkins Institute for Education Policy,
founder & director, The Living Water School, author,
The Black Intellectual Tradition and the Great Conversation:
Black Writers as Essential to an Education in Truth,
Goodness and Beauty

"*The Inferno* is lyrical, hypnotic, and insightful. I first met Winston in the depths of his despair, so I can vouch for the authenticity of his personal saga that undergirds the narrative. No doubt, this is why he captures human frailty and eternal misery with such empathy and understanding. Highly recommended."

—Timothy E. Gelion Floyd, author and pastor (retired)

The Inferno

A Novel

WINSTON BRADY

Fidelis Publishing®
Sterling, VA • Nashville, TN
www.fidelispublishing.com

ISBN: 9781956454260
ISBN: 9781956454277 (eBook)

The Inferno
A Novel

Manufactured in the United States of America
10 9 8 7 6 5 4 3 2 1

Though a work of fiction, the author has included important endnotes expanding, and in some cases, explaining some content. Since factual historical characters and events are part of the narrative, references to those have also been included at the end of this book.

Cover designed by Diana Lawrence
Interior design by Xcel Graphic
Edited by Amanda Varian

Fidelis Publishing, LLC
Sterling, VA • Nashville, TN
fidelispublishing.com

To Rachel, whose constant love, support, and encouragement have made the years of our marriage the brightest and happiest of my life.

All that the Father gives me will come to me, and whoever comes to me I will never cast out. For I have come down from heaven, not to do my own will, but the will of him who sent me.

And this is the will of him who sent me, that I should lose nothing of all that he has given me, but raise it up on the last day.

For this is the will of my Father, that everyone who looks on the Son and believes in him should have eternal life, and I will raise him up on the last day.

—John 6:37–40

Contents

CHAPTER I

A DARK WOOD

"I know I don't deserve forgiveness—really, I should go to Hell, and you would be right in sending me there because if I know anything about you, God, you are just: so go ahead and send me to a realm of endless torment since it's way too late for a sinner like me to repent."

That moment seemed so long ago. On remembering what I said, I put my hand over the pocket of my black fleece jacket. There I had stuffed a piece of paper I ripped from the Bible my grandmother gave me years ago. She hoped I would read it and it might help me stop drinking, and I did read it just before I tried to kill myself, but I couldn't make any sense of it. Now I have no idea where I am, and I don't see any trace of the Virginia farm country where I tried to kill myself—just a cold, dark wood. I'm definitely not in Virginia anymore.

I wandered into the woods, stumbling from one patch of moonlight to another. I walked beneath the branches of live oak trees, their bare limbs clawing at the sky like dead men rising from the grave as a cold wind tore through the branches. I trudged deeper into the woods, the air growing colder and the ground muddier with each step. The trees thinned and gave way to gray reeds and dark rills trickling downward like blood seeping from a wound. I followed the rills to the shores of a still black lake, tendrils of green mist hanging over the waters like a curtain. On the other shore, I saw the opening of a cave, a light flickering inside its mouth and bidding me to come closer.

I walked along the strand, avoiding the corpses of birds and fish at my feet. The pale light wavered back and forth inside the cave, trembling like the barest traces of a man from the darkness the thing displaced. I walked to the cave until I recognized what the thing was: the man whose life I had hoped to imitate, the man whose family seemed as cursed as my own, the man whose books I read and reread as my depression and drinking took over. Out of the cave and into the moonlight, bearded and in his hunting gear, stepped the shade of Ernest Hemingway.

"Ernest?" I stammered out. "Ernest Hemingway? Is that really you?"

He nodded, but this wasn't an Ernest I ever saw before. It wasn't Hemingway in his prime, days he could spin a fishing trip or a hospital stay into literary gold. Nor was it the Ernest who shot himself in his kitchen, wearing a silk robe and slippers.[1] It looked like Hemingway on safari, ready for one last adventure, dressed in a sweaty, white collar hunting shirt and a safari jacket, khaki pants tucked into tall leather boots. He wasn't breathing, and Hemingway's eyes, eyes I remember staring down a kudu or a typewriter, those eyes were as empty and black as the bottom of a well, cheerless and defeated, broken.[2] Only his thick white beard made him look anything like Papa Hemingway again.

"Are you Evan? Evan Esco?" the shadow asked me. "The boy who tried to kill himself?"

"I am," I answered. "But am I, am I dead?"

Ernest shook his head no.

"And you?" I asked. "What's happened to you, Ernest?"

"The damned hope that nothing happens when you die," Ernest answered, a look of sorrow passing through him like wind on the sea. "That was my hope too, but after death comes judgment, and now I am condemned to the Forest of the Suicides,[3] bound with other shades who took their lives to escape the pain of the world above until yesterday, when an angel came and released me from my place in Hell and bid me to be your guide."

"Guide?" I asked, backing away. "Where are you taking me?"

"Though Hell, Evan," Ernest answered me. "God would show you what he would save you from if you would repent of your sins and mean it and mean it truly."

Ernest leaned closer to me. He spoke in a low whisper like he was afraid someone or something was listening, and he placed a hand on my shoulder like he was talking to one of his sons. He came so close I saw through his shade into the abyss Ernest carried within him, yet stretched far beyond him. He did not breathe, but his words carried the heat of a powerful, unseen furnace. I did not feel cold anymore.

"I'll tell you everything I know about what's going on down there," Ernest said, "and everyone down there with me: the gluttons and the drunks, the murderers, swindlers, slave drivers, and whore-mongers, even a few bullfighters, anyone and everyone who did not get the chance you're getting now."

"But I should be damned to Hell too," I answered. "I want to die so bad, Ernest, and no one should forgive me, not after the life I've lived. I'm not worth it, and I'll never be one of the good ones."

"Maybe it's not about being one of the good ones," Papa Hemingway replied. "But you'll have to find that out for yourself."

Ernest turned back into the cave, his shade flickering like a moon-tossed sea. After years of self-destructive behavior, years of drinking, drugs, and depression, I finally self-destructed, and now I didn't have any choice but to follow the shade of my favorite author into the Inferno. Fearful and trembling, I entered a realm as dark as pitch, with only the shade of Ernest Hemingway to light the gathering abyss.

CHAPTER II

THE GUIDE

At first, the cave was just a tiny breach in the earth's surface. Ernest's shade provided only enough light to see the rock formations cascading out from the walls like fire inside a blast furnace. Ernest easily slipped through the passageway, but I had to squeeze between openings in the rock or crawl on my hands and knees while the roof dropped lower and the way tighter. Stalactites as sharp as dragon's teeth raked across my back, coated with acid that hissed whenever drops of the foul liquid fell to the floor.

"Evan Esco," Ernest said to himself. "An unusual name, kid, like Clark Kent almost. What does it mean?"

"It's Italian," I answered. "And it is kind of like a superhero name, but there's also a Latin word *evanesco* that literally means *I disappear*—the irony of it all, since I hoped I would disappear once I killed myself."

"Ironic indeed," Hem continued. "You know, I've studied death all my life—in the War, the Stream, the bullring—so I want to know, why did you go and try and kill yourself, Evan?"

"Life became so empty. I had been so depressed for so long and I started drinking and smoking marijuana to make myself feel something, anything besides the grief after my kid sister died. Evelyn was my only real friend, the only one who could have talked me out of doing what I did, faking a car accident in hopes I would just die, but she got leukemia and now she's dead, too, and all my efforts to make myself feel better made everything worse. A lot worse."

"The drink can be a good thing, if you can control it," Hem answered me in earnest, feeling along the walls until he found another narrow breach in which he disappeared, then called from the void. "And if you can't, it controls you."

"The more you feed the beast, the more food the beast demands," I answered, repeating a saying I picked up in AA—the *beast* now being the name I gave to this part of me that, no matter what, wanted to keep drinking.

"And then you become a beast," Hem replied, "The irony of it all, rejecting God to live however we want, but we end up living like animals."[1]

"I felt worse than an animal though. I felt evil, honestly, Ernest—evil, like I was capable of anything given the right circumstances. I was terrified I might really hurt someone when all I really wanted was to be a writer, a writer like you, Ernest, capable of real greatness—known, popular, admired."

"I did a lot of terrible things, kid. Things my writing never made up for, and while I thought it might bring some comfort to be remembered, to meet a fan, it doesn't, not here, not like this."

"So why'd you do it? Why would you commit suicide after the books you wrote? The greatest writer of the twentieth century? How did that not make you happy?"

"Work made me happy. But it couldn't keep me happy, not when work brought success, and success brings a different kind of hunger, a yearning, a thirst you can't satisfy like you're looking out across the ocean and wondering if you'll ever see land again, growing jealous of birds flying overhead."[2]

"Would you tell me how you died then? What happened?"

"I could write a good book about life on earth, now that I'm damned to Hell. The Forest of the Suicides reminds me of the woods at Ketchum where I shot myself, and Ketchum reminded me of summers up in Michigan, fishing for trout and looking at the moon and wondering what I would become in life. But we're almost to the gates of Hell."

Ernest led me to the top of a spiral staircase winding down into the darkness. He lifted an unlit torch from a sconce and held it inside his chest until the torch caught fire. A hollow gray light tumbled down the stairwell, bright enough for me to see scenes carved into the walls. The way down was adorned with demons, demons devouring the wings of angels, demons tempting man with sin, demons dragging the damned bound and chained to Hell, never to be seen again.

"What are these?" I asked.

"Scenes to terrify the damned. Scenes starting with Lucifer's rebellion, with war erupting in Heaven greater than anything we've put together on earth, more like planets slipping their orbits and going at it like bulls until God defeats Satan and hurls that demon headlong from Heaven. That blasted *galano*[3] falls for days on end until he lands in the pit just beyond these massive doors. But Satan doesn't stay down for long, and soon he's striking back at God by ruining God's new prized creation: man."

We came to the bottom of the stairs and out into a long hallway. The floor sloped downward while the ceiling rose higher and higher into the black expanse above our heads. The light from our torch faded as we pressed on, the flame moving about us like worms nibbling at the darkness. I felt like I hadn't awakened from a dream when the gates of Hell emerged from the abyss. Ernest knocked on the massive doors, and silence followed while we waited for Hell's gatekeepers to open and let us in.

"Once we go through this gate, Evan," Hem continued, "there's no turning back, not unless you get captured by some galano or until you reach the Lake of Fire at the bottom of Hell. Nor will the fiends make it easy on you. They know the more shades you speak with, the more likely it is you'll know what it means to repent and you'll actually do it, and the demons don't want that happening. So don't wander off."

"I won't," I nodded, noticing letters on the doorway I couldn't quite make sense of (you can't read in dreams, can you?). So I asked my guide, "Ernest, what is that written above the gate?"

"The words mean the same wherever they're written. But these are written in English: ABANDON ALL HOPE, YE WHO ENTER HERE.[4] The irony of it all—I lost all hope long before I came here but for your sake, I'll try and be happy and pretend we're fishing in the high hills of Spain, like you're my son and we're just out for a good time, or that the heat I feel is really the sun shimmering on the Gulf Stream and we're hooking some big monster from the deep. After all, in a way, that's all we're really doing."[5]

CHAPTER III

AT HELL

We waited in the darkness until the grind of locks and gears broke the silence. Then the doors opened wide enough for a single, solitary wail to escape the portal and dissolve into the darkness. The wail was followed by one scream after another and then laughter above the screams, a laughter I can only describe as joy perverted, a sickening glee, a cold wind blown through an empty wood. Then Ernest and I stepped over the threshold and into the first realm of the Inferno.

Beyond the portal stretched what looked like a massive marketplace, the kind where animals or slaves might be sold at auction, illuminated by the light of a thousand torches. The chamber was filled with the dead, great and small, known and unknown, numberless and hopeless, cast into Hell to be processed. The dead poured through a multitude of gates, their souls dragged by demons with long, sharp hooks as if they were doing no more than breaking a horse. While we walked through the hive of fiends, only one thought occupied my mind: *to fly my pain, this is where I would have flown.*

We walked beneath a vaulted ceiling, not unlike that of a temple or a cathedral. Serpent-like columns supported the roof, and the forum curled left and right like the horns of a crescent moon around the rest of Hell, as if we stood on the uppermost level of a stadium encircling the most horrific displays of human misery. The forum ended in a black stone wall separating the vestibule of Hell from the rest of Hell, punctuated by windows letting in the light of the Inferno—that is, if I could call beams of burning sulfur *light*. Ernest led me to the end of a long line of fiends and their charges, shades bound hand, foot, and neck, waiting for judgment.

"The rites of condemnation are reserved for fiends selected by the *arch-galano* Satan," Ernest shouted above the din, scarcely making himself heard. "Demons are not only given higher stations in the *abyssmalarchy*, the caste system of Hell, but also privileges they jealously guard from the lesser demons."

Ernest motioned ahead to the judge's tribunal at the far end of the forum. The tribunal was hewn from stone and looked like an altar, behind which the presiding fiend moved about like a shaman or a witchdoctor, complete with a headdress of long, jagged spikes running down the length of its spine to form a tail. Lesser fiends tended to a brazier built into the altar, and behind them gaped the eager mouth of Hell, outlined in flame. Upon seeing me, the fiends and their charges hastened out of the way and bid me to approach the judge.

"Evan Esco," the judge snarled, "the one who *tried* to repent. Surely, you have come to confess your folly?"

"God bids this boy to travel the lengths of Hell," Ernest declared, "and see the realm God would save him from. Let us pass."

"But the Enemy does not save people like you, Evan," replied the demon. "Do not believe he would, for I know your sins and the enjoyment you reaped from them—and thus, how much you really deserve to be here, how much you want to be here. Be assured, the first realm—that of *Eirachdam*,[1] the Sea of Lust—will indeed convince you of your rightful place in Hell."

"Are you going to let us pass or not?" Ernest snapped.

"Don't listen to your guide. He knows neither the Enemy nor the plans the Enemy hides from everyone but himself. Your guide is here with us, after all—how much can you really trust him? So be warned, Evan Esco, for the damned have wild and fanciful stories to tell, and they think they're right, even though they are in *Hell*."

The judge then bid the lesser demons to let us pass. We moved beside the altar, the brazier smoldering with burnt parchment and blackened flesh, and stepped onto the edge of a cliff. Stairs were carved into the black stone, stairs winding all the way down to what looked like a dock jutting out into the Sea of Lust, the realm the judge called *Eirachdam*. From atop the staircase, I surveyed the whole of this vast and horrible damnscape, adorned with features one might expect to see from the peaks of a mountain up on earth.

Below me, the sea curled around the seemingly limitless expanse of Hell. I surveyed the fiery waves until the sea broke upon a distant gray shore, a beach that gave way to a dense swamp cut by rivers of fire and brimstone. Beyond the swamp stretched wide, rolling plains ending at a range of black mountains barring me from seeing any deeper into Hell. The roar of gnashing teeth and the smoke of endless torment rose and settled in the heights of Hell, forming dark thunderclouds overhead.

But Hell had no sky. In its place, Hell was sealed with a great black dome and set in its center, in place of the shining sun, was the reflection of a burning lake, burning from somewhere deeper in the bottomless pit of the Inferno, dark red at its center with cords of flame convulsing at its edges. The image resembled in appearance a huge and terrible eye, perhaps even the Eye of Satan, and though the sun may obliterate anything that dares approach its orbit, I knew, deep down, if I was condemned to this burning lake, I would never cease to be. I would keep burning, burning forever, burning like the Eye.

And there was no turning back. So, with the wild and raging sea below, Ernest and I descended step-by-step down the cliffs and into the first realm of the Inferno.

CHAPTER IV

THE SEA OF LUST

We walked down a narrow stairway hanging over the Sea of Lust.[1] The cliffs looked as if they were made of obsidian and slate, with veins of iron coursing through them for added strength. I tried not to look at the Eye of Satan burning overhead, but the Sea of Lust was no better, for the Eye's matchless flame ignited the waves and made the sea one vast, fiery cauldron. If I dared to look over the edge and into the sea, I saw only shades clawing at the surface like sailors trapped in a sinking ship.

Finally, we came to the last step and onto a long, narrow dock. To the dock was moored a ship, reserved I assumed for the odd demon that could not fly. The sulfurous air filled my lungs and, mixing with the breath of someone still alive, began to burn. Maybe something like this happens inside the shades, or perhaps this was how temptation works on the soul, for I could feel my inner being begin to burn, my blood boiling and my bones hardening, the way I felt whenever I experienced the temptation to indulge in something forbidden and I heard the *beast* speak to me. So what would I find aboard a craft built for the seas of Hell?

The ship was long and flat, with oars like a galley or a pleasure barge, the kind that might have carried some pharaoh, king, or empress. The ship's prow was carved in the guise of a snake and adorned with jewels for scales, its stern shaped like a tail poised to strike the surface of the water. Hem walked down the jetty without saying a word, just shaking his head, a look of worry passing through him like the shadow of a great fish in the sea. Then he motioned for me to go up the gangway. I wanted to get away from the unrelenting gaze of the Eye so I hurried up the gangway with Hem at my heels.

The ship was indeed a pleasure craft, for I found a canopy bed covering the ship's entire deck. The bed was carved from smooth, ebony pillars and draped with golden and crimson silks. The smell of burning incense wafted out from the canopy bed, scents I thought were foreign to Hell but managed to smother the eternal stench of rotten eggs. I walked to the entrance like a lamb to the slaughter, and before I could pull the curtains aside, something drew them back for me. Then it grabbed me by the collar.

A trio of beautiful women lay waiting there, Siren-like, all of whom I recognized way too quickly. Lying across the bed, smiling and giggling, was an array of starlets whose work I knew too well: Aurora Shade, Bella Heat, and Amor Amoria. The shades wore white gowns, gold jewelry, and pearls, each adorned like a Greek goddess fit to be worshipped with the offerings of a sinful boy. They were in Hell, but they bore no trace of judgment, as if they were damned the moment their beauty began to turn. I had no idea any of them were dead.

A fourth spirit stood at the far end of the canopy bed. This spirit was taller than the others and while she also wore a white gown, she looked like something more than a shade yet still less than a fiend. Her green eyes were chased with even greener, sulfur-like threads, and her fiery red hair, hair seemingly kissed by hellfire, was braided and slung around her shoulders like a snake. Where was I? Was this really Hell?

At the moment she smiled at me, our ship unmoored from the dock. The Sea of Lust imperceptibly moved our pleasure barge forward, its oars barely turning the sea as our ship moved with the current.[2] Only then did the spirit in command of this fell craft begin to speak.

"Do make yourself comfortable," she said, "and come closer, for it has been too long since we have seen anyone still alive, and even then we have never seen a boy as cute as *you*."

"Is this really Hell?" I asked, entranced. "Who are you?"

"I have had so many names," she said, smiling, stretching toward me. "For I have long been worshipped by the mortal beings I serve, whose hearts I fill with pleasure, but you may call me Lilith. Our Father Herein,[3] my lord and prince Lucifer, gave me not only my beloved name but also my noble task: for it is I who fill the flowers with the fragrance that attracts the bees; the birds the sweet songs they sing out above the trees; and to the lovers among mankind, I give to them whatever their hearts desire.

"Indeed, an ounce of happiness from my embrace is often the only recompense for mankind's toil upon the earth. And now, though I am confined to this sea of fire and brimstone, I still watch over and tend to those shades who gave themselves to lovers and to love."

"Love? Condemned for love?" I asked and looked at Hem. "I don't understand—how can anyone be damned for love?"

"Do we look damned?" Lilith asked and smiled, cupping her hand behind a shade. "Do we not look free, free and happy to enjoy the heights of love without the rules God tries in vain to set upon human happiness? Love has no bounds, and even if love had such limits, God could not set them! Why, can anyone bind the stars that guide youthful hearts in love or stop the roses in mid-bloom, or bid the birds to cease their serenading once they wake from a night of bliss?[4]

"Of course not, my sweet, sweet boy. For when animals feel such a desire, they act upon it without fear or scruple. You should do the same whenever desire alights upon you, just like our ship glides upon this wondrous current without thought, care, or design. Truly, if you are to love anyone, you must break the bounds God jealously imposes upon human happiness and go beyond the silly rules God claims are there to *protect* love."

I heard something below clawing at our hull. Behind the shades I could see the reflection of the Lake of Fire churning in the vault over Hell while the reek of brimstone seeped across the deck. I tried to say something, but Aurora Shade, black-haired and giggling, brought a finger to my lips. Then with a voice still so sweet, Aurora's spirit began to speak.

"You cute, cute boy!" Aurora cooed. "We are *so* happy you came here and found us."

"But why have you come?" Bella Heat whispered next. "What's your name, sailor?"

"My name is Evan," I responded, stunned.

"And why are you here, Evan?"

"I don't, I don't know," I stuttered. "I tried to kill myself last night, and I—"

"Oh, we can help you with that," Bella answered me and put a finger to my lips. "You shouldn't feel sad now, and you need not feel sad ever again now that you're here, here with us."

"Are you a fan of our work?" asked Amor. "Surely you are—I can always tell when I've met a fan."

"I do know you," I answered sheepishly, "and I have seen your movies, I'm ashamed to ad—"

"Ashamed? Why?" Aurora asked. "We made them for you, silly boy, you and all our fans. And surely, our fans, they still remember us?"

"I don't know if they remember you," I answered with some pity. "Or if they even know you're gone—I didn't know."

"You mean you don't know how we died?" Bella asked despondently, as if she didn't know either.

"Oh, don't mind her!" Aurora cooed, ignoring Bella. "Come closer, sweet boy; it's been so long since any of us have seen anyone still alive, we barely know what to do with ourselves."

"Perhaps *you* should tell us what to do," Amor added, pulling me closer. "For we're so *desperate* for your help since you, and only *you,* can help us escape from here."

"Oh yes, help us!" Bella pleaded, regaining her fallen self. "For only a mortal boy, a living, mortal boy can help us escape. Oh please, won't you help us?"

"You're our only hope," Amor echoed. "Please help us."

"How can I help you?" I asked, my desire beginning to catch fire—how can I escape?

"Give yourself to us," Amor responded sultrily. "One real moment with us, Evan, could set us free, free from Hell forever, and free you, too, just like we freed you from your cares and troubles for a time up on earth."

"Won't you help us, Evan?" Aurora pleaded. "Like we helped you? Oh please, Evan, we need you."

"But if you knew about this place," I stammered, trembling, "would you have tried—to escape your troubles any differently? Would you have lived any differently if you knew about what happens when you die?"

"Hush, sweet boy," answered Amor Amoria, putting a finger to my lips, pouting, leaning closer. "We're not bad girls—in fact, God made us this way, and if God never wanted us to live the lives we did, then why would God give us so many fans?"

For years I acted upon my lust whenever I wanted it, however I could get it. Why should now be any different? But that freedom, the power to give into whatever desire chances upon a person, with whatever person the object of someone's lust happens to be—I knew somewhere this was wrong. But I only barely cared, the dilemma turning over in my soul along with fire and brimstone: should I give up whatever hope of heaven I could have if I repented so as to enjoy, *right now*, the pleasures my sinnermost self deeply desired, the shades I saw sprawled before me?[5]

"What's wrong, sailor?" Bella asked. "Are we not enough for you?"

"He's scared," Amor cooed, "scared to embrace the one happy lot still left to man, scared because then he'd be free."

"Oh Evan, like Adam and Eve's time in the Garden of Eden," Bella cooed, "you must reject God whenever he dares to restrain your freedom."

"This poor, sweet boy, he just needs some fun and cheer!" Amor whispered. "Won't you take my hand, and stay with us in here?"

The objects of my sad, lonely lust grabbed ahold of me, holding me tighter, my consciousness streaming on ahead of me while I tried to resist the temptation with whatever strength I had left, for if I yielded I would be damned to Hell forever, wouldn't I? But what was one little sin? Couldn't I give in *just a little* and help these poor shades, sweet as they are, misunderstood as they were in life, couldn't I accept their embrace and go back on my journ—*no, I can't*. I can't keep on sinning and expect to live even if I'm desperate for any sort of release from Hell and from the habits now so deeply engrained in me (and that's why I killed myself since I couldn't escape what I became); still, my mind raced to find some source of help, any help at all, until my train of thought settled on the page I ripped out from the Bible last night, in the final moments before I killed myself, so, maybe if I just touched that crumpled piece of paper, *I might really be free*: I reached for my pocket and the page and as soon as my fingers grazed its ink, I passed out, falling upon the deck as though I died while more shades escaped the sea and flew furiously by.

CHAPTER V

THE SHORES OF GLUTTONY

I thought I might have been dreaming again. But then I opened my eyes, and the image of the burning lake hurled me back to my new reality. The waves of the Sea of Lust were breaking upon me, soaking me in fire and brimstone, and I realized I was thrown onto the beach at the shoreline of Hell. I jumped up and looked around and saw a shade, the largest shade I've seen so far in Hell, eating what looked like tar. I tried not to move, afraid the shade might consume me too, but that shade was too consumed with its food to notice me. That shade was one of a multitude of the dead swarming the beach, all of whom were devouring the pitch-like sand and mingling their food with their tears. I didn't move until Hemingway grabbed me and pulled me up from the sands and shades.

"You did all right on that ship, kid," Hemingway said, pulling tar off my shoulder. "I wouldn't have lasted that long, especially if we were on the *Pilar* and I had them to myself."

"Did you know what was going to happen?" I asked Hem, shaking. What would have happened if I didn't pass out? Or if I yielded to my fantasy and my lust—would I have been damned? And why did I pass out when my hands simply touched the piece of paper I ripped out from the Bible?

"I was told the route to take and the shades you'd have to speak with," Hem answered. "But I was not told of every trial you would have along the way, though I had my suspicions heading into that boat it'd be a trap. The demons want to devour you whole, after all—just like a galano—and they won't make your journey easy on you. In that way, we're more like fish in the Gulf Stream, the demons trying to hook *us*."[1]

"What happened to those shades?" I asked. "Do you know?"

"Why they were damned?" Hem answered me in earnest. "I don't know, but if they were anything like the women in my books, women I subjected to a fate that didn't care how pretty they were, they had sad, lonely lives, families that split apart, fathers who left, their looks the only thing to get them through a world otherwise indifferent to them."

"I watched their scenes without ever wondering who they were." I hung my head in shame. "Could they have been saved, Ernest? If they repented?"

"I think you'll find out, if you haven't already, why most people don't want to be saved."

"Where are we now then?" I asked my guide.

"The Shores of Gluttony," Hem responded.[2] "A realm filled with gluttons—the fiends call them *bingewraiths*—shades who gave their lives to eating and to drinking, but their real sin was not so much in what they consumed, but in what they turned to *instead* of God—food, booze, drugs—to comfort them, feed them, strengthen them, until there was nothing left in them except an empty shell, a *wraith*, like an abandoned tent set up by a hiker lost in the woods."

"This is where I belong, Ernest. I had so much potential, Ernest, and I wasted it, all of it. I grew up with too much money and freedom, and I spent it all on alcohol and drugs, and all because I hated myself so much, hating myself and hating God for making me the way I am."

Hem motioned for me to follow him through the gluttons. As we moved, the bingewraiths would rise en masse and bear down upon us like a tidal wave, pulling me down with them. I've lived my whole life looking for joy at the bottom of an empty bottle, and while the pleasure I might find in binge drinking or overeating felt good for a while, my pursuits always left me emptier than before, the bites and draughts draining my soul of the strength I needed to face my problems. That pattern continued until I killed myself.

I could barely keep up with Ernest. The Lake of Fire burning overhead made the black, tarry sands unimaginably hot, so we made our way through the realm as quickly as we could. Occasionally, I stepped on the backs of the gluttons like I was crossing a wide and ravenous river one rock at a time, always hurrying onto the next shade. Then Ernest led me to one massive glutton perched upon a mass of wraiths, bearded and dressed (despite the heat) in a black woolen suit.

He took no notice of us at first. In spite of his place in Hell, the shade was singing with whatever remained of his lungs:

In my speech I said my motto
an old one, tried and true;
"Do unto others as you wish
They'd do to you."

Thus, we lived to feed the masses,
The great joy of our Hall,
Out o' lack of faith
For God to feed anyone at all.

Oh, I swear I'd keep my word
My oath I made by St. Paul,
But things did take a horrid turn (I'm here, aren't I?)
Since I joined Tammany Hall.

Still, we lived to feed the masses,
The great joy of our Hall,
Out o' lack of faith
For God to feed anyone at all.[3]

Finally, the shade saw me, stopped singing, and bellowed, "Why, hello there! And who might you be?"

"My name is Evan, sir," I answered meekly. "And who are you?"

"Boss is fine," the shade answered, raising his hands in the air. "A boss I still am, after all, if only of what I see from my noble perch, and boss I once was—indeed, Grand Sachem of the noble Society of Saint Tammany. Those were the days, and that's all ye need to know! Now, what brings ye to these parts?"

"I killed myself last night, but God, for reasons I don't entirely understand, is letting me see the Hell I would have sent myself."

"And what do you think of our accommodations?" the shade, whoever he was, replied. "I do miss my evenings at Delmonico's, but this tar has quite a kick to it, doesn't it?" laughing and kicking the shades beneath him.

"This place is terrifying," I said, feeling the Eye bearing down on me. "But why, if you were a saint, why are you here in Hell?"

"Argh! A saint!" the shade guffawed and reeled backwards. "He thinks me a saint! Indeed, in many ways I proved a saint for the charity and the alms I gave the poor—but of course, I did a lot of other things too."

"So, why are you here then?" I asked him again, staring in horror at his throne of shades and remembering *how much I deserved to be here*.

"Now, I've wondered that myself. But I suppose my gluttony drove on all the rest of my sins, so base and powerful as that one sin is. And as the rivers surround Manhatt'n, so I stood at the confluence of three powerful currents, so extolled in my refrain: the feeding of the masses, the joys of the Hall in feeding them, and the diminishing faith that God would feed anyone at all.

"Let me tell you a story, my lad," the shade began, "of a poor oyster, a poor, poor oyster, tossed about by the waves of fortune into New York harbor. He heard everywhere he was equal to the other animals in town—even if clad in a shell and lacking legs and all—and yet this poor oyster was oyster-cized by all his peers. The *established* animals wanted nothing to do with him, nor with any of the untold masses of freshly arrived oysters in the city! And what is this poor creature to do?[4]

"That oyster wandered about town, looking for food, crying for help, shedding briny tears inside that cold, tiny shell of his. No one heard him, *no one* helped him, *no one cared for him* until the day that oyster chanced upon a walrus who, being a walrus, was also shunned by all the creatures of New York. Mind you, a walrus is built for the sea, built to withstand the cold, cruel Arctic currents, and thus this walrus built up the means of taking care of cold, little animals lost and on their own, this oyster being one of them. And what did our friend the walrus do? Why, he did all he could to help that little fellow, finding him a job, housing, even so little a boon as a lump of coal to warm that shell of his through the winter."

"And what happened next?" I asked. "Did they live happily ever after?"

"Well, the walrus certainly did," the shade replied, whose massive girth and bushy mustache made him look very much like a walrus himself. "For a time, that is."

"What does that story mean?"

"That, I suppose, you'll have to figure out for yourself!" the shade guffawed again. "Once you figure that out, you'll have figured out everything else."

The shade plunged his hand into the mound of shades, pulled out a mass of sticky tar, and stuffed it in his mouth. Then, in between bites, the shade proclaimed, "I wish you the best of luck upon your journey. Huzzah, and good day to you both!"

Ernest motioned for me to follow him and, once we were far enough away from the Boss, Ernest turned to me and said, "I recognize that shade, at least by reputation. He stole untold amounts of money from New York to support the lifestyle that drove him to this place, as if theft alone was not enough to damn a person. But that admission—the three currents—that might be all he had to tell you . . ."

But I had already stopped listening to Ernest. Up ahead, I saw a shade, a shade who was my *idol*, my favorite actor, and my model for how I could become famous for the one real talent I felt I had: making people laugh. I was always the class clown. No matter how much trouble I might get into, if a joke popped into my head, I had to tell it. I *lived* for making people laugh even if that joke might distract the class, hurt one of my peers, or reveal just how little regard I had for myself or for sacred things. But how could he be here in Hell?

His name was Everett Man, and I loved everything he did—his movies, his skits, his characters. On the days I dreamed of becoming a writer and making it in television or movies, I looked to Everett for inspiration and a plan to become famous—that is, until he died. I thought I could be happy if I succeeded in the one, real talent I thought I had, just as he was so successful in what he did. Everett's life, his physical comedy, and his career provided the template for making it on TV and in Hollywood—although not necessarily how to *stay* there. For Everett Man died of an overdose from speedballs—a mix of cocaine and heroin—and that was not the end I wanted. Unless, that end might cement my legend, as his drug overdose helped to cement *his*.

He still had something of his boyish grin. But now he was crawling on his huge hands and knees, sifting through the black sand for choicer food. I know Ernest warned me not to pity the shades, but I couldn't help but cry when I saw Everett ahead of me, mostly because in him I saw what I wanted to be. Hem kept the shades at bay, so I could speak with my idol.

"Are you Everett Man?" I asked, a few tears streaming down my cheeks turning at once to steam.

"I am," the shade replied and tried to smile. "And who are you?"

"A fan, a huge fan actually. I love all your work and the hilarious movies you made. I loved everything you did while you were alive."

"It makes me happy to meet a fan, someone who remembers me," Everett replied. "But you don't *really* know me—otherwise, you'd hate me, too, for all I did."

"Well, I don't know you. But I know some of the people who did know you, and those people certainly don't hate you."

"But look at me here," Everett said, throwing his hands up in frustration. "My friends, my family, they all hoped I'd get clean and sober, but I could never do it. Just look at where I've gotten myself! You didn't do something like that, did you? That's not why you're here, right kid? Alcohol? Coke? Heroin?"

"No heroin," I answered, voice quivering. "But I tried everything else in hopes of gaining a happy life. And now, although I don't understand why, God is giving me some kind of second chance,

Everett, to let me know what could happen if I don't repent—but I don't know what repentance *is*."

"A second chance?" Everett pleaded with me. "Whoever you are and whatever repentance is, you've got to do it the best you can to keep from coming here. Do you have any idea what made you so unhappy, why you would kill yourself?"

"The depression's always been there. In high school, kids made fun of me for being so awkward, having this huge bird-like chest and rail-thin legs, so I look like a stork or a pelican, and I got nicknames like 'The House on Stilts' or 'The Goblin' because of how weird and awkward and ugly I look. And for as often as people mocked me, I burned with a desire to be successful, as if that would make me happy. I usually settled for getting really drunk."

"I know what that's like. My life wasn't so bad, growing up in Ohio. Other people had it worse, and I had real good parents actually, parents who did the best they could despite the circumstances. But I hated two things: the fact I was so big, so big and so fat, and then how cold the world was—and winters in Ohio, when your dad is underemployed your whole childhood, those winters were cold, very, very cold.

"I had some sense God existed, but I hated him for the life, the body, and the world he threw me into. People were always fighting each other, ruining each other, and then God made me so fat I could never have a real relationship. If I hugged a girl, she disappeared into the folds of fat, and I felt like some sort of cosmic joke, an accident, and a fool.

"I hated God, and I hated myself for being so big, and I tried to smother these sad, lonely thoughts in jokes about my weight while that seed of self-loathing just grew and grew. I found success in standup and on TV and movies, sure, and that success brought some money and fame—but never any real happiness or contentment or peace. But I doubled down on drugs and booze and kept buying 'em even as they destroyed me, emptying me of what little joy I had before I got famous. They promised happiness and delivered chains," he said, holding up his hands as if I should see the bonds he put on his soul.

"I should have stayed in Ohio and settled for a normal life. That would have been the life God would have had for me, I guess, but I wanted to make something of myself. So I chased after fame and the hope that success would give me happiness. But all success gave me was money—money for better drugs and more prostitutes, the only real relationships I could afford, so the gulf between the love I got from strangers and the hatred I kept for myself kept growing bigger and bigger. No one told *me* how to repent or how to free myself from the beast—the beast I'd been feeding all my life. The more I fed the thing, the more it demanded of me, until the beast was strong enough to push me over the edge."

"The beast?" I asked, my heart racing. "What are you talking about?"

"You don't know?" Everett gasped. "*The beast is us*, the worst parts of us, our flesh or the demons Satan assigns us or maybe both working to ruin everything in our lives. I don't know what else to tell you, what to say so you can escape from here—except repent and don't make the same mistakes I did, kid. Money, booze, drugs, girls, trappings of fame, they're all just that—a trap, a lot of meaningless bright lights leading us on like moths to a flame.[5] So whatever repentance is, do it and do it now to avoid this fate, then turn from all your sins before it is too late!"[6]

CHAPTER VI

THE SWAMPS OF GREED

I was put on probation my freshman year at the College of William & Mary. That probation would have lasted until I graduated two years from now if I hadn't, well, you know. I was arrested on two separate occasions for the same crime: being drunk in public and the destruction of public property. William & Mary forced me to attend Alcoholics Anonymous, so I could see the effects of lifelong alcohol abuse writ upon the faces of old men the bottle ruined. I didn't stop drinking even while I attended those meetings, not when I could bundle myself into the void of being black-out drunk. Then, one day, a wise, homeless, bearded old-timer named Elmo, between endless drags on his cigarette, warned the group, "The more you feed the beast, the more food the beast demands."

The beast—the same words Everett uttered to me, the same phrase Ernest said outside the cave, the same thought flitting through my mind whenever I woke up after a night of drinking: *the more you feed the beast*. For years, I wanted to be a *beast*, someone who got the girls and the lacrosse scholarships and seemed happy enough. The more I tried to live like the cool kids whose popularity I envied, the more I drank the more I acted like an animal, living only for the pleasures I reaped from the empty hook-up culture of Washington, DC, but I built up such a dependence I couldn't stop drinking. And if I tried to resist, I heard this voice, the voice of the beast, the beast talking to me—a creature as fiendish as I was, living inside my heart like Gollum inside his cave, searching for his *precious* and influencing my choices. The voice of the beast urged me to drink harder, smoke marijuana more often, and care less for the future. The more I fed the beast, the more of my life the foul thing demanded, and the longer I tried to satisfy this creature, the more I lived just to serve its needs.

"I should be suffering here with you, Everett," I gasped.

"But you're not, not yet. And you have a chance to escape this place so go—go and leave me to the only comforts I have left."

"Good-bye, Everett. Please know I am so sorry for what has happened to you."

Everett said nothing in reply, and Hem motioned me to move forward. We hurried across the Shores of Gluttony, and I tried to stick as close to Hem as I could. At times I tried to lean on my guide, but I would fall straight through his shade and onto the beach. I thought I might pass out from the heat and collapse somewhere in the Inferno, lost wherever my mortal body landed, but then the shoreline ended in a mound of black dunes covered with gray grass and thorns. There I saw the beginnings of a huge and hideous swamp rolling out ahead of us.

This great dismal swamp resembled the undeveloped land around Williamsburg. The countryside around William & Mary remained the same swampy shoreline that swallowed up Jamestown's first settlers, woods I loved to explore on the odd days I felt bold enough to leave my apartment, albeit probably high or a little drunk. This swamp may have imitated the world above, but it was still a grim reservoir of ruin with creeks and inlets and streams of fire cutting through the clusters of gray reeds.

Growing from the flames were trees as tall as the cypresses lording over Jamestown Beach. "Writhe oaks," Ernest called them, on account of their broken limbs and exposed roots twisting in the heat like a bed of snakes. They formed a thick canopy blocking the view of the Eye but trapping its heat, leaving the floor of the swamp even hotter than the shores we just passed through. Green mist curled upward from the swamp to form a curtain so thick I could barely see the flames in front of me like city lights often hide the heavenly stars from view.[1] And everywhere we looked, we saw huge shades fighting each other for some prize the likes of which I could not see.

"We've made it to the Swamps of Greed," Ernest told me, scratching his white beard.[2] "The demons call these shades the *Beruqtai*, the *heaps*—heaps not only of gold and silver, but heaps of bodies as high as the mounds of men after a bad day in the Great War. For this is what greed does to a people.

"These shades are condemned for sins of greed and profligacy, either hoarding their gold or wasting it, using their wealth to ease the burden God wants man to feel for him, to trust in and lean against and depend on God and not do everything by your own strength. These shades gathered up their wealth so they would need not ever ask God for *anything*, and now they are condemned to fight each other with all the fury they gave to their pursuit of riches up on earth."[3]

Ernest walked ahead with me following close behind. I tried to keep from being spotted by the shades, but they were too consumed with fighting each other to notice me, consuming as much fire and brimstone as they could. They jumped into pools and drank it; broke boughs off the oaks and ate it; and ripped open smaller shades and gorged themselves of it. Even though Hell was one vast, open flame, the shades of greedy men deemed fire too precious a commodity to permit anyone else to have it.

And the more sulfur the Beruqtai consumed, the bigger they grew. Some of them had become titanic, troll-like monsters rivaling the writhe oaks in size and the demons in savagery. They in turn attacked the smaller shades, tossing them about like rag dolls; for defense, the smaller shades moved in packs like wolves, climbing up on the bellies of larger shades and clawing at their stomachs. And even if the titans of Hell escaped the smaller, hyena-like wraiths, demons, walking spider-like amongst the flames, would strike down any of them who grew too big for the confines of the Inferno.

The shades didn't seem to notice me. Still, for my safety, Ernest led me into a lonely and seemingly abandoned section of the swamp. We had not walked for long when I tripped over the roots of what I thought was another writhe oak. But then I heard the sulfurous leaves rustling in the canopy overhead, and the entire tree moved, boughs and all, to see what small creature was scurrying about its trunk.

The shade, or whatever it was, was tall enough he could eat the ashen leaves off the tops of the trees. This strategy allowed him to reach the heights of an oak or even an Ent, those giant, talking trees from *The Lord of the Rings*. This strategy allowed him to avoid (at least for the time being) the destruction of the other Beruqtai so he stood as tall as a redwood. His shade had hardened into a cracked, bark-like substance not unlike tar or pitch or even the center of a smoldering tree stump, a stump that hardens even as it burns. The shade's leaf-like hair and trim, albeit mossy beard rustled as he shifted his gaze down toward me. After a long, long pause, he gave me a puzzled look. Then the shade bent and scooped me up by the waist.

"You are a strange creature," the shade said after an interminably long time and with unbearable pauses between his words. "Are you alive? Do you have a name?"

"Evan," I gasped, trying to recognize the shade. "My name is Evan, and I'm just a kid, a kid who killed himself last night, but God saved me from—"

"Saved you?" the Ent-like shade replied, raising a puzzled, barky eyebrow. Then he looked around and asked, "Are you sure?"

"Yes . . . well, I think so, although, I don't really know what it means to be alive in a place like this."

"Maybe it is a test," the shade slowly, steadily said after another long pause. "Or a trick, for God, God often looks at man more like a . . ."

"Like what?" I asked when I gave up hope the shade would finish his sentence.

"Why, a prize," the shade finally answered, "a prize to be won or lost, a prize in wagers made with Satan, like Job or Joseph or some other person from that book of his, the name of which I have forgotten, the one that describes God leaving people to their own devices just like God left me—and you, too, it seems, that I am sure of."[4]

"Evan," I heard Ernest calling out from far below me. "Are you alright?"

"And who is that?" the Ent looked down, large flakes of ash falling to the floor like leaves in autumn. "A friend?"

"My guide. The shade of Ernest Hemingway, who's taking me through—"

"Oh yes, I know him," the Ent interrupted and slowly, steadily bent again and picked Ernest up in his other hand. Ernest did not look happy or impressed until the giant shade told Ernest he was a fan of his work. Then the shade offered, "Say, would you want me to take you to the end of the swamp?"

"Yes," my guide replied for us. "We are heading to the shores of the River Bane."

"The River Bane," the talking tree answered and took one long, slow, measured step forward. "Good, good, you'll meet more shades there who will confirm the truth of what I am telling you."

"And who are you?" I said, holding tight to the long, smoldering brands this shade had for fingers. "What happened to you? What's your name?"

"What use is a name down here?" the Ent replied, lumbering through the swamp as slowly as he spoke. "But I will give you a word of advice: do not think God will protect you. That is not what I saw in the world above, and it is a feeling I have long since thought on here in Hell."

"And why would you say that?" I asked.

"Why, because God doesn't care about you," the tree replied, raising a barky eyebrow again. "God does not care about anyone—not unless they get on their knees and beg him to notice them, and even then, God hardly does. But you did not need to travel all the way to Hell to figure that out, not when the world above is full of cancer and warfare and meaningless, bottomless hatred. It should be—it should be—indeed—it should be . . ."

"Should be what?" I asked, afraid he might never finish his sentence.

"Obvious," the shade continued, drawing deep sulfurous breaths between each word. "It was obvious when I was young, obvious when I was old, and that truth only grew more obvious as the cancer grew worse."

"You died of cancer?" I asked, remembering the day my little sister Evelyn complained her feet were cold, and we fell into the abyss that was Georgetown's "amazing" cancer center. Once the funeral was over and I was alone, I smoked a cigar. When it was nearly finished, I put it out on the back of my hand, grinding the nicotine and the ash into my skin and leaving a quarter-sized wound large enough to remind me I should have gotten leukemia—not Evelyn.

"Cancer, terrible cancer," the shade replied. "Death is terrible, every form of it, but cancer may be the worst—the pain, the pain of its treatment and how random it is, like lightning or a car wreck. But, of course, those things are quick, and the pain is over soon. Not with cancer."

"If it was slow," I asked, rubbing my scar, "and if you knew you were going to die, why didn't you repent?"

"I knew it would be no use," the Ent replied. "You see, I went on a pilgrimage too, not unlike yours, it seems. And there I saw the truth for myself, a pilgrimage to . . ."

The Ent took several giant steps through the woods before I gave up hope he would finish his story, and so I asked, "Where did you go?"

"To India," the shade replied, "where I walked barefoot, lived like a brahmin, meditated day and night, prayed to everything I could, and sought out truth, real truth. In this, I did not reach enlightenment—that state of perfect being—when you realize your soul is at one with the universe—knowledge, sublime and perfect, flowing into the inner recesses of your mind and spirit—illuminating you from the outside in—oh, God barred my way to such a state—such bliss—but I did see the world for what it really is, for what that is worth."

"And what did you see?" I asked him after waiting another intolerably long time for him to tell me.

"Ah, yes. I saw this: if you want purpose, you have to make it up for yourself. The only thing that comes from God is suffering, so you cannot depend on God to take care of you, and we are fools to believe he will—well, you are. You are the fool to believe God will help you."

"But God *is* helping me. I mean, he sent Ernest to guide me, and perhaps even you to carry me."

"That is what I said," the shade answered, furrowing two immense, barky eyebrows. "Ernest is guiding you, I am carrying you, and God is toying with you. I will try and speak more slowly if you do not understand what I am saying.

"And you are lucky I found you," the Ent continued. "The other shades in this swamp did terrible things to gain their wealth, and they do awful things now, but I left the world much better than I found it—and all at a salary of a dollar a year. Now, I tend to the writhe oaks until the demons find me and once they do, I go back to where they found me and pick up where I left off. If a man has to make up his purpose for himself when he's alive, then I will make up my purpose in Hell too. It's what I did in life, and it's what I do now in death—and both this world and the world above are better off for what I do for it."

"What did you do then, when you were alive?"

"I dreamed," the shade answered, parting two massive oaks to make a path. "Yes, I dreamed, dreamed up as many dreams as I could, dreamed up gifts leading to other dreams helping man either overcome or at least forget the suffering that comes from . . . comes from . . ."

"From what?" I asked, still wondering who this shade was.

"From God. Many things, many gifts, but always one dream, that man could find purpose and joy on his own, and in this dream all mankind would come together and pool their knowledge (and their dreams too) for the good of them all."

We didn't pray for Evelyn, I thought, *except that science would heal her, as if science was a person. Maybe we cried out to God every once and a while in moments of weaknesses—but did he listen? Grandmasco prayed for Evelyn to be healed and that healing never happened either. Maybe she should have prayed we could keep going after Evelyn died. That might have been more useful. I didn't make it two years.*

"Indeed, God toys with man and bars from us *the knowledge* we need to escape suffering—knowledge to make the world what we need it to be. Then, in our ignorance, we fight each other for the scraps God throws down from Heaven. And yet—out of the human mind comes treasure most men cannot fathom—for no one knows what they want until a dreamer and a doer (like me) either shows them a future they could not dream, or unlocks the door and frees them from the cage they did not know they were in. And usually—for most people—it's both."

The Ent parted two more writhe oaks and walked between them. Then he paused for a moment and sighed when he saw the river separating the Swamps of Greed from the next realm. Then the shade slowly, steadily bent to the ground and gently set Ernest and me onto the banks of the river.

"The River Bane," the Ent said, scratching his mossy beard. "I must leave you here. But do think about what I said and try to take care of yourself, because . . . because . . ."

"God will not take care of me?" I couldn't wait for him any longer.

"Do not be so impatient," the Ent barked at me. "But yes, yes, you are right. God does not care—he left us to our own devices—but me—I dreamed up such devices to improve man's awful lot—or, at least, distract us—from seeing how absurd life really is until—we are crushed under the realization that nothing really matters. Not many could live how I lived or dreamed what I dreamed, but I did what I could to help man all the same. For God may have barred our way to real, true enlightenment—to keep mankind in a state of miserable ignorance—but I freed us all through a device which contained all knowledge within it."

CHAPTER VII

THE RIVER BANE

The shade slowly stood again and headed back into the swamp. The sulfur, leaves, and twigs composing the shade melded into the forest until I couldn't see where the Ent ended and the boughs began. Soon, he disappeared amidst the writhe oaks entirely. At that, I turned to my guide and asked, "Who *was* that?"

"He may not even remember anymore," Ernest answered me.

"Where are we now though, Ernest?"

"The River Bane[1]—the word *bane* meaning 'poison' both in English and in fiendspeech. It is indeed a river teeming with poison—poison and sulfur and bloated flesh. Be careful not to fall in, for I don't know what would consume you faster, the flames or the shades, or what would happen to me if I jumped in after you."

"I'll be careful," I said, stepping back from the edge. "Where are we heading next?"

"We'll walk along the riverbank here," Ernest began, taking off, "until we find a place to cross the River Bane and then we'll make for those mountains off in the distance."

Ernest pointed to our left and into the darkness where I saw a mountain range, capped with volcanoes vomiting fire into Hell's wrathmosphere.

"The demons in fiendspeech call that mountain range *Kilijiarchago*," Ernest continued, "the 'Crown of our Prince' and to us the damned, the mountain is just the Crown."

"The Crown?"

"No crown fits Satan better," the old shade answered, pointing at the mountain as he walked. "The summit of Kilijiarchago not only exalts itself over Hell but also keeps the galanos from rising above his prison, the likes of which was made for him after all.

"My parents raised me with enough religion,"[2] Hem continued in earnest, "I remember Paul calling those who belong to Christ *his* joy and *his* crown.[3] But Satan's joy derives from what he *destroys*, and he delights in the destruction of those damned to his kingdom—don't you forget that.[4]

"So shades composed that mountain from its peaks to its roots, shades who gave themselves to Satan to better serve themselves. And so many people have made such a deal with the devil, that Kilijiarchago is taller than the Rockies, Mount Denali, even the snowy peaks of Kilimanjaro all put together."[5]

We walked along the banks of the river, the Swamps of Greed on our right. On my left, within the River Bane, I saw shades fighting on the surface of the water. Those condemned at the surface fought for air while below them I saw shades chained to the riverbed, their arms free only to scrape at the surface overhead. Oil or ash or venom poured out from them all like Old Faithful and added to the poisonous current. Serpents slipped in between the shades and tore at their limbs and frames, while other demons, tightening the chains of those down below, periodically came up for air and then down to the bottom again they'd go.

Finally, we reached some point in the river suitable enough for us to cross. The river looked as wide as ever while the current grew comparatively calmer, and the banks fell onto a beach large enough to accommodate a raft or a skiff. Here, Ernest stopped short and jumped onto the sand, and I followed him. Then my guide signaled in, or to, the darkness.

Soon a raft appeared to ferry us across the dismal current. Wraiths clawed at its timbers while the shade skillfully steered his ship around them all until he reached us. The pilot jumped off the boat and heaved the raft upon the shore, then leaned against his pole and scowled at me. A solitary lantern on the deck outlined the shade's leathery face, his shock of ghastly gray hair, bushy gray eyebrows, and an even bushier gray mustache. I recognized the shade immediately and fell back with shock of my own.

"*Are you Mark Twain?*" I gasped and looked over at Ernest who seemed as surprised as I was.

"Indeed I once was," the shade sighed, perhaps annoyed at being recognized. "Not much left of who we once were once we get down here, you see. But what is that to you? And what's *your* name?

"Mr. Twain, this is Evan Esco," answered Ernest, still trying not to look impressed.

"Evan *Esco*?" Twain muttered with surprise. "What kind of an odd and pe*cul*iar name is that?"

"It's Italian," I replied.

"I'm sure you'd like to think so," Twain answered, cocking an eyebrow in disbelief. "How come you're in Hell then, if yer still alive? You are alive, ain't ya? Surely, if yer smart enough to recognize me, you must have wits enough to tell me how this all came about."

"I killed myself last night," I answered, "but then I woke up in a dark wood and found my guide, Ernest Hemingway, a writer like you, prepared to take me into Hell to see and speak with the shades I'd find down here."

"Well, I'll be damned *again*!" Twain exclaimed, slapping his thigh and ushering us aboard. "We got ourselves a little Dante here! Maybe you are Italian after all. Come aboard, boy, come aboard. And who are *you* then, and how *did* you get picked for such a choice assignment?"

"My name is Ernest Hemingway, and last night, I was released from *Erium*,[6] the Forest of the Suicides, by an angel who chose me perhaps because I was a good enough writer—like Virgil for Dante—to lead the boy through Hell. Or maybe the angel thought I'd get Evan safely through Hell since Evan looks too much like my own boys to let him down, to let anything happen to him, even if that's not the kind of father I was on earth."

"You're a writer, eh?" Twain asked. "What kind of books you write?"

"Ones that bled. Works as true as I could make them, books I hoped would finish, finish and further, what you started in *Huckleberry Finn*, the best piece of American literature since every other piece of modern literature that's any *good* derives what makes it good from *your* work."

"Two generations of writers aboard this raft," Twain tried to smile, then settled for pushing our skiff offshore. "I wonder what's going to come of you, boy? Perhaps you've figured something out since you've been down here? Aside from the sad and lamentable fact this place—this Hell—is *real*, after all?"

"The only thing I've figured out," I started, "is I have to repent, but I still don't understand what that *means.* Do you know what it means to repent?"

"'Fraid not," Twain answered in his Missouri drawl, hitting a shade with his pole, "aside from rec'gnizing that repentance indeed is a mighty big provision and that by it, a man gets in good with the Lord God whoever. How to do it though—hard to say, because it is much harder, in word and deed, to trust in such a being. Nor do I know too much about trusting in this God of yours since I am (after all) damned for speaking up on all my doubts.

"You see, Ol' Halley's comet brought me into the world and when I died, her tail dragged me down to Hell.[7] Such circumstances befell me because I believed trusting in God makes fools of men and leaves the doubters of his so-called goodness dead—dead and down here. And it does seem mighty unfair of God to do away with his critics in such a fashion, sending folks like me to Hell not for murd'dring or thieving, but for speaking our minds upon the issue of God's ostensible, questionable, and erstwhile re*prehensible* goodness.

"But at least my place in Hell leaves me some semblance of my life on earth. Indeed, I'm in the job I liked the most out of all the occupations I had on earth, even with the success I found in the craft of writing."

"How *are* you piloting a boat up and down a river in Hell?" I asked. "How did you get up here, and not—in the current?"

"Devil sure thought it'd be funny," Twain replied, scowling, his black eyes smoldering like coals, "given my experience 'pon the mighty Mississippi.[8] For sure, there may be no real cessation of punishment or even the most temporary abatement of my anguish, but it does feel mighty free and easy and comfortable being onboard a raft again."

Twain hit another shade and continued ferrying us across. His was a difficult task since the current moved against us as if it were alive and intent on stopping us. Like the Mississippi curls out from its icy heart in Minnesota, then gorges itself on the rainfall of an entire continent and swallows whole villages built too near its banks, so the River Bane moved as if it enjoyed consuming the shades condemned to its wake. Still, I was almost happy, indeed too happy, to be onboard the same craft with Mark Twain and Ernest Hemingway I nearly forgot where I was for a moment. I stared at them both in awe, until Hem finally broke the silence.

"Evan, look into the river here and tell me what you see."

I looked into the river for a long while, staring in horror at the shades within the current. I saw the shades of men I admired, comedians and actors whose routines mocked God for his rule and religious people for their folly. I stared deeper into the eddies made by shades chained to the riverbed, but then I saw her—I saw Evelyn, or some shade *like* Evelyn, for her form was brighter even in Hell, an angel of light immured in a realm of death—but what was she doing here? I jumped backward to get away, knocking over Twain's lantern in the process. Our pilot howled with laughter.

"Must have seen something good!" Twain said, fixing his lantern. "What'd you think? Recognize someone down there?"

"I saw Evelyn! Ernest, I saw my sister, my sweet kid sister, chained to the riverbed! What is she doing here?"

"Please stop the boat," Ernest asked Mark Twain, who stopped the best he could given the current. "Evan, what did she look like?"

"Like her old self, before cancer but brighter, and not like the other shades."

"Evan, I don't see any girls at all in the River Bane. You said she was twelve when she died?"

"Yes, that's right."

"I don't see anyone who looks like a twelve-year old girl in the river, Evan, and no shade any 'brighter' than the others."

"But what did I see then? I know I saw *something*."

"A trick, maybe. I told you the demons didn't want you to get out of here, and I wouldn't trust everything you see down here."

"Now if I may get us moving again," Twain said, "and ask you what happened to your sister, this sister you say you saw down there?"

"My sister Evelyn. She got cancer right as I started high school, and she died the day before I graduated, although I can't remember much of senior year, drunk as I was for almost all of it."

"Now Evan, I am sorry for your loss. I may be a boatman, a ruffian, and now a shade, but I still got some semblance of proper principles. I lost a child too, a sweet baby boy, and my only consolation in his passing was the fact he didn't suffer anymore or any longer than he did—unlike me or you and your younger sister down here (or wherever she may be). Thus I better understand where you are coming from now, my boy.

"This realm contains the shades likewise crushed by that suffering, shades condemned for taking the Lord's name in vain. A man like Job might have kept the faith he had despite what happened to him, but these shades never had the faith Job possessed, and frankly, I can't blame 'em. Terrible things of one kind or another befell them, and they cursed God because of them. Then they died, and now they're here.

"Now ya see," Twain said, continuing to ferry us across, "at the bottom, you got the shades who cursed God out o' sadness an' melancholy. The shades nearer t' the surface, meanwhile, mocked God from anger, pride, malice, and all the like. Enraged they were by the very thought of your God's frankly-sacredly-ridiculous name, they spent every breath they had to render it in vain. And even in Hell, they're still cursing God up above because the God they hoped did not exist, sadly enough, turned out to be our *Judge*."

Twain pushed back on his pole. He remained the expert riverboat pilot even in death, steering around fiery whirlpools and islands seemingly made of shades. When the shore came into sight, Twain dropped a knotted rope into the water to gauge the depth.[9] Twain let the current carry us downriver while he pulled up the cord and counted the knots.

"There we are," Twain said after a long pause, then pointed to an inlet flowing into the River Bane. "I'll let ye out there—the current should be deep enough, and the banks firm enough, to handle someone still alive like you, Evan.

"Now, not that I ever done this," Twain began, "but once you get off, walk along the riverbanks until you reach the Falls of Contempt. There you'll find a pool fed by a waterfall of fire and brimstone and a tall gorge encircling the pool. There's a path cut into the gorge that'll take you safely in and around and through the Falls of Contempt.

"More important, that path leads to a tunnel, and that path'll be safer than walking out in the open," Twain motioned overhead to demons circling in the vault of Hell. "The fiends built a fortress over the falls and at times, they go after shades who might merit some specialized attention. Take the path, head for the falls, and go down the tunnel running under the fortress, and it'll put you out and into the next realm, that I promise you, fellars. You just take care the demons don't see you since you don't know what they'll do if they catch you."

"Thank you, Mr. Twain," I said.

"It was nothing," Twain cocked another eyebrow in the dying lamplight. "Indeed, it was a pleasure ferrying the likes of you since, after all, Hell's the only place a man's intellect is ever *valued*.[10] It might be too late for regrets and wish-dids and what-nots, but I'da come here for company like you—although to be sure, you haven't come *here* yet, not *yet* at least, Evan.

"And I wouldn't mind knowing, if only for my curiosity, why'd you kill yourself, if ye don't mind me asking? Was it your sister's death, or something worse?"

"I realized how evil I had become," I answered.

"And how'd you come to understand *that*?"

"There were a few things that pushed me over the edge, but one that happened a few days before I killed myself was this:

there's a man who works at our school cafeteria, a dishwasher named Clifford, who has special needs. At least, my friends and I think he has special needs because he makes these announcements in the cafeteria, standing on top of a milk carton, wishing everyone good luck with their day, that make it obvious something is amiss with him.

"Well, my friends and I make fun of him every time we eat in the cafeteria, but last week I took it too far: I wrote, in ketchup, on a dish, for Clifford to wash back in the scullery, the words, U R STUPID. Clifford saw that and came running out of the kitchen, asking who would do such a thing and that he is in fact *not* stupid. His response haunts me.

"And why did I do such a thing? Why did I write such a mean and nasty thing to someone who is as low down on the totem pole as you can get? I did it because Clifford is happy while I hate myself, and so I tore him down for the joy that comes with ruining someone who is *happy*, *happy* despite his handicap, happy even if he doesn't have gifts the world values, happy in all the ways *I was miserable*. I wounded him, insulted him, for the pleasure that comes from doing something wrong for no other reason than it made *me* laugh."

"Well, I scarcely know what *ketchup* is, after all," Twain said, "but if you struck down another man with such slander for no reason at all and if you felt such guilt you'd kill yourself, there is much more, and much worse, beneath the surface of that particular deed in that there heart of yours. I certainly saw that kind of malice time and time again during my own time on earth."

"What do you mean?" I asked, hoping I could keep one of the best writers of American literature talking.

"Oh Evan, the whole system of morals was irretrievably overturned in the years I was alive," Twain said, grabbing his lantern and leaning in closer to me. "Slavery, and the desire to rationalize it, to justify it, to keep it going and keep certain people on top, it turned the whole world upside down.

"Then things only worsened with th' Jim Crow laws. Those laws kept blacks as close to slaves as their former masters could get 'em. Across slavery and segregation, and I saw both up close and personal, well, anyone who had owned a slave, or kept some sharecropper in a state akin to slavery, or just hated blacks and wanted to keep 'em down to make 'emselves feel good—perhaps a feeling not unlike what you describe—those folks made good things appear evil and evil things appear not so bad at all.[11]

"Men of my day indeed committed acts of such vehement violence, all of it under the cover of the darkest night and the whitest robes: burnings, lootings, shootings, lynchings of poor black folk because they stepped outside of some godforsaken line. They did everything they could to keep blacks down as low as possible, even used the Bible to justify it all.

"That was in part why I could never repent. In my day, I saw around me shysters and slavedrivers pretending to do God's work and promoting that book o' his, for it was indeed the slavedrivers, the hypocrites, and the fools who were the *most* vociferous supporters of the Lord I ever knew. So I couldn't, I wouldn't trust in anything they were saying or put any stock in the book they claimed God had written. How could I ever dare do so?

"So *o'course* any free-thinking man *like me* could easily assume, God was in the dock for all the problems I saw in the world, problems he wasn't fixing, evil he wasn't doing anything about. If God was all-powerful, why *couldn't* he do anything? If he was all-good, why *wouldn't* he do *something*, anything?

"Just like my infant boy died not less than a year old, and I buried him in that awful little coffin, and your sister there, Evan—Bible's full of stories of God healing the sick and giving sight to the blind. Couldn't God have done something about them both? Would it have been so hard getting my sweet boy walking and talking and enjoying life with his dad, or your sister through whatever hardships God just dropped on her? If he could do it, why didn't he do it? Why won't God stop all this evil?"

Twain ushered us off his raft, still holding his lantern. He spat on a shade and leaned in even closer to me, his lantern outlining the dark furrows on his face, his shock of scraggly, ashen-gray hair, and the smoldering black coals that remained of his eyes.

"And if God don't care about that evil," the shade of Mark Twain continued, his voice barely audible above the din of the Bane, "why should he care how I live my life? What's it to him if I live my life unto myself and enjoy a cigar every now and then? The conundrum was enough to drive a man like me to hell which, in part, it did—though o'course, maybe, I'd found the perfect excuse *not* to give my life to him.

"You see, I always had too much of ol' Huck in me. I know that now, for as soon as I was grown, I was cutting into trouble and lighting out for the territory,[12] just like my boy Huckleberry.

"For I made the same the choice I gave to Huck: I'd rather go to Hell than float along the current of a corrupt and callous culture, not as bad as this here river but close, too close, and the likes of such a culture puts *shackles* on people, both real and metaphorical. It's hard not to reject God and everything he made or does in favor of the freedom that comes from being your own damned self, and I didn't see much point then in giving up my freedoms for so little in return as a hard seat in church, a set of rules, and one *long* book.[13]

"Course I know *now* God exists, so maybe there's more to knowing God than that and I had it wrong. That's fine, I'll take it—but you, you Evan, you got a chance I don't, maybe never did, and thus I *hope* you'll figure out what it means to repent and you do it. But before you do, you make sure you figure out what's *really* going on. For if all morality was overturned in my day to support lynching and slavery, there's something deeper going on, something worse, something making *everyone* so weak, immoral, and crazy.[14]

CHAPTER VIII

THE FALLS OF CONTEMPT

With that, Mark Twain bowed his head and trudged back to his skiff. He leaned on his pole and slowly pushed his craft back into the current. The river caught hold of it while the shade of Mark Twain slowly merged with the flames and fumes of the River Bane, lantern fading into the darkness. Then he was gone.

"Was he lying to me?" I asked, remembering Ernest's warning.

"Mark Twain would never lie," Hem answered, indignant. "We're about to find out though."

Ernest motioned for me to follow him, and we walked beside the River Bane. As we walked, I noticed large rocks and boulders piercing the surface of the river, rocks which would have broken our raft to pieces. We came to the fall line of the River Bane, the furthest point we could have traveled had Twain been strong enough to ferry us against the current. Then Ernest pointed up ahead, past the rocks, where the riverbanks rose into what Twain called the Falls of Contempt.

The gorge rose upward and curved like the horns of a bull around a massive, shade-infested pool. The gorge was tall and steep, its sides like the slopes of Georgia's Lookout Mountain hanging over this veritable river of death. The slopes came together in a fiery waterfall at its center from which fire and brimstone cascaded into the pool below. A fortress stood over the gorge, its two guard towers flanking the Falls of Contempt and with its signal fire for eyes and fiery waterfall for a mouth, the fortress looked like the very jaws of Hell vomiting out the contents of its dungeon-like innards. The only way through was a set of stairs cut into the side of the gorge.

"You go first," Ernest told me, "because if you fall, I can try and catch you. Just take one step at a time, Evan."

I walked on ahead, expecting to find the stairs slick with sulfur or poison from the River Bane. Instead, the stairs were covered in a bird-lime-like substance that made them sticky—sticky enough I had to pull my feet from the stairs with each step. That effort, combined with the narrowness of the stairs, made it more likely I might fall into the burning pool below. But any time I came too close, Ernest grabbed me and help me back upon the path, as if his shade was given substance enough the moment I needed him.

Still, we were safer here than on top of the gorge or out in the open. I could see demons standing guard over the firefall, their signal fires occasionally obscured by fiends pacing the walls. Other demons flew in the vault overhead on the lookout for escape attempts—not that any shades could escape from Hell. But perhaps the demons needed something to do, someone to hunt.

Nor were Ernest and I alone on the path. Whenever I leaned against the rock for support, I could feel the sides of the gorge moving behind me, trying to push me off the edge. If I looked over my shoulder, I saw only the barest outlines of a shade moving within the walls, writhing, wracked with guilt, crushed by the falls of Hell. The shades looked as if they composed the rocks even while they struggled to bear the weight of Hell upon their shoulders.

"The shades behind you," Ernest explained, "the ones condemned to the Falls of Contempt are punished here for dishonoring the Sabbath: the very rocks contain the shades who looked to their own pleasures and their own interests every Sunday, all while ignoring the God who made them.[1]

"If man should trust in God and thereby rest on the Sabbath, these shades trusted in their own works, living as if their works could make them happy or, even less likely, fill God with pleasure, so now the falls of Hell are a burden they bear forever."

I nodded but didn't respond. All around me the shades were whispering or uttering blasphemies or pleading with me to help them escape. I heard their sad, hopeless cries until some shade or demon who could move within the rock dragged them deeper down within it. Others lamented how they spent their last years engaged in idle ways: scrolling, trolling, posting, fronting, streaming, shopping, snatching trinkets and trifles, boating and hunting, golfing and fishing, all the while giving themselves to their work or their leisure. None of those condemned within the rock had made any plans to meet their Maker, and now all they could do was curse the burdens placed upon them by their Creator.[2] If I hadn't done anything at all—no blackouts, no mindless destruction, nothing—but lived a good life without repenting, this is where I would be.

Finally, we arrived at the falls, the path ending six, seven feet, maybe more from the landing behind the firefall, and I saw I'd have to jump. I looked to Hem, who shouted, "You can make it, kid."

I walked to the edge and foolishly looked down, seeing the shades at the bottom of a long, lonely drop. Then I leapt from the last step—not a great leap, but a leap in the dark on earth I never would have tried.

And I barely made it onto the lime-lined ledge. My legs swung dangerously in the air, trying to find some footing in the rock. Ernest jumped over me and landed on his feet, then dragged me up onto the landing. I got to my knees, coughing and struggling to catch my breath, my deep breaths filling my lungs with oxidized sulfur smothering my soul in Hell's matchless flame. Perhaps this reaction went on inside the shades I've seen in Hell, for the fire did not weaken, abate, or dissipate. But I was getting used to the burn.

I walked around the landing, waiting for the flames to smolder. Just like Twain told us, there was a narrow tunnel behind the firefall leading under the fortress of the demons. Growing on the canyon walls, I found what looked like strange plants—thick, accursed brambles or the exposed roots of the ruined trees I've seen elsewhere in Hell. But then I realized the layers of briers covering the gorge were really the exposed legs of shades, each leg twisted around another and covered in ash and thorns. The rest of their bodies were immersed in the black rock, hidden from view.

"What is this?" I asked, walking over to Hem standing near the edge. "What sin did they commit on earth, that they would be exposed like this in Hell?"

"These shades dishonored their father and mother," Ernest instructed me, brushing ash off his safari jacket, "and as they exalted themselves in life, so they are humiliated now in death, bound within the kinds of rocks that would have been thrown at them had they lived in the days of Moses."[3]

"But these legs look old enough to be a parent, not some unruly teenager like me," I said, pointing to the wall of wrinkly, writhing limbs.

"God gave the commandment not just to the young, but to adults to care for parents in their old age. Those legs you see belong to some soul who cared about themselves so much they refused to care for the ones who raised them—but if they were anything like my parents, I don't blame them."

Ernest turned away at the thought of his life on earth. He leaned over the edge and spat into the darkness, resting on bended knee like he were taking a break on safari. But then, looking down from this height, Ernest's face dropped like a stone. I could tell he saw something moving against the shadows and the spray of the firefall. I dared to look over the edge too, and saw only the barest trace of a shade or something worse, a little more than a wraith yet still less than the darkness, displacing flakes of fire and climbing straight up against the rocks, undeterred by Hell's continual pestilence. Something was following us.

"It's time we left the Falls," Ernest said, standing up quickly. "The fiends may have sent something after us, and it's never safe to stay too long in one place down here anyway. Nor can you ask these shades any questions, not when their faces are buried deep within the rock and right above a layer of unending fire.

"That tunnel should lead us right under the fortress," Ernest said, walking to the tunnel's black mouth and pointing to a flame at the tunnel's far end, the only light to guide us through the darkness. "No choice but to take it now, not when the alternative is to ask the demons for passage, and I'm not asking the galanos for anything ever again. Then, once we're out of the tunnel, we'll head straight for the Plains of Murder."

CHAPTER IX

THE PLAINS OF MURDER

Ernest and I followed that single, slender flame for miles while the spider-leg-like limbs of damnlight crept toward us, growing larger until we neared the end of the tunnel and finally, the Inferno with all its fumes and fury appeared before our eyes. I felt as if I stood on one of the hills overlooking Richmond, looking across the piedmont to the Blue Ridge Mountains just beyond the horizon—except the Crown of Satan dominated the skyline here, its peaks as black as everything else in Hell.

The tunnel ended at the top of a hill, and the hill sloped down to a wide plain sown with wheat, corn, or some other staple grain. Meanwhile, the River Bane, like the River James up above, wound through the fields like a serpent and divided the plains into two immense halves. Looming in the distance was Kilijiarchago, the Crown of Satan, whose slopes began as soon as the plains ended. After surveying the damnscape, I turned to my guide and asked, "What's waiting for us?"

"The Plains of Murder, called *Ragaltim* by the fiends, a realm ruled over by Apollyon, prince of destruction,[1] arch-galano—one of Hell's Big Five—a demon I would love to bring down, if only we had the guns big enough to do it."

"Big Five?" I asked.

"I thought you read my books?" Hem harrumphed, then stroked his beard. "Africa has its five big game animals—lions, leopards, elephants, rhinos, buffalos—and Hell has its own Big Five atop the abyssmalarchy: Apollyon, Mephistopheles, Beelzebub, Belial, and Lucifer."

"Those demons are real?[2] I've heard of them from books I've read in high school, but will I have to speak with them, like I have to speak with the shades?"

"If you knew everything," Hem replied in earnest, "what God planned for you on your journey, you might well give up and yield to wherever in Hell you happened to be. Try and take it one step at a time, Evan."

"I'll try, Ernest," I said, nodding, gulping, trying to look tough. "What's the plan now?"

"Apollyon and his demons are working the fields somewhere on the other side of Kilijiarchago," Ernest answered, pointing to the black peaks ahead. "There, in the fields below, the demons harvest the dead, continually cutting down the shades condemned to Ragaltim. The fiends would cut us down, too, but with some luck, we can make it through the killing fields before the galanos come back again—if we run fast enough. Are you ready, Evan?"

I had hardly nodded *yes* when Hem took off down the hill. The demons overhead screeched and wheeled on their wings to follow us, being tasked, perhaps, with trailing us as we wound our way through Hell. Nevertheless, we ran until we reached the edge of the plain and ducked between the furrows raised by Apollyon's minions, for whatever grew in the well-tilled fields of Hell was tall enough to shield us from the fiends. Still, the demons circled overhead like sharks around their prey.

But this was no cornfield. In place of some staple grain grew the shades of violent men, condemned for committing cold, calculated, ruthless, unrepentant murder. They stood fixed in the fields, arranged in thick, serried rows stretching ahead until the rows were swallowed by the base of the Crown. Growing amongst the human wreckage, the shades of violent men continually cast their eyes back over their shoulders for fear the demons were coming for them again. And the shades never ceased to gnash their teeth.

"What is going on here?" I whispered.

"Just or unjust, this is our punishment," answered a feminine shade from behind me, clad all in black, her hair cut in a bob. "Isn't it obvious, boy?"

I looked to Hem, who nodded and motioned for me to speak with this shade, culled from all those condemned to Hell to tell me what I needed to know about God's plans, man's pride, and Satan's wiles.

"But what does your punishment mean? Why are you here, like this?"

"We took life on earth," answered the shade, her feet firmly fixed in the furrow, eyes firmly fixed on me. "So here, the demons take what little remains of us."

"But it looks like a field of wheat, like the farm my grandpa Esco worked as a child back in Sicilia, in the old country, or the farm in the Shenandoah Valley that my mom's family settled after the Revolution."

"Oh my, an immigrant," the shade replied, interest piqued. "An Italian, truly? And marrying into a line that stretches back to the founding of my country—English, though, surely?"

"I guess so, but what does that have to do with you? Why do you care? And what have you done?"

"Indeed, I suppose it means nothing. But rarely does meaningful, reliable intelligence come to us from the world above.

"But as for me, do not worry about my name, for it rouses too much contention, and you could never look at my deeds with right judgment or right mind once you know it."

"What happened to you then?" I asked, stung by some sirocco-like blast sweeping through the plains, rustling the shades along the rows. "Why are you here?"

"I am condemned for answering Job's prayer, for those who could not utter it, the poor souls who did not know Job's lot was their own."

"The prayer of Job? What did he pray for?"

"To never have been born so he might avoid the days of suffering and misery allotted to him. I indeed answered this plea on behalf of the masses up above, for they suffered as Job did and worse. For them, the earth is indeed a kind of Hell: they have too little food, too much cold, too small a reprieve from life's manifold hardships. I would contend I never took life but freed it, freed it from a life of toil, turmoil, and tumult to which God would condemn the poor little thing.

"Such was my life's work. The work began with thought, thoughts racing through my mind any time I was up with a sick child: 'My poor babe, love it though I may, and miss it though I would, this child and any other like it should never endure such pains. This lot need not have fallen on the poor thing, if only I had known the sad days awaiting it.'

"And Job could not prevent his birth. Nor could we go back and forestall our own once we knew the world's cruel ways—but we could save others from being born to a life where surely they would, one day, lament their own sad existence. Such thoughts raced and raced while I worked and spoke and taught and founded clinics and institutions and professions that would answer Job's prayer long after I was gone. Who would not want to escape such a miserable lot? Or receive some help in doing so?"

People said this about Evelyn, I thought to myself. *She would not feel any more pain if she died, and if there was anything we could do to ease her suffering . . .*

"And that choice, indeed, could be painless, harmless if done under the right conditions. That way, the poor thing might feel nothing but the sweet and tender bundling into a void where there is no suffering, no hardship, no lack, no want, only darkness and nothing more—and is that so bad a thing?

"And for those who live, the greater share of everything else. The earth would groan a little less for one less pair of feet striding upon it, the father toil a little less for bread to cast upon the waters of his household, the mother fewer burdens to bear. Such burdens should not be overlooked, for if neither father nor mother can raise the child, the duty, indeed the privilege, of parentage falls to the magistrate, and the magistrate, that enlightened representative of the state, must act for the benefit of society as a whole and never for the privileged few."

"So in you let a little air . . ." Hem whispered to himself.[3]

"I did what was needed," the shade replied. "For indeed, few individuals are as privileged as the one with no means to provide for itself, for they keep the living from ascending to a lot higher than the one God assigns to a wretched man or a harried woman. This I realized walking amidst the strikes and rallies and sit-ins in Boston and New York and Detroit, anywhere the workers pressed for their just rights. Such were my efforts to bring about some meaningful change that might alleviate the plight of the workers up above—at least, before I realized what really held us back and precluded our success: our children.

"Indeed, the utopia we wanted was crowded out by the needs of our babes. The workers could not endure the sacrifices needed to achieve our aims, not if they also had to sacrifice for hungry mouths at home. Neither group could be fully satisfied without the needs of one being snuffed out, and one group could be snuffed out with hardly any pain or duress. And in so doing, we could realize our ambition—to enjoy the fruits of our labor and then some, to have some semblance of the life the idle rich withheld from us—if we only had the power to choose who would enter the ranks of the living. If we, not God, had this power, we might one day be *free*."

The feeding of the masses, the refrain of the walrus-like shade from the Shores of Gluttony came back to me, *the joys of the Hall in feeding them, and the lack of faith that God would feed anyone at all . . . but what was the Hall? Is the Hall the magistrate, the state, now tasked with feeding everyone who has lost faith in God to take care of them? And to choose who gets fed?*

"Pay attention, boy," the shade snapped at me, recognizing I stopped listening. "For men like you, our husbands, the workers—they are fools. They never saw the connection *I* saw between our broods and our failures; instead, they worked by day, drank their wages by night, and multiplied our burdens by their lust. Nor did they bear the twin-fold curse God laid upon Eve: cursed with Adam's toil, for Adam's lot would inevitably be Eve's also, and cursed in childbearing, a curse that goes as long as the child lives. But one single moment could change it all, our lives all the better should they avoid a world unfit to support them anyway.

"One choice could free men, women, and children all alike from their pains, if only we had the tools and will to deal with life unworthy to be named: so now, having fulfilled my grand ambition, I suffer gladly my endless, just perdition."

CHAPTER X

THE HARVEST OF DEATH

"But go on," the shade commanded, "and speak to the damned, listen to their stories, and learn why they made *their* choice."

The shade raised her arms as if she were offering an incantation. Then the other shades along the rows ceased to gnaw the air and turned to me at once. Ernest motioned for me to follow him down the furrow while the shades of ruthless men clawed at me and gnashed whatever remained of their teeth. They all looked too much like me, teenagers dressed in jeans and flannel, angst-ridden, easily-vexed, as if we all grew up together and were shaped by the same influences, albeit in the disparate states of America. Then, all these loathsome words they began to speak.

"Life on earth," one shade hissed, ". . . an infinite, miserable sadness . . ."

"So we shoot up our school . . ." the shade beside him crowed, ". . . and started our own movement . . ."

"I carried my hurt for years," another shade shrieked triumphantly, ". . . so I went ballistic . . . brought the misery of it all onto everyone else . . ."

"I got more than anyone else *here though* . . ." another wraith gloated, his empty voice reverberating down the rows.

"You wish . . ." another shade hissed in reply. "My spree was longer, better planned, better *executed*."

That boast spurred the other shades along murderers' row to cry out even louder. They crowed their evil deeds on earth as if they wanted more, and not less, credit for what they did before they killed themselves, fighting each other as to who inflicted more hurt, more pain, more anguish in the last few hours or moments they spent in the world above. Then they began calling out numbers.

"58 . . ."

"49 . . ."

"32 . . ."

"27 . . ." the numbers trailed behind me, falling like ash.

"26 . . ."

"23 . . ."

"22 . . ."

"21 . . ."

"13 . . ."

I killed myself in part because I was terrified of what I was capable of. I saw I was liable to snap and lash out at a godless universe and take down whoever happened to be too close to me. But these shades committed such unbounded evil in the world above and only then did they either kill themselves or will themselves be killed. The grief for those left alive, left to make sense of it all, was nearly limitless, and I chose to die rather than risk getting myself so far gone I might ever do something like that. I've seen in myself the same pit of evil from which such evil thoughts arise and drive evil men onto their evil deeds. But was it any consolation they were here in Hell, and that the universe is *not* godless?

And as we walked down murderers' row, I noticed how the clothing the shades wore began to change. The jeans and flannel, trench coats and boots, changed to coarse, loose-fitting linen shirts, white robes, or even fine black suits. When these shades began to speak, they described different crimes, different victims, and different means but always the same motivation as that of the other shades within this realm: no regard for neighbor, no fear of God, no thought of judgment.

"Can't tell you how many blacks I lynched . . ." one shade announced. " . . . or even why I did it . . ."

"I bombed a church . . ." another shade boasted while behind him another hissed, "and me several more . . ."

"I beat some black boy to death . . ." a long, lonely voice trailed out from somewhere along the rows, ". . . looked at my girl funny . . ."

"Ah, the time I spent whipping 'em all . . ." more shrill voices called out, ". . . and the joy I got in doing it . . ."

"But don't think you're better than us," warned one shade, his red eyes as piercing as firebrands. "I can tell you have the same fire raging in *you*."

At once this shade, who seemed to be their leader, shoved me back across the rows. I fell into the embrace of violent men who bellowed in approval and gnashed their teeth. They pulled on my outstretched limbs and held me upright, digging their claw-like hands into my body and roaring, "We got 'em now!" Ernest tried to break their grip but the shades seized my guide and held him back while Hem struggled to break free. Then their leader, whoever he was, his long, white hair so dry and cracked it looked like the splinters of a broken bone, proceeded thus to speak.

"Don't let this boy leave her' alive!" he bellowed, his broad, heavy chin supporting a mouth that roared like a furnace. "For he is one of us, *I know it*—I can see it in 'em, the hatred and the loathing and the contempt for a world that treats him so. Stick around, boy, and you might learn something!"

"Let go of me!" I cried, struggling to break their grip.

"Oh boy, you do have that fire in your belly, don't you?" the shade roared again. "Why, you got to live with that fire, harness it, make it do your bidding! If you're wronged, you don't forgive, you don't forget, you only *feed, feed* the fire, *feed* the beast and make it stronger. That's the only way to live, boy!"

"Who are you?" I cried. "Let go of me!"

"Only someone who did what was needed," the shade crowed, his long white hair sparking like embers with every word. "I fired the first shots on Fort Sumter, shots that began the War of Northern Aggression and would have freed the South if *only* we had more men *like me* resolved to do whatever was needed.

"Even when defeated, kowtowed, humiliated at Appomattox, subjugated beneath that terrible Yankee yoke, I draped myself in the stars and bars and put a bullet in my own head, so that I would never share my bread with blacks and never endure the rule of hateful Yankee overlords!"[1]

"Boss," bellowed another shade. "The demons, they almost here!"

Ernest tried to free me, but the wraiths kept him back. Nor could I free myself from the grip of these murderous shades tearing at my hair and my limbs. I started to lose both hope and consciousness: no wonder Mark Twain became so skeptical and cynical,[2] seeing the horrors of slavery and the irrational violence of lynch mobs. And no matter what I might think of them, I actually deserve to be here with them as much as I deserve to be anywhere else in Hell. How was what I did to Clifford, writing in ketchup that he was stupid, striking him down because he was happy and I was not—how were my deeds any different in spirit from the crimes of these wraiths? What is in a man that makes him so cruel, that he would let his sin wield him so and be its tool?[3]

My reminiscing was cut short by a troop of demons coming over the amber waves of pain. They worked a long line stretching from one end of the plain to the other while they reaped the shades of violent men. The demons had the wings and the appearance of giant locusts outfitted for war: their jaws were filled with lion's teeth, each tooth larger than my head, their bodies covered in gray scales harder than plates of iron, and their hands gripped massive scythes they swung in deadly unison.[4] The roar of their wings rolled across the plains like a vast multitude heading into battle.

Then all I saw was one enormous demon standing in front of me, scythe raised, and scorpion-like tail poised to destroy everything in its path. The shades threw up their arms, hoping to forestall the unstoppable blade from slicing them in half again. I breathed in deeply and resigned myself to my fate, for I deserved to die for my sins, sins differing in degree but not in kind. The fiend held that long, tortured scythe in the air just long enough for me to see my reflection in its blade. I was sure I was going to die right then and there, where I belonged.

Then finally Ernest reached me. My guide broke the grip of the fire-eaters and threw me to the ground so I barely missed the scythe tearing through the rows of wraiths. One swift, unending stroke spilt them all in two and scattered their limbs across the plains. The demons never stopped for me, so I had to duck and roll this way and that to avoid their massive hooves pounding across the murderous plains. Then more lines of demons came up behind them, working the killing fields with shovels and spades, heaping the human wreckage into ridges, and scattering the mutilated limbs across the ground like seed. Then the ground cried out in the tumult of their judgment, screams worsening as the shades took root in the Plains of Murder. Finally, the last line of fiends disappeared.

I hoped the danger might be over. But when I opened my eyes, I saw another demon standing over me. In appearance, the great demon looked like a locust clad in chainmail and plates of armor, except the armor was his skin, skin hardened over centuries of residing in Hell. Horns twisted upward like great columns, and between those horns hovered a scorpion-like tail dripping with blood or something like it. Then the huge galano drove two huge, spiked hooves into the ground and pulled me up by the scruff of my neck. The demon could only be Apollyon, prince of Hell, a demon near the top of the abyssmalarchy, Hell's dreadful caste system.

The fiend smiled and stretched his wings wide enough to block the reflection of the Lake of Fire. Now, with the only light coming from the fire in Apollyon's eyes or reflecting off his scales, which are his pride,[5] Apollyon moved to question me, so any faith I had would now be tried.

CHAPTER XI

A DUEL WITH A DEMON

"Evan Esco," Apollyon bellowed, his voice tearing into me as the wind might grind down the side of a mountain. "Evan, after all the years we've spent in serving you, responding to your cries for help, why would you attempt to quit our service?"

"I've hated myself for so long, and I can't live anymore, not like this."

"Yet you would abandon the side of Lucifer, your rightful lord, after all he has done for you?"

"But I can't keep going like this. The drinking and the drugs and the humiliating myself day after day when everything I've ever done to get out of my depression has made my life so much worse."

"And you think God would help you?" asked the demon.

"I can only hope so, even though I haven't done anything to deserve it."

"No indeed, you have not," Apollyon snarled, his jaw unhinging like that of a shark's. "Nor did God help your little sister, who deserved God's help far more than you. Yet, God did nothing for her either. Still, you think God would *save* you, help you, deliver you from this place and from what misery you say you experienced on earth?"

"I know I do not deserve any mercy from God," I answered, struggling to breathe, my hand scraping over the page I ripped from the Bible. "But if God did not hear my sad, lonely prayer—my sad attempts at repenting—wouldn't I be dead already and burning in Hell by now?"

"God is not as quick to hear as we demons are. Nor can you mend your life by turning to God, but my gracious prince, Lucifer, Our Father Herein, would give you the life you desire and all the happiness you crave, *for Lucifer would make you strong*, and it is strength you need to be happy."

"He'd make me happy?" My cigar-wound ached, and I moved my hand away from the page I ripped from the Bible, thinking of the funeral and that awful little coffin.

"Of course he would. Lucifer would preserve the one gift, the one precious gift you would lose if you turned to God instead of us."

"What is that?"

"Your freedom, Evan. Freedom you have possessed but have never truly used, freedom that comes the moment you seize the rightful rule over your life from a God who would only hold you back."

"I can't handle that freedom. I've tried so many times to change, and I've only gotten worse, like there's some evil thing inside me making me do things that leave me more miserable and more ashamed. And whatever this thing *is*, this beast, it grows stronger by ruining me."

"A problem common to all mankind. Let me explain, dear boy, the way the world works and the way you should work within it."

Apollyon held his massive hands aloft, almost like a theater, and from his claws threads of flame appeared. The flames formed a puppet and its strings moved alongside the counsel Apollyon now gave to me, his talons raising and lowering to make the puppet move.

"This beast does indeed live inside your heart. You are, and all humanity is, at heart, a beast, yet you, and other humans, pretend you are something more, and so your pain arises because you struggle against your very nature instead of embracing what you really are.[1] If human beings are no more than animals, mere beasts who live to satisfy their needs for sex or food or ruling over weaker creatures, then humans may be happy should they indulge in such desires whenever the opportunity arises.[2] You are unhappy not because of what you have done but because you have not accepted what you are and lived accordingly. Ought you not be true to yourself?

"Evan, cease this pointless struggle and return to us," Apollyon continued, the fiery puppet kneeling. "If you retract your claims at repentance, you may take hold of all the choice gifts, pleasures, and freedoms we can give you. In contrast, submission to God is only the first step in a life of idle servitude, for humans are but a speck to God, a speck so easily ignored your life would be that of a slave just toiling to catch his attention. Your hope lies not in yielding to God, but in seizing power from him. That way, you may live however you wish and take everything you want—and is not that the life you really want?"

Apollyon's voice grew lower and deeper, like a rift forming at the earth's foundations, or the low rumble preceding an earthquake. He expected me to kneel.

"Turn to us and let us serve you, for you cannot trust God to give you the things you need, not when he has so far ignored your every plea. Yet the yoke of Lucifer is both light and easy in our kingdom, so curse God and claim your freedom."[3]

"Don't trust him, Evan," my guide reminded me, standing by my side. "If he's anything like his father Satan, then he's a liar and a very good liar at that. This is the matador coming out, leading you on with the cape work, smooth and pure, natural."[4]

"I don't believe you, Apollyon," I answered, still holding my hand above my heart, feeling whatever page I ripped from the Bible. "I may know very little of God's ways, but I don't think God is anything like you say."

"A pity," Apollyon snarled and lifted his scythe. "We had such high hopes for you, but if you will not accept our help in life, you will feel our wrath in death."

I had no time to catch my breath or collect my wits before Apollyon plunged his scythe into me. The demon aimed for my heart and tried to plant the blade deep inside me but only struck the page I tore from the Bible. The blow knocked me backward, and it should have cut me in half, but something about the page made the cruel steel of Apollyon's scythe shatter into a thousand pieces as soon as it made contact with it. All I felt was the page press that much harder against my heart.

The loss of his scythe enraged Apollyon. Red eyes blazing, he instinctively unfurled his wings in a fit of mindless rage. The demon lunged for me with his huge, clawed hands, and I scrambled over the remains of violent men, trying to get to my feet but unable to keep my balance. I fell over and over again until Ernest, who could stand on top of the shades with greater ease, pulled me to my feet. He dragged me over and across and in between the furrows to escape Apollyon, making for the tree line at the far end of the Plains of Murder.

Apollyon bounded after us, sweeping whole ridges of shades with his massive tail. He shouted for the demons to cease their reaping and stop us while the scattered limbs of violent men tried to grab me as we ran over them. Finally, we reached the edge of the netherfields and into a dark, tangled forest where Apollyon seemingly could not or would not pursue us any further. Belting curses and mortal epithets,[5] the demon pounded the ground with his fists and then leapt into the skies. We hid at the tree line and watched him disappear, safe for now amidst the brambles and the thorns and the darkness of whatever grim new reality we just entered.

CHAPTER XII

THE FOREST OF THE SUICIDES

"Where are we now?" I asked, out of breath, looking around the godforsaken forest providing us with some refuge from Apollyon.

"My home," the old shade said, shaking his head. "The Forest of the Suicides, which the demons call *Erium*, a word in fiendspeech that means only 'the Void.'[1] Erium contains the shades who killed themselves, shades whose souls are bound up in the very trees surrounding us, trunks as twisted and as cruel as was our last choice on earth, the choice to kill ourselves, Evan, and leave our families to deal with whatever bloody mess we made of our lives."

Ernest held out his hands as if he could still see the blood upon them. Then, with a look of regret swelling up within him like the shadow of a fish in the sea, Ernest buried his face in his hands, the whole of which he blew off with a shotgun. I had never seen Ernest look this depressed in photographs on earth or during our time in Hell, like he wasn't just mourning his own end but mine too. Evelyn would have been ashamed of me. Soon, they would find my body mangled and ruined inside of my 4Runner and could only guess my soul was lost to Hell—not that they believe in this place, but deep down they'd suspect that if I was anywhere at all, it would be here. But still, I have a chance to escape and spare my family from the grief, if I could only just repent. But how could I do that?

"And there are other shades wandering through these woods," Ernest said, collecting himself and continuing to describe his home. "They lived their lives with such abandon they may as well have killed themselves too. Now we're all damned together for taking death by the horns, condemned to woods as empty and dark as was the void we *hoped* we would enter once we died, a forest of trees bearing only poison for fruit and supporting throngs of demons in place of birds, demons whose teeth give us our only break from the suicidal thoughts we still have every moment we spend in Hell—we killed ourselves, after all, to escape the ruin we made of our lives, only to fly to a realm where pain never dies."

Ernest shook his head again and headed into the void. He walked slowly, deliberately, trying to avoid the thorns tightly binding each branch. These short, stumpy trees grew to a height barely above my head, like an olive grove across a mountainside, but their boughs created a canopy of gray leaves and limbs thick enough to veil the Lake of Fire burning overhead. Not even a single shaft of flame hit the forest floor. I relied on Hemingway to guide me through the woods, his pale shade lighting our path like we were on a night safari. The woods seemed empty, but I got the feeling we were being watched.

And Erium was deathly silent. The woods consumed both the shades within and the wails without the rest of Hell; even the poison collecting at the tips of each thorn fell to the forest floor without a sound. The fruit was poisonous, the leaves ashen, the darkness unlimited, but the silence of the wood was unbearable, for the silence reminded me of the empty void I hoped I would enter once I died. Here, I had no distractions to make me forget the guilt, grief, and loss permeating my every thought until I finally killed myself. In its own way, the silence was worse than the flames.

Hemingway led the way through the wood. Without him I could not see my hand in front of my face, let alone the long, sharp branches hardened to a point like the pit of a peach raking me whenever I came too close. I wondered if Ernest was taking me to his tree or the furrow his shade occupied in Hell until yesterday. Or the day before yesterday? How long have I been here? Or perhaps Ernest's trunk still stood there but split in two, like a bolt of lightning might cleave a tree in half.

I saw some trees like this. The trunks were rent down the middle, as if the shades had been split in two and cursed to bear the wrath and void of Erium two times over. Yet, some trees that should have had two trunks had but one missing, with one part on earth and the other down below, and at times, I was sure I saw what was missing growing in leaps and bounds and boughs appearing out of the grim air.

"What is happening to here?" I asked my guide.

"These trees are growing as we speak," Hem answered me in earnest, "albeit slowly, shades who thought God gave them the wrong names and bodies and life and everything else so they went beyond what God had given them, pursuing happiness apart from himself so now they're here. What could answer you is up on earth and since we cannot ask them any questions, it is best we keep moving through the woods."

But I couldn't move, trembling with fear, seeing myself bound in the trunks now twisted and torn in two. I've hated every part of me for so long—how awkward I am and how ugly I feel every waking moment—I would have sold my very soul to the devil to be popular, one of the cool kids who got everything they wanted, *a beast*. I've tried everything to feel happy or, at the very least. at peace with who I am, pursuing happiness in anything apart from this repentance the shades have spoken about. How sad and tragic it all is—but then Ernest kept motioning me forward, leading me along a hard, demon-beaten path through the woods and up the slopes of the Crown. Finally, he stopped at one tree as black as ash, with branches cruel and twisted from whatever soul it held within its grasp.

"Go on and tear off that branch in front of you," the old shade said, leaning against a tree, stroking his beard, anxious about something.

I did as Ernest asked and with both hands, broke off a large branch, carefully avoiding the thorns. Then I waited until I heard a voice oozing out from where I snapped the limb, a sound not unlike air escaping from a live branch set over an open flame. Then, from the bleeding sap, emerged the face of Kurt Cobain.[2]

I knew too well the story of this rock star from Seattle. Kurt Cobain lived a little before my time, but I and so many of my friends loved his music, music that spoke for a generation of kids like me who gave up on life before any of us even got a chance to do anything with our lives.[3] He died when I was in elementary school, long before I started listening to grunge and punk music, but his band Nirvana was still popular when I got to high school. His music played almost continuously in my head during the whole of Evelyn's chemo.

And Nirvana was popular in part because of Kurt's suicide at the age of twenty-seven. That was the age past which the so-called gods of rock-and-roll like Kurt Cobain and Jimi Hendrix and others do not live for manifold reasons. In high school, I loved Kurt Cobain because he wrote songs about the same doubts and depression I long suffered from, angry over the meaninglessness of life and the injustice of it all. And with his music, I could drown out what idiotic sense my parents tried to make of what was happening to our family. Evelyn hated Nirvana and everything like it, and she tried without success to get me to stop listening to it. But I didn't have too long to think, because once the face of my teenage idol was fully formed, he began to speak.

"And who are you?" the shade snarled.

"You're Kurt Cobain," I exclaimed, surprised. "I can't believe it."

"Oh my God, oh my God, you're Kurt Cobain! Kurt Cobain!" he parroted back in a shrill, high-pitched voice. "Can I have your autograph? My God, you are so pathetic. Do you not have any idea where you are? Who in this crazy Hell are you?"[4]

"His name is Evan," Ernest answered for me. "He is here to speak with the shades in Hell and ask them why they're here. He tried to kill himself just like you did."

"Is that so?" Cobain snarled again. "Did you kill yourself so you could come here and tell me you're my biggest fan? Or did you just look in a mirror and realize what a loser you are?"

"I've struggled with depression for a long time," I answered, fighting back some tears. "I've tried so hard and failed to get out of it but no matter what I do, I just seem to make my life worse, a lot worse. I couldn't take it anymore, so I killed myself."

"I hate to tell you," he sneered, his unkempt hair already starting to fade, "but you look alive. So it seems like you failed even in trying to kill yourself. Maybe the world would have been better off without you, just like the people I cared about I'm sure are better off without me. How *are* you still alive then? Oh no, did you make the rookie mistake of going across the street and not down the tracks?"

"I tried killing myself in a car accident," I said, "but I don't know what's happened to my body. I do know I deserve to be here, here in Hell and nowhere else, so I tried to repent before I died. I was scared to face God if he exists, which now I know he does."

"Sad story, really," Cobain said, "especially the part about God. None of us really counted on that part being true, did we? Who would have known? Not a lot of evidence up there if you ask me. But if you're done, go ahead and tear off another branch, if you want me to keep talking to you."

I did as he asked and broke off another poisoned limb. I let it fall to the ground, where it smoldered in the ash heap of the forest floor. The fire caught the tenuous light of a pair of eyes moving through the woods I thought were empty. Cobain closed his eyes and sighed with relief.

As Cobain collected himself, a new kind of shame arose in my mind. I listened to Nirvana because their songs nourished the same loathing I long reserved for myself, and now I felt ashamed I idolized someone who hated himself so much he wanted to die. That was actually the name of one of Nirvana's songs, the words for which I actually wrote on a pair of shoes, as if I was being cool by walking around in Cobain's suicidal tendencies.[5] No wonder then I ended up this way, but how many more kids are out there turning to things that bring no joy or solace or relief, only self-destruction, like the branch I tore off from Kurt Cobain's poisoned tree?

"Now kid, a question for you," Cobain sighed with relief, his shade returning to his ashen blue eyes. "Do people still listen to

Nirvana? Does anyone still buy my music or talk about what I accomplished in my life? Has anyone tried to make a movie about my life yet?"

"Documentaries, yes," I replied, trying to collect myself. "And I personally loved Nirvana in high school."

"Great, great kid," Cobain answered and breathed in deeply. "Now, what about people who *matter?* You know, smart people, people who understand music and not, well, you."

"People still compare grunge, your music," I answered, "with the music of the 1960s and among those bands, Nirvana is still considered the best, almost like the Beatles of the whole movement."

"Better than Pearl Jam?" Cobain asked as his shade was ebbing away. "And tear off another branch, a bigger one this time, will you?"

"Yea, bigger than Pearl Jam," I snapped off a larger limb. "They may be fading away now but because you killed yourself, you never had the chance to sell out or grow old. Instead, you burned out so even if people are sad, you're gone—you died when people still admired you. They remember you just like you were."

"Then it worked," Cobain smiled, looking more relieved than had I cut his tree in two. "People remember the genius I was when I was at the top, not the junkie screwing up his life more and more with each passing day."

"Now that's why I killed myself," I said. "I feel exactly like that, that I have hurt so many people already and as long as I am alive, my problems and my life will only get worse. So I killed myself."

"You have no idea how worse life gets," Cobain replied, his voice crackling like embers. "Once you've made it, there's nowhere to go but down, and down for me would have been too much for me to bear. I would've been forced to go back home to Aberdeen and get a nine-to-five job, stocking shelves or something else unworthy of my genius, so I blew my brains out instead.[6]

"Sometimes I wonder what would have happened if I was content to be a loser, a loser like you maybe, if I wasn't so driven to get really rich and really famous, or if I wasn't so scared that I'd have to go back to Aberdeen a failure and work the drive-thru or the lumberyard. Maybe then I wouldn't have ended up here. But whatever."

"I know I can't understand what you went through, but would you tell me how you died?" I asked, snapping off another limb in hopes he would answer. "What made you choose a solution so final, to relieve a pain that may have been only temporary?"

"Don't talk to me about pain," Cobain snarled again. "I was given a slow, ugly life, growing up in an awful town filled with drunk lumberjacks and unfit parents, where it rained every day and if it didn't rain I got picked on at school.[7] The only way I could escape a life of sad, white trash conformity was making music that said 'f— you, universe,' music that let everyone know life outside the womb was a barren, empty wasteland. But when I first started making music, I didn't really want to be famous: I just wanted to detach from the orbit of a meaningless life and spin out of control. And then the dream hit me.

"That dream got me the first few times I stepped out on stage. I felt free, free for the first time in my life, lost and free in music and in the darkness of the stage, the parts of my life I loathed so much going up with the smoke of a few dozen cigarettes. It was great. I hated living, hated who I was, and hated everyone responsible for me, but on stage I could feel my soul, whatever the hell that is, bundle itself up in the darkness and disappear and take with it all my pain, all while I heard the crowd cheering, cheers that were the closest thing any human being gets to being worshipped, worshipped like a god and not a man because your music is taking people into the darkness with you—'cause that's what God does, after all, God takes *everyone* into the darkness. So I gave myself to the dream of making it big and the more I gave my life to it, the more of my life the dream took from me.[8]

"And then Nirvana blew up. We got on MTV and got bigger venues and got to tour all over the world. But I felt like the man I had been was blown away like a candle and the dream went up in smoke with it. Guess that was the universe saying, 'f—you' back, which is what Nirvana means anyway—a snuffing out, a blowing up, just like a candle.

"I gave every moment of my life to the dream and sacrificed everything to make it happen, only to figure out dreams aren't real and to see everything I wanted in life—fame, success, genius, money, maybe a family—passing by me like a shadow marking time on a sundial. Heroin and cough syrup were really the least of my problems, not when I'd be getting hassled by corporate hacks so I missed out on all the fun things that came with being a rock god, things I gave my life up for to begin with."

The tree was fast drinking up the shade of Kurt Cobain, so I snapped off another limb and Kurt, sighing with relief, started talking again.

"The dream made me a slave once I blew up. Soon I was hating myself more than ever, even hating my music too, since that came from me and I hated everything about me. There I was, dancing for nickels in front of a bunch of snot-nosed Republicans too stupid to see how sad and unoriginal *Nevermind* really was. I had to make something better. I couldn't let my best work be one mediocre album, especially when *that album was behind me*. I couldn't eat on the fact my music defined a generation, whatever that means, not when music was all I had, music was my release, music was my *Nirvana,* my very reason for being or not being.[9]

"Then God took the two things I loved: my music and my daughter, my sweet little bean. My daughter went first since all social services had to do was listen to Nirvana and figure out I was an unfit parent. But then God reached down and snatched up my ability to write and play what few chords I knew.[10] But unlike my music, my daughter wasn't foul and ruined, not yet: she was perfect, sweet and innocent, and I loved her like nothing else in the world above—really, I couldn't love anything else, *never* loved anything else.

"Deep down I knew it couldn't last, *I* couldn't last, not when I screwed up my life shooting drugs and guns and anything else I could get my hands on. It was just a matter of time before I *really* failed, and my little bean would be the one paying for it. I couldn't ruin her the way I ruined myself, but I also couldn't just *start* being a dad either. Was there a way to give my life for her, just like I gave my life to the dream?

"I had to figure out something because I couldn't, I wouldn't stop with the drugs. Heroin made me more creative, creativity I desperately needed for new songs, new songs for new albums, new albums for new tours, new tours for more money and more money to buy more drugs. But playing wasn't fun anymore,[11] and the words to new songs weren't coming either.[12] The hope I had of a future that was whatever I wanted it to be was slipping away, the drugs consuming all my thought until one thought appeared to consume them all: I would fail, and I would ruin my sweet girl's life unless I left the world on the highest note a rock god like me could ever play.[13]

"I remember holding her and swilling the thought about in my mind: either I'll die, or I'll live just long enough to ruin her. If I lived, I'd amount to little more than a junkie until I ran out of money. Then I'd try to support my family some way else, but I would fail at that too. But if I burned out and killed myself when I was still like a god to my fans, those fans would keep buying my records. My memory, my music, my image would be preserved when I was at my peak, my fans interested enough to keep buying my records long after I was gone.

"Sure, my daughter would grow up without a dad. But even if she grew up in the shadow of my suicide, it wouldn't hurt her as much because she would have my fortune to live on in place of her miserable failure of a father. And really, either way, I wasn't meant to be a dad.[14] Of course, Hell is other people, and now I'm surrounded by all the fans I tried to escape while I was up on earth."

"Your fans?" I asked.

"You aren't the first to follow me down here,"[15] Cobain said, motioning with his eyes to the trees on his left and right. "A lot of kids figured it out too, and saw how meaningless and stupid the world up above is, so they followed my lead and came down here after me. After all, it is better to burn out than to fade away, right? People on earth just assumed I was a jerk and had a lot of nerve—but me and my fans? You see, we're just ahead of the curve."

CHAPTER XIII

THE 27 CLUB

The one real fight Evelyn and I ever had was about Nirvana. She saw how their music nursed my self-loathing, and she didn't want me to feel that way about myself anymore or talk about dying so often. She knew it would help if I just stopped listening to this kind of music. Evelyn was right, and I could see now just how selfish my suicide truly was. Maybe I was too scared to face the consequences of my actions and used my depression, severe though it was, as an excuse to seek a solution that helped only me. I am so deluded, self-deceived.

But those suicidal thoughts are lifting. Slowly, surely, they're being replaced by the realization that God has let me survive my suicide attempt and that maybe, truly, God loves me. My journey through Hell, with Ernest as my guide, is part of God's plan to lead me to something the shades have been calling repentance, and I have to figure out what it means to repent, how to do it, and do it right. How else can I be spared from this terrible realm? And where is Evelyn now?

I had a long way to go before I got out of here. Perhaps, too, if I can figure out what happened to me, why I lived each day as if there was no God and no hope but also no Hell. Maybe then I could share my experiences in the world above about what God did for me, they'd turn from the way of ruin leading to this awful realm. If God would save someone like me when I called out to him, dead in my sins as I am,[1] surely God would save anyone else who cried out to God and begged from him his strength[2]—that is, if they repented.

But why would anyone refuse to repent? The shades I've spoken with, Ernest especially, all had some knowledge of God and of God's existence, and yet they discarded the possibility God not only *is* but is our Judge: a few moments of pleasure or power for an eternity of suffering seemed wickedly foolish. Then these shades spoke of the injustice or the unfairness of God, but they also abandoned hope long before they entered here.[3] If God is just, aren't these shades rationalizing their sins? But why would they not repent? Why would anyone risk being condemned to this terrible place?

I had to know how all this fits together. But, before I could think any longer about God's mercy or his plan, I heard terrible screams tearing through the woods. I looked up and saw shades running through the Forest of the Suicides and ripping branches off the trees, fleeing from a pack of fiends.

"The shades of profligates," Ernest whispered. "Do you recognize any of them?"

The three profligate shades ducked beneath the branches of Kurt Cobain. The demons in this realm were smaller than the fiends I saw elsewhere, nimbly jumping from tree to tree like monkeys in the jungle. The shades sighed with relief upon seeing the demons pass them by and move on through the woods, looking for easier prey.

I gasped as soon as I recognized them. The three shades were rock gods of the 1960s, their pale shades dressed in the remains of wild, psychedelic hues, colors once the blues of luscious skies or the greens of rolling fields now turned to ash and bands of varying degrees of gray, black, and a pale green that looked like death. My parents were proud hippies, and they loved the Beatles, Hendrix, the Rolling Stones, the Doors, and the other bands that provided the soundtrack of a new and glorious age opening in the Sixties. Our living room was filled with their records, and my parents' stories continually pointed back to high school and college when they saw them play live in concert—with certain choice details omitted. Evelyn and I found our parents' attempts to be cool laughable, silly, but Grandmasco never looked on approvingly, knowing what her son gave up to attend a concert. But the shades before me looked nothing like the pictures on their records.

The shade of Jimi Hendrix[4] stood the closest to me. He was obviously their leader, and I recognized him by his wild hair, dead velvet pants, and the loose-flowing clothes that made him look like he had been a pirate up on earth. In a way maybe he was. Next to him stood Janis Joplin, her hair adorned with wormwood and a fiendish grin across her face. Next to her was Jim Morrison, whose own hair, rich and thick though it may have been on earth, drifted up toward the vault of Hell like the tentacles of a jellyfish. They were all members of the 27 Club, whose membership extends only to celebrities who died in godforsaken circumstances at the age of twenty-seven. They relaxed their guard and turned around, only to startle with surprise upon seeing me.

"Check it out," the shade of Jimi Hendrix said. "This boy's alive—y'all see anything like this before?"

"Nawh, not since I've come down here," the wraith of Janis Joplin said, accompanied by sick laughter. "Let's eat him!"

"The boy is with me," Ernest said and moved between us. "And he is not to be harmed by the likes of you, not when he has been sent to speak with various shades in Hell."

"Ernest, I admire you," said the shade of Jim Morrison.[5] "But I also know you and your stories too well, so I know you don't care about anything apart from fishing or your writing. What then is this boy to you? Why not just leave him to us?"

"You don't know me," Ernest said, unmoved.

That admiration turned to contempt as Jim Morrison and Ernest Hemingway sized each other up. Morrison's tongue darted in and out like a lizard's as he steadied himself against a tree and eyed me down like a snake sliding toward an egg.[6] The silence was finally broken by Jimi Hendrix, leaning against the trunk of Kurt Cobain and prying off one damned sprig from Cobain's boughs. His interest was piqued.

"So now, you here to interview people?" Jimi asked, picking his teeth with the branch. "I'll answer your questions, long as you tell us whether or not people are still listening to our records up in the world above. I have my doubts, but still I got to know. What do people say 'bout us, kid?"

"Yes, they must," Joplin said, her voice bubbling like a cauldron, "oh yes, they must listen to our music!"

"As if our fates are worth it," snarled Jim Morrison, still staring me down, "even if people remember us."

"All three of you are regarded as some of the greatest musicians of all time," I said with fear and trepidation. "You died before you could have gone downhill—*could* have but didn't—so people still remember you as musical geniuses. My parents loved your music and got me into your songs, and many people still listen to your albums today, but the American people also crave new styles of music and flashier forms of entertainment, so as time goes by, the less your tracks are listened to, except by a handful of people who really appreciate the music of the caliber you created."

"He lies, the boy lies," Joplin screeched. "I know my fans, and I know they would never abandon *me!*"

"But your fans are getting older too," I replied, "and dying."

"Nah, the boy's right," Jimi Hendrix replied, turning the sprig in his long, bony fingers. "I knew it on earth, and it is a shame the crowds just want to be entertained and get their money's worth, but it's the truth. I remember now how I had to play the same three hit songs for them and then burn my guitar, or else they'd move onto someone new."

"Do you want to know anything more about the world as it is today?" I asked, hoping to keep him talking.

"Nah, not really," Jimi Hendrix answered for the group and broke off another branch. "Best not to dwell in the past too much—just adds fuel for the fire. We got enough fire around here, don't we?" he tried to smile at Joplin and Morrison.

"Could you tell me about your life then?" I asked. "People think of you as the *greatest* guitar player of all time, but what was life really like for you? Did the crowds and the songs and the records and everything else that comes with fame make you happy? Or was it not enough?"

"Fame's an odd thing," Hendrix answered, breaking off another sprig. "Not that it made me unhappy, but fame's like a groupie following you and asking you to come on back to her: take more drugs and drink more alcohol and experiment with new ways of thinking so when you played, you could walk through the doors of a new way of being. And, of course, all the old doors weren't opening anymore, so by the time I made it big, it seemed a new world was coming on and I was the closing act, just like at Woodstock.

"And for the fans who got me," Hendrix continued, "I gave up part of my soul for 'em every time I played on stage. I'd take enough of the purple[7] and time my trip just right so I would peak while I was up on that stage. Then I'd feel those crowds and their praises lifting me higher and higher until I was up there in the clouds straight next to God, and the more I sat next to the Majesty on High, tripping on LSD and scouting out the plains of Heaven, the closer God brought my very soul to death—I could feel it happening—because no man should be up there all on his own, not when equality with God is something God does not allow,[8] and as I came down from tripping near the throne, I could feel something like worms gnawing at my soul, because I accepted a kind of fame fit only for God and not for any mortal man. And I loved it."

"Stop talking about God," Joplin hissed. "Don't remind us how we're *here*."

"But if you want to know the future, I can tell you," Jimi ignored her and continued. "I saw it before I died."

"We all did," Jim Morrison moaned. "It was the last thing we saw before we broke through to what was *really* on the other side."

"What did you see?" I leaned in closer to hear him speak.

"I remember that last night too well," Hendrix began. "I did a lot of crazy things in my life, but the night I died I only took a handful of pills, just enough to help me sleep and no more than usual—and still I went on a crazier trip than anything I ever took on the purple. As I lay there dying, my soul hov'ring over that gloomy deep, I saw each and every show I ever played from my boyhood in

Seattle to the Chitlin' Circuit down South and finally to London and Monterey and Woodstock and all the shows in between.

"I was flying over each and e'ery one of those crowds and looking into the souls of the people in 'em. I could see how they lived and who they were and whether they grew up hard like me and if they took to my music because my life was better than the garbage everyone else'd been feeding them. Old values in America were falling away, but ol' Jimi was there with his friends to show them a better way. And we could all go together beyond the bounds of old-time morality, heading through the doors of experience and getting ourselves full of free love, endless drugs, and good ole' rock 'n roll.

"You see, I knew these kids were fed up with the generations—and their values—that came before 'em, their parents and grandparents and all the fussy people in Washington and everywhere else. Maybe the masses were all ashamed of segregation, or they were scared of fighting in Vietnam, or just tired of sitting in the hard pews at church and hearing some old preacher-man talk why they should vote Republican and shouldn't be chasing pretty girls or dancing or some other such nonsense.

"Whatever it was, the life their parents gave them is not the one they wanted. The life they wanted was *mine,* the life of a rockstar or something like it, up there on that stage in front of fans who worshipped me, women who waited on me, and all the drugs you needed to get through the day 'cause that was the life, man, and it sure was *fun.* God doesn't exist, we thought, so why not do whatever we want?

"But we were all so focused on that stage none of us saw the pit op'ning up its mouth and forming right below us all, crowds of hopeless youth sleeping in the mud when that mud began to churn and the earth split open and the grave got bigger and bigger until it swallowed up whole all the people waiting on me to play. And finally, that big ol' black abyss pulled me down with them."

"So on that final trip I saw what was sure to be America's future: life would be one long, Woodstock-style jam fest, its people strung out on sex and drugs and pursuing a godless happiness; and they'd be ignoring God as an old and crusty superstition, living free and easy, with none of that ol'-time religion."[9]

The feeding of the masses, I thought again about the refrain of the walrus, *and the lack of faith of God to feed them . . . did the masses, ordinary people like my parents, want to be free from God to feed themselves—and more things than just food, indulging their appetite with drugs and alcohol and sex, things to make you forget God may exist and ease the pain of our existence, all the things I embraced to make me happy because I did not know God either?*

"Jimi, we can't stay here any longer," Jim Morrison interrupted. "The demons are making their way back through the woods, looking for us."

"Aw right," Jimi replied. "Interview's over."

Janis Joplin and Jim Morrison took off through the woods, ripping more boughs off the trees as they went. While this may have alerted the fiends to their presence and left a trail for the demons to follow, it didn't seem like the profligate shades could help themselves as they raced through the woods. Jimi coolly finished chewing on his branch, even while his companions left him far behind, but before he turned to leave I asked him one more question.

"Jimi," I asked. "What's the quickest way out of here?"

"Aw really, man?" Jimi asked, sighing. "Do I look like I know how to get out of here?"

CHAPTER XIV

THE DEVIL'S CROWN

Thankfully, my guide knew the way out. But now we were heading into regions of Hell even Ernest hadn't seen before, with the slopes growing steeper and the climb harder and the fire hotter with every step. Without anything to hold onto I slipped constantly on ash and scree, the heat and the height making breathing difficult and climbing almost impossible. The peaks of Kilijiarchago still seemed so high above me, piercing the vault of Hell like a crown of thorns. How much harder would I have to work to escape from Hell?

"Don't get discouraged," Ernest said and, despite being a shade, helped me to my feet. "Take it one foot at a time and don't give up. You can make it, and I'll be of any help to you I can."

"Ernest, though, why are you doing this?" I asked. "I mean, why do you want to do this? Can you feel anything? Or remember much of who you once were?"

"I have some memory," Ernest answered me, sorrow welling up in him again. "You remind me of my boys, and I see you've got that same death awful loneliness I saw in them—I helped give to them, after all. That sickness makes you feel alone, like you've got no one looking after you, just like I never looked after them. I was always off fishing in the Stream or cheating on whoever their mom happened to be and leaving my boys to raise themselves. And now that I'm in Hell, I'm not getting out, but I'll help you however I can so you can escape this place."[1]

"Thank you, Ernest," I said, sitting down on one of the spurs of Kilijiarchago. "Ernest, can I ask, what did you really know about Christianity growing up?"

At this, something within my heart begin to stir. I've long called this feeling *the beast*, for it felt like a real thing, with a mind and a nature all its own. I've felt it move like this before whenever I considered not binge drinking, not smoking marijuana, or not indulging in anything else that could ruin me, the lust consuming my thoughts of self-restraint until I gave in to whatever sweet release of pleasure the creature demanded. I read *Pilgrim's Progress* in school, and I remembered Christian struggling with that great burden upon his back, and I remember even from a few Sunday school lessons that Paul had some kind of thorn piercing his side. I, meanwhile, had this foul, Gollum-like little thing living inside my heart bidding me to serve its needs, never retreating or yielding, always waiting.[2] And now the beast felt threatened.

"Too much and not enough," Hemingway replied and sat down next to me. "I grew up in Oak Park, right outside of Chicago, and my parents were wretched little churchgoers who made Christianity a kind of prison, filling their religion with petty rules and silly clothes. My own dumb pig of a mother[3] even dressed me up like a girl and dared to tell me the way I was living went against God's commands—commands she mistook for her own opinions. So when I became a man, I wanted my own life and nothing to do with whoever this Jesus was. Still, if I knew up above what I know now in Hell, I would have repented, I know it. I would have kept myself out of here."

"Can anyone keep themselves out of here?" I asked. "What would you have done differently?"

"I've had a lot of time to think about that, down there in Erium," Hem replied in earnest, pointing to the Forest of the Suicides. "On earth, I reasoned that if God existed, he was a tyrant, like my parents. God's existence was unlikely anyway, what with all the evil and misery I saw in the world above and the advancements man made in science and technology since the days of Darwin and Freud and Ford. Science and suffering confirmed what I long suspected, chaffing under my mother's rules: God was an illusion, a story told to frighten children like me into obedience.

"But no more. Slowly, surely, I found happiness on my own. That happiness came in going beyond the rules God laid down in the Bible so I could create all the meaning for my life I needed, as if I was writing another book. The best writing comes from the truest sentences,[4] and the best living, the kind of living I aimed to live, came from willing the freest choices, from experiencing anything and everything that happens under the sun, whether or not God permits it.

"So I lived the most authentic life I could, writing my books and fishing the Stream and occasionally moving onto a new wife. And if I couldn't live the life I wanted, I didn't want to live at all. I would rather die than embrace the life my parents lived, and I killed myself to spare myself their fate."

"What happened the day you died, Ernest? Why did you do it?"

"I had it all," Ernest began, sorrow passing through him like the wind on the sea. "I had a boat, the *Pilar*, and a good wife, the blonde one,[5] taking care of me, and more books I could write. But then I went to Africa to learn something about lions before I died.

"There I was in not one but two plane crashes. One crash might have been an accident, but two crashes, one right after the other, made me realize something was coming for me,[6] leading me on like a matador with only the best cape work, smooth, natural, pure. That made me the bull in the arena, distracted by fame and fortune and my Pulitzers.

"After those plane wrecks, whole sentences started drifting away. It was like I went too far out to sea writing the very best sentences I could, and now the galanos of my own mind came to feast on what little remained of my thought. And that arch-galano Satan knew I wouldn't grow old or weak like my dad who shot himself too,[7] my mind as blank as the pages I could no longer fill with words. If I couldn't give my thoughts to a piece of paper, I would lose them inside a gun barrel. That gun I remember well. I loved that gun.

"I didn't sit for long in my kitchen foyer that day, holding my double-barreled, 12-gauge pigeon shooting gun, pressing it against the shiny linoleum tile,[8] peering inside its dark grooves that looked like hands reaching up from the grave and watching my life pass before the barrels: the days my mom dressed me up like a girl, the times I went fishing with my dad, the moment I held the gun he used to shoot himself, my divorces from decent women, boys I abandoned, and the parade of characters I killed off in childbirth or sent on suicide missions, every bit of misery I either endured or authored or inflicted on someone else all came together so any thought I had of turning away from this, my last free choice on earth, was drowned in the loathing I had for a life without words: so in I let a little air[9] and blasted the top half of my head clean off and blew the other half of me to Hell—and why not? All the meaning I wanted was in my work, and once my work was gone, I would just as soon be dead—and then I was."[10]

"Do you regret it now, what you did?"

"What's the point? The fact that Hell is real makes me admit God exists, my choices really mattered, and Christianity is true even if Christianity became a big stinking nada when I was alive—but how could Christianity seem like anything else with everything my generation either did or lived through?

"The time I lived saw one human catastrophe after another: abroad there was the Great War, then the Second World War and the fascists, then the Holocaust and the atom bomb, and at home in America, there was two hundred years of slavery, then segregation, Indian removal, and the reality we threw the slaves and the natives into the machinery of empire and ground them up until we enjoyed the highest standard of living the capitalist world ever saw.

"Men like me, we see the evil in the world," Hem continued in earnest, "and we abandon hope, hope in God, hope that choices really matter, hope that anything matters. And we abandon it willingly, gleefully, because then, and only then, can we live however we want and truly, that freedom is all we really want."

"Is that why people don't want to be saved then?" I asked Hem. "Why they won't repent? And who was this Jesus, really?"

"I've studied death all my life—I can tell you now this Jesus conquered it, taking on the life of a slave and enduring more evil than I could experience in a lifetime or capture in a story. Crucifixion by the Romans was the most painful way a man could go, but Jesus embraced the cross and took on himself the curse that falls on anyone who dies in his rebellion. And if we turn to the cross, we're brought near to God, so what God wants from us is something now we *freely* give him.

"Still, I can't figure out if God works in us before we can believe—since, as far as I know, God didn't do such work in me, but I know now man's redeemed state is much better than simply being *free*."

At this I doubled over and grabbed at my heart, gasping for breath. Whatever the beast was, it was thrashing more violently than ever and mixing its screams with my thoughts. As in the days leading up to my suicide, the beast moved out of my heart and into my head to strangle any thoughts of hope it could find. The longer I sat, the more I thought about giving up and throwing myself off these peaks to take my rightful place in Hell.

"Ernest, I can't sit here any longer," I cried, gasping, struggling to breathe. "I can't look at the abyss anymore—I just, I still want to die so badly."

"Let's move. You first, and I'll be right behind you."

I nodded and started climbing again, frantically clawing at the scree covering the slopes. I slipped occasionally as I neared the top, but Ernest was always behind me to make sure I didn't fall too far. But would I ever be free of the beast? Could I kill something living inside me? Isn't that why I had to die? Who would deliver me from this body of death?[11]

Finally, we made it to the top of Kilijiarchago. I tried to catch my breath but took in only sulfur. Lava poured down from the peaks of the Crown, the molten rock oozing over the edge and down the slopes to form the rivers flowing through Hell. The vault of Hell was still miles above my head, but now I had nothing to obstruct my view of the reflection of the Lake of Fire. I saw how the burning lake, the terrible Eye of Satan, continually drew in and tore apart threads of light like a black hole devours anything daring to approach its grim gates. That left the summit of the Crown shrouded in a darkness unique to Hell—dark because one could not see anything except the ancient malice of Satan.

Soon my eyes grew accustomed to the upper, and not just the outer, darkness while the Eye, meanwhile, grew still. Flames lapped at its edges while the deep thoughts of Satan concentrated on the single thread of hope I had within me, the hope I could be saved. Where had Ernest led me?

"What's wrong, Evan?" Ernest asked, still holding me by my black fleece.

"I don't know. I've always felt this evil thing inside me, a beast or a demon in my heart, and now it's crying out I have to kill myself again. I know I deserve to suffer in Hell, and I haven't done anything to earn God's forgiveness, but I also have no idea what I should do now. Ernest, please help me—what should I do to be saved?"[12]

"You don't need to do anything," Ernest said, pulling me up. "At least, not now, except rest."

"Ernest, does it help at all, what you've learned about God?"

"No, it's too late. But you're not in Hell, not truly, not yet—in fact, you've only reached the summit, so rest here for a while."[13]

I stood there in the darkness until something like trees emerged from the shadows. We walked between the spurs of the Crown and the springs of lava. The trees ahead looked more and more like men, rows of gnarled, black trees covering the twists, the turns, and the slight hills rippling through the defile of the Crown. As I walked forward, I saw they were not trees but rows of silent, wooden crosses.

Once I realized this, more pain shot through my body. Upon seeing the cross nearest me, I doubled over in pain again, but this was not my own hateful sin assailing me and tempting me to ruin. Instead, I felt the beast writhing in agony like it had been nailed to the cross and left for dead.[14] The pain I felt was that of the beast unable to endure the sight of the cross, whose presence was wounding, hopefully killing, this evil thing dwelling inside me. Those hands were really those of some gracious spirit extirpating the beast from its hiding places throughout my body. In its place, the cross was imparting a joy I never experienced in my life before.

Slowly, the pain dissipated in the sight of the cross. I found myself kneeling in bliss before this barren tree and saw, for the first time, how much God really loved me, for if God did not spare his own Son[15] to save me from my sins, neither would God abandon my soul to Hell.[16] But I grew quiet once I realized I wasn't alone before this wonderful, dreamy rood,[17] which appeared so beautiful even if it was so crude, for in gazing upon the cross, I saw something begin to move.

CHAPTER XV

THE GROVE OF HERETICS

"Where are we?" I whispered, surveying the shades hanging in the darkness.

"The Grove of Heretics," Ernest answered.[1] "These shades committed acts of violence against God, having embraced false teachings about the nature of God or believed Jesus was more human than divine or more divine than human or a teacher of morals and nothing more. Now these shades bear the curse for embracing these other gospels instead of trusting in the cross."[2]

"Other gospels?" I asked, now noticing the wraiths were crucified backward, their faces bound against the wood. "What other gospels?"

"Many more, many, many more, and anyone who preaches another gospel is accursed. This is just what that curse looks like.[3] Even I remember from my days in Oak Park[4] Paul warning of a time when men will not endure sound teaching but instead follow teachers who indulge their lusts. Now their fate in death merely reflects their sin in life since these shades trusted in their own works instead of in the person of Jesus Christ."

What "works" was Ernest talking about? I thought. *Was this why, in all the attempts I made to save myself, I always failed? The times I tried to quit drinking through sheer force of will, had I been trying to save myself through whatever these "works" are?*[5]

"Ernest, what are 'works'?"

"Filthy rags, but ones which we think will please God.[6] Works are our attempt to establish the grounds of our own salvation, and the heretics occupying the Crown added to the cross all kinds of deeds that may have served them well in the eyes of men but did nothing to help them once they died."[7]

"They tried to save themselves through works? Like I tried to do from time to time?"

"You'll have to ask the shades for yourself, Evan. For the sinners you see in the grove ahead, they belong to the sect of the Deists, filled as it is with shades you wouldn't believe are here until you've seen them."

"I do know what Deism is," I said, looking at the crosses but unable to recognize any of the shades. "But how is Deism a heresy?"

"Heresy is nothing new, but the freedom we enjoy in America lends itself to doing and believing and embracing the newest ideas that may keep a man from bowing before a man like Jesus, hanging naked and ashamed upon a tree like this.

"Deism arose during the Enlightenment," Ernest continued, "an age that exalted the rational powers of mankind over and against God's revelation of himself in the Bible, and the Deists made a god not unlike themselves, strict and disciplined and rational, a god who wound up creation like a watch and let it loose without much regard for anyone actually living in the world.

"So even if they believed in a kind of Providence, well, this is still the faith of demons, and the fiends do not care if a man believes in God so long as he does not think of asking God for help."[8]

Ernest led me by the pale light of his own shade through a narrow pass in the mountain, occasionally pointing to a cross to emphasize his points. The shades tried in vain to free themselves from the crosses, the one thing they would not experience in life now the only thing they could see in death. I was walking upon dried blood that crackled like embers, terrified now that I've realized our deeds on earth, no matter how great they seem, can never save us from our sins. But if I couldn't save myself through the good works I could do—well, what should I do instead? Is repentance a good work, or is it something different?

"Now, the next shade may be better suited for your questions than I, Evan," Ernest said, pointing to the shade nearest us. "For of all the shades you've met so far, and the questions you have asked them, none may be as esteemed or as significant as the one before you now, the shade of Mr. Benjamin Franklin."[9]

I walked in front of the cross nearest me and saw the face of a gentle but broken man, bald on his head with tangled white hair strewn across his shoulders. He shifted his weight and craned his neck around the cross to look at me.

"I thank ye for the introduction," the shade of Benjamin Franklin said, "and for any reprieve in my condition that your conversation may permit."

"How are you here?" I asked, barely getting the words out, so sorry upon seeing him as I was seeing Everett Mann. "Is that really you, Mr. Franklin?"

"Surely, there can be no doubt of that now," Franklin said, struggling to raise himself by his legs. "But who approaches? Are you from Philadelphia or New York, or do you hail from regions on the frontier, or some realm even further west, perhaps?"

"My name is Evan, and I'm from Northern Virginia," my voice trembling.

"Ah, of course, Virginia, always the Virginians," Franklin simpered. "Perhaps the Virginians do have God's peculiar favor after all, a favor your fore-bearers of the Old Dominion wanted all of colonial America to acknowledge. But, indeed, God is permitting you to walk through Hell unharmed, so perhaps they were right on some account. So indeed, my boy, truly, you are alive?"

"I think so. Last night, after years of drinking and depression and all kinds of sin, I killed myself, only to awake in a dark, lonely wood with my guide here prepared to take me through the realms of the Inferno."

"I am sorry, my dear boy, to hear you tried to take your life when your youth betokens nothing but promise, potential, prosperity. Such is a hardship I would not wish upon anyone, man or woman.

"Indeed, poor boy, you look not a little unlike my grandson Temple, who pursued the very same vices you mentioned and perpetually scorned the advice I proffered him.

"I tried to keep my loved ones from walking in paths of idleness and ruin, whose consequences in worlds above and below are more terrible than this tongue of mine can describe. Thus, I will yield what wisdom may remain to me to aid you in your pilgrimage. But pray, tell me, what do you know of my life?"

"Almost everything," I replied. "We learn about you in school, how you did more than any other American so our country may be *free*, whether it was in editing the Declaration of Independence or in negotiating the alliance with France that helped *win* our independence. And as if that wasn't enough, you left behind inventions and institutions that have helped every American prosper: the lightning rod, the first library, the first fire department, daylight savings time, bifocals—the list goes on with all of the things you either did or invented that have improved the lives of literally millions of people."

"You speak truly," Franklin sighed. "Yet, hearing my works recounted only makes my cross that much harder to bear."

"I still don't understand how you're here. What happened?"

"I shall try and explain as best I can, dear boy. You see, in life, I considered the only worship the Deity wanted—and note the word I used—was that I do good works for his creatures,[10] the kinds of works you so ably recounted. Thus, I devoted my time and energies to serve my country, its people, and indeed the whole of mankind, but my ruin came in my attempt to save myself, a feat no man can achieve. Sure, I tamed the baser parts of my condition much as I bested the lightning, but I went too far.

"You see, I ventured upon a quest for moral perfection. In this, I took upon myself a new virtue each day: temperance, sincerity, justice, and the like. I recorded my progress on one day to improve upon that virtue on the next, all while striving to cultivate good character and subdue my passions in a manner I thought pleasing to the Maker. Humility was the hardest virtue to cultivate, and the passions I found hard to subjugate, for it is our passions that so often lead us into ruin. But of course, so does our reason.

"Indeed, I came as close as any man to sinless bliss through the realization of one noble virtue at a time.[11] But alas, it was all for naught, seeing that no work, not even the ones you listed, could ever impress the Deity.[12] There is but one duty that God requires, of which I would not comply: repentance."

"I've been warned by other shades to repent of my sins, and I tried to repent last night," I said, "or at least I think I did, but I still don't really understand what repentance really *is*."

"I do understand only as far as the reasons why I would not do it," Franklin simpered again and shifted his weight on the cross. "For repentance means to bend the knee, bow before a holy God, and admit I am a sinner, in plain need of God's Son who died for me for reasons, while living, I would not consider.

"I remember such a time when I felt an urge to repent. It was upon hearing no less a preacher than Mr. George Whitefield, an evangelist who traveled the length of the colonies, preaching before massive crowds and in the open air no less, a man whose sermons I printed and from their dissemination derived a nice and tidy profit.[13] But I digress.

"I remember hearing Mr. Whitefield preaching one such day, berating his hearers they were all but half-beasts and half-devils.[14] Thus they needed the cross of Christ more than anything else in life if they were to be saved from sin and ruin. I felt as if he were speaking directly to me, or at least at me, perhaps even about me, and I considered for a moment if I too was composed in the manner he both described and decried.

"So I looked within every nook and cranny of that foolish heart of mine, but within its chambers I saw no such beast—a few follies hither and thither, forsooth, but no worse than anyone else in Whitefield's herd, nor indeed in Whitefield. Indeed, the few such errata I did find I weighed carefully and found they did not merit prostrating myself before him or before anyone else."

The beast? What did Franklin say about a beast? I asked myself. *Did the same beast or some similar monster dwell in Mr. Franklin's heart, the same creature which has long lurked within my own?* I felt the beast stirring again, wounded though the beast had been in the sight of the cross. *Was Franklin telling the truth, claiming he saw no such beast dwelling inside his breast, or did he prefer to serve this creature instead of seeking heavenly rest?*

"All my life I heard humanity was so depraved in mind and body," Franklin continued, "that man had no hope apart from daily church attendance. Perhaps I would have shared these views if my livelihood depended upon the tithe, as did Mr. Whitefield's, but I could scarce believe God endorsed such doctrines. As any rational creature like myself can find a reason to justify almost anything, it was easy to assume God did not share the opinions of Mr. Whitefield. In fact, it was easier to believe he favored *me*.

"And why not? For indeed, as far as I know, God never tried to turn me from my folly. And God easily could have done such a thing and at any time—why, during my famed experiments with electricity, for instance, flying a kite as I did in a thunderstorm and using a key that could have unlocked the veritable wrath of God and brought it down upon my foolish head. For surely, if God was not pleased with my life and works, God should have blasted me for my pride right then and there.

"Ah, if only he had! Instead, God adorned my foolish head with honors from kings, the friendship of *philosophes*, and stirring tributes from those whom I esteemed the best of all, the common people. As I grew older, it became harder to see what need, if any, I had for Jesus, not when I convinced myself I was living each day just like Jesus would, imitating Jesus as a teacher of morals and a model of humility.[15] Such is all I thought he was, and so I would neither live my life *for him*, nor give my life *to him* as my Savior. For this, I did not want him.

"I affirmed the existence of the Deity and spoke often of his goodness, sometimes even in public, but so do these demons.[16] I pledged my life, my fortune, my sacred honor, but I never thought I would give my soul for American independence. So you must warn our people what is happening to me, for if they follow my example, an example I know is but folly now, they and their posterity shall reap the consequences I in part may have helped to sow for them."

"But they'll never listen to a boy like me," I said. "No matter what I say."

"Let that not deter you from making the truth your aim in every endeavor. I lived in an Age of Enlightenment—a time of tolerance, goodwill, and reason—and we aimed in all we did to promote the commonweal of mankind, whether it was in founding a republic or a fire department, or by composing our founding documents which provided the foundation upon which to build a better world. But these are not enough to save anyone.

"Even in life, deep down within that witless heart of me, I knew this to be true. Yet I buried this conviction beneath my good fortune and my pleasures. I indulged in the finer things of life I so often warned others against partaking, whether it was fine French food, Parisian life, perhaps a tryst or two as my life neared its end.[17] These were but trifles, and now that I have been hanging upon this cross for so long, I have realized the singular erratum from which all the other errata in my life did since derive: I long assumed I was right with God because of *my* works, and not those of this Jesus. And the folly of this I should have known, even while I was a man upon the earth.

"For you see, when I was but a youth, before my adventure in Philadelphia began, I read Bunyan's *Pilgrim's Progress* over and over again. I loved that book, and I considered my own life to be a pilgrimage not unlike that of the work's good and faithful Christian. And yet I so thoroughly missed the point so plainly promoted by its maker, that of Mr. John Bunyan.

"For if you know the book, you know Christian was turned aside by the wiles of a Mr. Worldly-Wise Man. That rogue urged Christian to seek a life of ease and gain instead of going through the Wicket Gate, the way of repentance and faith. In my folly, I neither went through the Wicket Gate nor followed the plain example of that good Christian.

"Instead, I indulged my preference for simple pleasures and easy morals and long-dwelt in what I believed was the 'very good' town of Carnal Policy. I kept my company with men as worldly-wise as I was, and while Christian turned back from his sin, in heart and mind and body I never went with him. Such was my folly.

"Truly, truly, I lived no differently than that scoundrel Mr. Worldly-Wise Man,[18] and I fear our people will fare no better if they follow the example of Mr. Benjamin Franklin, who hangs backward upon this tree now that his life is lost—and all because in life, I wholly, I willfully, I completely ignored the cross.

"So it cannot help me if great things of me are said, not when I have only this barren cross to rest my foolish head.[19] Evan, you must draw from my fate the most tragic lesson of them all: to assume we're right with God, apart from faith, precedes a most-horrific fall."[20]

CHAPTER XVI

THE CLIFFS OF FAITHLESSNESS

"But now you must continue your journey," Franklin sighed, "as you must have a great distance to travel, and much to discover before you leave—if you leave, that is. I hope you do."

"But, Mr. Franklin," I said, "I don't understand how your warning and your advice fits in with the other shades I've spoken with."

"Nor do I, I'm afraid," Franklin replied. "But it was plain to me on earth that if our people ever abandoned virtue so as to follow their instinct or their appetites or allow both to usurp their reason, the basest parts of mankind would be released—perhaps the very same beast Whitefield warned me of, whose presence in my heart I dismissed so quickly. For once the animal lurking in us all is loosed from its cage, the creature will destroy both reason and passion, soul and body all alike. But as to such an agency that may make people forgo the path of virtue, even *if* they suspect such a path leads to Hell, that I do not know."

The feeding of the masses, the refrain of the walrus drifted through my mind again, *and the joys of the Hall in feeding them. Somehow, somewhere, someway, the spirit of the normal, average American broke, just like my spirit finally broke, broke for good, when Evelyn died, people like me who didn't believe in God and exchanged good deeds for easier pleasures—and all because they believed nothing mattered, either? But what is the Hall that it might take some joy in feeding the masses?*

"This is all why we have to keep moving, Evan," my guide replied. "On this journey, you are to learn not only why God wants to save you, but why so many others would not want to be saved, and the more shades you speak with, the more likely it is you will discover how to repent and do it truly and so escape this awful place for good."

"And on that account, I wish you all the strength the Deity may permit," Franklin said, looking down at me from the cross. "For in surveying the darkness of the human heart, you will most certainly need that strength, lest you be destroyed by what you see or worse, tempted by what it offers."

"Good-bye then, Mr. Franklin," I said and turned to Ernest, who motioned for me to follow him.

My guide led me through the twists and turns of the narrow path through the mountain. Finally, we came to the summit's edge, and there I saw the peaks atop the Crown rising in agony from the damnscape of Hell, like a man broken upon the rack. Along the range of the mountain came a downcast arm, elsewhere a tortured limb, and everywhere defiles cutting through the ranges like gashes across the mountain's back. I leaned into the darkness, as if I were standing on some lofty spur of the Alleghany Mountains and looking as far west as mortal eyes would allow. But instead of snowcapped peaks and valleys shrouded with trees and leaves, cut only by mountain streams trickling down from cooler heights, I saw a sprawling wasteland of fire, despair, and death.

First, the cliffs of the Crown plummeted into darkness. I could not see the base of the cliffs, shrouded as they were in ash, but in the distance, I saw a series of desolate valleys that looked like the Grand Canyon if that national treasure had been carved by demons from the interior of a volcano, an interconnected series of ravines and slopes and gorges all blackened by eons of fire.

This damned canyon spiraled downward to the Lake of Fire, burning in Hell's grim center. I felt as if I were looking into an immense and inverted volcano larger than anything in the Ring of Fire, the chain of volcanoes surrounding the waters of the Pacific Ocean, except I would not be climbing out of this furnace but down and into the flames that composed its source. And no volcano on earth could ever compare with the Lake of Fire, a pit of matchless flame that appeared greater in size, circumference, and swells than the waters of the Pacific Ocean heaped together and which are themselves only *ringed* by fire.[1]

"What's next?" I choked.

"The Cliffs of Faithlessness," Ernest answered, stroking his beard, "where those condemned for adultery and sexual immorality are cast about on the winds of their immorality for all eternity. A man shall leave his father and mother and be joined to his wife, and the two shall become one flesh.[2] Sexual immorality destroys this bond, and now adulterers are ripped in two with both halves hurled about by the winds of Satan around these cliffs. Nothing can stop a man's willful descent into sexual immorality, and nothing can save either half of a man when the demons hurl him down these cliffs. Now come on, Evan, we don't have much time."

Climbing up was easy compared to our descent. Ernest went down first in case I fell and he needed to grab me, providing he, as a shade, could hold onto me. I desperately needed his help, for I could barely see the clefts in the rocks I held onto, the wind having ground down the cliffs so fine and smooth it was nearly impossible for me to hold onto anything. And the Eye of Satan was fixated upon me again like a searchlight. What would happen to my soul if I fell since my body was already traveling through Hell?

If I dared to look left or right, I saw the winds tossing about the shades of adulterers. They were torn in two, thrown about in one endless circuit around the cliffs of the Crown, hollowed out like a shucked oyster. Fire and brimstone continually unfurled from the wind and tore at the shades in as many parts as they now existed. The shades tried to hold onto the cliffs wherever they could but should they succeed, the winds only intensified and flung them that much faster about the cliffs.

I stopped climbing to catch my breath. I looked into the darkness below while the wind tore at my fingers, trying to pry them lose.

Then the winds stopped. Perhaps the mind of Satan was considering some other way to dislodge me from my hold, because the simoom suddenly picked up speed again and hurled a shade at me. Now I finally lost my hold and fell through the darkness, unable to grab onto anything since any hold I might gain crumbled to ash in my fingers. I heard Ernest calling out my name, but I could do nothing but slam against the rock and plummet farther and farther down into the shadows of despair, slipping in and out of consciousness as the slopes of the Crown closed in around me like the jaws of a trap.

The shade, meanwhile, held onto me with all the strength still left to it until we landed on my back on a rocky ledge and the blow jolted me awake. I tried to pull the hot, cobweb-like shade off of me, but whatever was left of it held on even tighter. Through the shade, I could see the entrance to a cave behind us, leading deeper into the bowels of Hell. Then the wraith began to speak.

"Help me, help me . . ." the shade hissed as if some other part of him was uttering half his syllables. "Whoever you are—help me escape—and my family—my family—what may be left of them—will reward you beyond your wildest dreams."

"I don't know how I could do that," I said, still struggling against the shade. "I'm not even sure *I'll* return alive. But who are you?"

"Not so fast then . . ." the shade, half-consumed and half-bespectacled, answered, normal speech returning to him. "If you won't help me—escape,[3] I can't risk you ruining my name—that I'll keep to myself . . ."

"What can you tell me about yourself?" I asked. "What did you do, that you ended up here?"

"I wagered everything I had to build a house for my family."[4]

"A house? You were condemned for building a house?"

"A legacy, you nitwit," the shade snarled. "In my life, I reaped such a fortune, my children need never work themselves . . . devote their lives instead to serve their country."

"Would I know them?"

"Of course you would," he answered with waning patience. "My sons—with my direction—reached the highest levels an American can aspire to, and our name soon outstripped even the glory of

Camelot—all going according to plan—*my* plan—until the day God just snatched it all away from me—the grief—the grief . . ."

Grief, hardship, sorrow, I thought to myself, *so many shades have cited some loss they suffered or injustice they endured. Is this why the masses don't believe God would care for them, to quote the walrus? Is this how their spirit breaks, and then they turn to something other than God to mend it? I drank in part because it was fun and it helped me forget that Evelyn had cancer, a cancer that killed her as slowly as I let alcohol and depression kill me—so is that what happened to this shade?*

"What happened to you then?" I asked. "Did you cheat on your wife because of that grief, so now you're here, with the adulterers? Is that what you turned to instead of God?"

"What is it to you how I lived? Sure—I discarded the one rose that in marriage I was meant to cherish—but you had no idea the *pressure* I was under—I had to pluck other roses if I was going to survive that pressure at all—and do for my family what was *really* needed . . ."

"Plucked other roses?" I asked, desperate to keep him talking. "Do you mean cheating? Adultery? Is that why you broke those rules against adultery?"

"Rules?" he laughed. "Look, I never cared much for rules—well, aside from knowing how to twist them—like my years working the stock market—so sure, I strolled through any garden I set my eyes on—and got from other girls whatever joys my wife wasn't giving me.

"Now did I reap what I sowed? Watching my boys' funeral on TV—my boys—buried with every honor for their deeds—and all the joy—I had in raising them—my boys—my boys—to the heights of power—lowered to the grave with them? No, I didn't deserve that—no one does, kid."

"Did you try and repent? Did you know what repentance was?"

"Kid, I repented all the time," answered the shade, his face half-crestfallen. "Repentance doesn't work—at least not for me—but perhaps I should I have remembered from old Guido,[5] you don't repent for sins—especially sins like mine—you want to commit again."

"Wait, who are you?" I asked, looking through the shade at the Lake of Fire burning down in the center of Hell.

"If you can't figure that out, I shouldn't tell you," the shade replied and shook his head. "Besides, time's up, kid—so it'd be best if you just let me go—and I'll take my place upon the winds of the Inferno . . ."

With one arm he pushed himself off me. The winds of Satan filled his shade like the sails of a boat and carried him off across the cliffs of the Crown. I took a deep breath and scanned the cliffs above for any trace of Ernest. When I couldn't see him, I dared to look over the ledge to see how much farther down we had to climb. I could barely gauge the depth in the darkness, but it looked as if we had a few hundred more feet to go until we reached the bottom.

I couldn't see Ernest on the cliffs above, so I decided to wait for him rather than risk going through Hell without my guide. I sat with my back against a rock and proceeded to wait, feeling safe for once until I heard something stirring within the cave. But as I turned and looked behind me, something leapt out from the cave and grabbed me, knocked me unconscious, and into the darkness dragged me.

CHAPTER XVII

UNDER HELL

"Now I gets my wings," something whispered. "My wings . . . wings . . ."

I slowly regained consciousness to the sound of something rapping its knuckles against the ground as it walked beside a still black lake. My captor, walking upon its hind legs, may have been an angel once but now looked like the shell of a once-powerful demon.

The creature's sick, lamp-like eyes provided the cave's only light and by those eyes, the size and color of a dirty fishbowl, I could see it should have towered over me in height. But the creature was wracked and broken, with chipped tusks jutting out from a sharp, horny beak and two jagged stumps from either side of its disjointed spine. Whatever life it possessed was drained from it—its remains left for dead in a realm already made to punish fallen spirits. All the while, the thing whispered, "My wings, my wings . . ."

"Your wings?" I gulped.

"Indeed," the creature hissed, "for Lucifer will give me back my wings and let me leave for the world above again, once I bring *you* to *him*."

"Who are you?" I asked. "Or what are you? I feel like I've seen you somewhere—or felt you—like the shadow of a nightmare."

"Indeed, I am the spirit assigned to you," the demon hissed, sibilant syllables slithering across his speech like a snake. "I am your caretaker and you my patient, and long have I watched over you in the world above."

"Do you have a name then?" I stammered, terrified. "What do they call you down here?"

"*Reif*," the fiend answered, "for the *fire* hidden within my name and inside my very being."

"And what's happened to you?"

"Only what I deserve," Reif snarled, casting his eyes downward in shame. "My lord and prince Lucifer tasked *me* with tempting *you*, believing you were safe enough for a worm like me to bring here once you died. But then you tried to repent, and when Lucifer discovered my failure, he cast me down to the very bottom of the abyssmalarchy and let angels more worthy than me devour my wings. But all my fortunes will change now that I have *you*."

At that Reif set me down and proceeded to tie me up. Then he reached into his heart—or whatever equivalent demons have for such an organ—and pulled out threads of his fallen spirit while flames (and not blood) lapped at the opening Reif made in his chest. He used the strands as a rope to bind my hands and feet. This demon had already fallen once from heaven, once from earth, and once through the ranks of demons, and now the desperate hope of regaining Satan's favor turned this galano into a bristling, spider-like monster. Reif finished tying me up while flames seared the wound shut. Then he threw me over his shoulder and made off into the darkness.

Far behind us, I could see a small opening, outlined in flame, high on the wall at the far end of the cave. That opening may lead to the rocky ledge where Reif found me, but if we left this cave and descended any deeper into the bowels of Hell, I might never resume my journey. Ernest told me the more shades I see, the greater the chance I could escape from Hell forever. If I would leave this realm for good, I must take up my pilgrimage again and speak with the shades who could tell me what it means to repent. I wasn't strong enough to physically overpower Reif, but maybe I could trick him, and if I could climb up to that opening, maybe I could escape. Then I had an idea.

"No, you can't do this," I gasped, trying to break free. "How can Satan take me if you haven't given me any terms?'

"Terms?" Reif stopped. "What 'terms'? We spirits do what we want with our charges."

"No you don't. You snuck up on me and overpowered me sure, but you demons never just take a mortal for yourselves—at least not in the books *I've* read. People ask demons for help and then the demons make a deal with them, and those deals have *terms*—and where are my terms?"

"Go on," the fiend replied, arching his cruel back so I could see the bony stumps where his wings once grew.

"It might be a contest where if the mortals lose, you demons take their soul, or you demons give them something they want like musical talent or knowledge, or maybe you offer the human some years of service. Then, only when the terms are completed, do you take them to Hell.

"Those are the rules and even the demons play by them, and if you want Satan to give your wings back, you've *got* to give me a deal like that—otherwise you'll have to let me go in Satan's presence once he realizes you've failed him *again*."

"And what terms do you propose?" Reif said, throwing me to the ground and propping me up against a boulder.

"Well, you obviously are too strong for me," I said, feeling sharp, jagged rocks against my back. "So it wouldn't be fair to fight for it, but maybe Satan would accept the loser in a game of wits?"

"Perhaps," Reif answered, tapping a claw against his brow.

"Then what about a riddle contest?" I asked, remembering such contests in a few of the good books I read. "One riddle each until one of us guesses wrong, and whoever loses the first riddle stays in Hell and the other goes free."

"Agreed," Reif answered, agreeing too quickly for comfort. "You may even go first."

"All right," *I hope this works since I actually don't know too many riddles.* I paused, thinking of the wording, remembering the book where I got this idea, then finally offered my first riddle.

What has roots nobody sees,
Is taller than trees,
Up, up it goes,
And yet never grows?

"The mountains," Reif answered quickly—too quickly. Then Reif smiled, tail whisking behind him, thinking of his time on earth, and with a touch of scorn, the demon spoke,

Something worthless inside the shell,
Outside its worth too great to tell;
Wager your life to buy and sell,
On its own, sends you to Hell.

I thought long and hard about the possible answer. The fear of being condemned to Hell while Reif regained his wings made the contest much harder than I anticipated. I looked out at the still black lake, wondering if other fiends were swimming in it, until my thoughts seized upon the word *shell*, and I answered, "*Purple*, the color purple, which comes from a dye taken from a seashell."

"Clever mortal," Reif snarled. "Your turn."

I immediately regretted suggesting we have a riddle contest. I did not know many riddles, and I assumed—wrongly, it turns out—a demon would know even fewer riddles than me. Maybe Reif gleaned them from other souls he tempted in previous ages, ancient Greece or the Enlightenment or something because Reif never tempted *me* to engage in such a contest. Of course, Reif probably needed to tempt me very little, since my friends and I already considered drinking to be a competition entirely worthwhile on its own. We boasted in how much we could drink, in the damage we wrought upon our bodies, and how fast we could consume our spirits, the irony of which was not missing from me now that Reif intended to consume my own.[1] No wonder Satan assigned a demon like him to me, believing my soul to be such an easy target.

The only riddles I knew came from the right books I read, thanks in part to my classical education (although I wonder now if some of those books only nurtured my fiendish imagination), but all the same, I posed this riddle to Reif,

Out of the eater came something to eat.
Out of the strong came something sweet . . .

"Sweeter than honey? Stronger than a lion?" Reif snarled again. "Or better known than Samson? Surely, you know Lucifer and his angels can quote Scripture too—better than you, at least."[2]

"Yes, I realize that now," I replied, feeling stupid, but hopeful Reif was growing overconfident. I rubbed my birdlime-like ropes against the rock, hoping he wouldn't notice. "But you're next."

The creature tapped a claw against his brow. His tail whisked behind him and his face tightened as he searched the depths of his own malice for a riddle. Then his face sank like a stone and dragged his snarl down with it, as if the thought of something he lost, something he could never get back, something not completely consumed in misery appeared in his mind. Not his wings, nor the esteem from his peers in Hell, but maybe the memory of a choice he made long ago. Then whatever it was, the snarl returned and Reif offered this riddle,

What master sets his servants free
In hopes they'd sooner his loyal subjects be?

I couldn't think of an answer. Instead, I pictured what my place in Hell would look like once I was cut off from the knowledge of true repentance, and Reif brought me bound before the prince of fiends to answer for my sins. Perhaps the Sea of Lust, or the Shores of Gluttony? Or the Forest of the Suicides, since killing myself was only the most recent sin I committed? Finally, I whispered a prayer, "O God, please—"

"Most clever," Reif rapped his knuckles against the ground in frustration. "But go ahead and offer another riddle if you hope to leave this place."[3]

"Of course," I realized my prayer saved me, that God was the master in the riddle, and I could feel my ropes just beginning to break when I offered to Reif the only riddle I had left,

What walks on four legs in the morning,
Two legs in the afternoon,
And three legs in the evening?[4]

"My lord and prince Lucifer himself," the fiend exclaimed, rapping his claws with glee. "He crawled on four legs in feigned obedience to Heaven's dreary tyrant; then upon two legs in his valiant cause to seize the throne of Heaven; and now, having been cast from Heaven to the depths of Hell, Lucifer walks upon three legs, his crutch being the host of men who have joined us in our rebellion against our eternal Enemy and all his host, the being you men call God."

Reif was wrong, but he provided an intriguing answer. So I paused to think about the fiend's response for just a little, thinking of the shades I've met so far in Hell who regarded themselves as masters of their fate. Thus, they did not repent and were never freed from their chains, their fetters forged from their worship of worldly esteem, their love of earthly pleasures, or of the idle loathing[5] they held for their Creator.

But Satan has more snares than what I've seen so far in Hell. I remember from the few good books I read that Lucifer also tempted Jesus to serve himself instead of trusting God.[6] Only when Jesus refused to turn stones into bread or put God to the test did Satan offer Jesus the glory of all the kingdoms of the world.[7] Had mankind, or at least a portion of us, accepted this temptation Lucifer hurled at Jesus? Is this how mankind became the "crutch" of Satan, exchanging a relationship with God for worldly power and dominion? Were the shades awaiting me in Hell damned by such ambition, shades who, unbeknownst to them, were vassals of Satan, wraiths who gained the world but lost their souls?[8] But I would not risk staying in this place of woe, so facing Reif I boldly answered, "No!"

"No, it is Lucifer!" Reif shouted and reared back on his hind legs. "Lucifer, the bearer of light, the lord of all this realm!"

"No, that is not the right answer," I said, standing up to the fiend. "The answer is *man*: man as a baby, man as an adult, and man in his old age walking with a cane. Now you have to let me go, and it's *you* who will be staying here!"

My ropes snapped free and I jumped to my feet. Reif tried to seize me again, but perhaps the demon had no more soul from which to spin his web and tie me up again. Reif clawed unsuccessfully at my back and my legs, leaving long bloody gashes where his claws raked across my limbs. I punched Reif in the nose[9] and stunned the demon momentarily, then I hit him again and again near the bony stumps the other fiends left of his wings. The demon doubled over and fell backward against the stony floor. Now was my chance.

I raced for the far end of the cave and the small, orange opening I hoped would lead up to the Cliffs of Faithlessness. The opening was high off the ground, but not so high I couldn't climb for it. Or at least try. But the edges of the cave wall were as smooth as the cliffs of the Crown and I couldn't get a decent grip. I might gain a few feet above the ground until the rocks gave way and I fell as far as I climbed. Then I saw Reif slowly regain his composure, like a tree stump hardening even as it burns, and with a few long strides, the fiend would easily overtake me. I was just beginning to abandon all hope when Ernest appeared in the opening above and threw me a rope.

CHAPTER XVIII

THE VALE OF THIEVES

Reif tried but failed to follow us. I looked below and saw the fiend clawing at the cave walls, his screams filled with a despair I had thus far heard only from the shades. The demon could neither climb nor fly; soon he gave up and slunk away into the darkness, and I was left alone with Papa Hemingway on a spur jutting out from the Cliffs of Faithlessness. I let out a deep sigh of relief, feeling safe for the time being, until I realized the rope Hem tossed me was actually made from his fallen spirit. He looked like he had been mauled by some sick galano, the strands blowing in the wind like banners, like the tattered sails of a ship washed up on shore.

"Ernest, what's happening to you?" I asked, my voice trolling with fear.

"I was married four times," Ernest answered, the wind grinding down his pale beard. "I went from one woman to another and if I hadn't shot myself, I'd be condemned to these cliffs with the rest of the adulterers. Now my former sins are giving these hellish winds strength enough to afflict me too."

"We should hurry off from these cliffs then," I said.

"I do not mind the pain," Ernest replied. "Pain reminds me of what it means to be a man, and the best thing—next to repentance, that is—a man can do is stand against the tragedy of life and still remain the man he is. If something broken and sick inside me moved me to abandon one wife after another, and the winds of Hell are bringing it up to the surface, and if the Devil is heaping more torment upon the pain I always feel, it only makes my punishment seem more real—and all of that pain I deserve. But let us hurry for your sake since there is much more for you to see and many more people for you to speak with."

Ernest went down first, and I followed my guide over the edge. I groped about in the darkness for clefts in the rock large enough for me to hold or place my feet, and inch-by-harrowing-inch we made our descent down the cliffs of the Crown. I was exhausted, as every realm we crossed was the size of three or four states. Still, I tried to hurry for the sake of my guide. Finally, we neared the bottom, where the cliffs turned to foothills rippling outward from the foul roots of Hell's great mountain range.

These foothills I could walk upon, although it was hard. They were made from the ash drifting down from the heights of Hell so it was like trudging through deep layers of snow. Soon I was covered in black soot, and Ernest's pale shade merged wholly with the darkness we traveled. For the time being, there was no one to interview, and I had no questions for my guide, so we walked in silence—well, we were silent, but the more progress we made, the more a dreadful, sibilant din rolled out over the hills. The *hiss* of some unknown torment drowned out even the wailing and gnashing of teeth otherwise dominating the background noise of Hell.

At last, we came to the crest of a hill and below us stretched a series of narrow gulches curving outward from the foothills. They twisted and turned like snakes crawling across black sand. Some of the gulches contained ash and shades; others, rivers of fire and molten rock flowing from the peaks of the Crown, winding their way downward until they reached the Lake of Fire. Each depression looked as if Satan himself had raked his claws across Hell's grim damnscape and made long his furrows to house the wraiths tormented here. And whatever shades were condemned to these black hollows, they were moving.

The realm looked as black and heartless as death, and I thought of Ben Franklin's last words to me. What would make someone abandon whatever life God would have for them and live only for themselves? Could the dream of Jimi Hendrix explain what Benjamin Franklin was talking about, that people rejected God, hated Christianity, and abandoned any semblance of traditional morality because of their guilt over slavery and segregation, the horrors of World War II, the fear of endless war and nuclear annihilation, and the myriad forms of suffering, evil, and hardship we see in the world? *We lived to feed the masses*, so ran the refrain of the walrus, *the great joy of our Hall, out o' the lack of faith God would feed anyone at all*. Did the Hall take the place of God, to care for people who rejected Him and lived to serve the beast until they ruined their lives, just like I ruined my own? Did such things break the spirit of several generations of Americans, just like Evelyn's death pushed me over the edge? Or were those just excuses?

Wherever that evil came from, I'd find it in the gulch in front of me. I stared into a pit filled from one end to the other with snakes: snakes writhing in agony as if tortured by unseen flames, coiling and recoiling about themselves, the bellies of snakes nearer to the top scorching the backs of serpents beneath them. The sound of hissing and rattling and striking was so deafening even I gnashed my teeth, and as my eyes grew used to the newest shade of darkness, I saw every size, color, and kind of snake from copperheads and diamondback rattlers to cobras and asps fighting in the pit. I saw a few scattered shades trying to escape like dead men rising from the grave, but soon enough they were brought back down to the level of snakes again. There was no way out.

"Where are we now?" I gasped. "What is going on here?"

"We've entered the Vale of Thieves,"[1] Ernest replied, "in fiend-speech, *Saraiqtai*, and as these shades are condemned for stealing, so now their bodies and any trace of who they were in life are stolen from them, over and over again,[2] the snakes stealing from their fellow shades the form they need to become a wraith again. Once they become a snake, they lose their memories, personality, even their rationality, so the beasts they imitated most in life continually overtake them in death, a process repeating itself for as long as the shades suffer here in Hell—that is, to say, *forever*."

I stood and watched their punishment unfold. First, serpents coiled around the shade until their scales merged with the damned. But only one snake could take the form of a wraith, one seemingly chosen at random by the demons once all the snakes had sunk their fangs into the shade. Then, as venom drains the life of a man on earth, the shade's features ebbed away while the poison ran its course: the shade's hair recoiled into scales, his eyes receded to thin, fiery slits, his head reduced to a shell of his former self. His lips dissolved and his teeth bulged forward until they formed a point suitable for a long, forked tongue to dart in and out. Then once his legs and arms grew together and the shade sank among the snakes, the transformation was complete. The man, who became a wraith condemned for sins meriting this awful fate, disappeared and, in his place, was crawling another loathsome, crafty snake.

"Does this valley contain all the thieves in Hell?" I asked.

"There are two more valleys not unlike this one," Ernest answered. "This pit contains the shades who stole from their neighbors, while the next is another narrow gulch filled with the shades who stole from the church, a pack of sinners called the *simoniacs*. The last valley contains those thieves who stole from the state—the barrators—greedy pigs who plundered the public treasury for their own enrichment. But they are not all filled with snakes, for each kind of theft turns that thief into a different animal, the beast best suited to steal their very selves from them."

"Good, because I am terrified of snakes." I admitted, looking across the vale of serpents.

"Try not to look down then," Papa answered, "because there is no getting around them here. We'll have to go through; come on and follow me."

I let Hem lead the way through the valley. Our progress was constantly beset by snakes coiling around my ankles, slithering around my legs, raising themselves upon their serpentine folds to try and equal me in height. They hoped my life could provide the form they needed to become a real, living human being again, so the mass of snakes followed me everywhere as we walked. They stared at me with both envy and despair because I was what they could never possess again. But when the serpents lunged at me, Ernest hit them with the back of his hand to keep them at bay. He seemed to enjoy doing that.

"Why snakes?" I asked.

"A snake might live in the roots of an oak, and steal eggs from the birds nesting in the branches, just like the thieves here stole from their neigh—"

Ernest stopped short when a shade grabbed his ankles. The shade was still in the guise of a man and begged us for help while serpents sunk their fangs into him. The longer the snakes held their bite, the more human features the serpents sucked out from him. Finally, as the wraith resumed the form of a snake, another serpent undertook the transformation to take his place.

This snake had red and black scales, each one hardened to a point like the pit of a peach. These scales slowly dissolved back into its skin while its long, serpentine body quartered into legs and arms. Soon a head emerged out of the sinuous frame, slowly, fitfully, as if the shade was pulling himself free from a nest of baby snakes. When those snakes gave way to a head of unruly brown hair and his mind took control of him again, his eyes widened just enough to signal they belonged to a man and not a beast. But those eyes still sized me up, like a snake spotting a nest in the high branches of a tree.

"We have a visitor," said the shade in a slow, Southern drawl. "And who might you be, and your purpose in visiting our home?"

"My name is Evan, and I have been given some kind of a second chance to see this realm and speak with the shades condemned within it."

"Then I do hope our accommodations prove respectable," the shade remarked, a very human tongue darting in and out of his mouth. "I presume you would soon be joining us here, for God sends so many people to *see* this realm—it just so happens they do not leave."

"Careful now," Ernest admonished the shade.

"I meant no harm," the shade replied with feigned courtesy. "We receive so few visitors in Hell, I seem to have forgotten my manners, and for that, I beg your pardon. Now, where are you from, dear boy?"

"Northern Virginia," I answered.

"I see," the shade sneered. "A little too north, for my taste, but I hail from regions much further south, although not as far south as where I am right now."

"And who are you?" I asked.

"For the moment," the shade replied with speech as smooth as a Savannah lawyer, "or at least until I become a snake again, I was once a governor, governor of the great state of Georgia. My name is Troup, George M. Troup,[3] and I began my career in politics a proud Jeffersonian and at the height of my power became an even prouder Democrat, my heroes, models, and patrons being the venerable statesmen Jefferson and Jackson. These great men not only composed the grounds of my freedom, but also did they impart to me the reasoning and the wherewithal to exercise both my liberty and my power to their uttermost, both for myself and for my people."

"And what are you here for?" I asked. "What did you steal?"

"I, steal? Hardly," the shade snapped indignantly. "Why, I never possessed anything that, by the rights of sovereign states, did not already belong to me and my people. Indeed, in life, I earned the sobriquet the 'Hercules of States' Rights,' for as Hercules bested giants and hydras, I fought a series of savage, hardy foes bent on holding my people in bondage and, indeed, in the very worst kind of chains, such chains bound upon a people not permitted to fulfill their full potential."

"What are you talking about?" I asked him, as Ernest hit a snake to keep it from attacking the shade.

"Why, the riches and blessings I secured for my state and my people," he replied, hooking his thumbs on his grim gray coat. "For I seized only what was rightfully *ours*, our land from the brutal, deceitful Cherokees—a hateful nation who took on a mere veneer of respectability even while they plotted our violent overthrow. Oh, they saw their hills and fields teeming with gold and countless riches, and they continually made their plans to attack the weakest of Georgians, scalping the women and children and retreating back to the pits from whence they came. And should I let such a terrible fate come upon my people?

"Hardly. Never would I permit such violence to befall the hard-working farmers, craftsmen, tradesmen of my great and noble state. With Gen'ral Jackson's help, then president, we moved quickly to seize what was rightfully ours: gold, our gold, gold discovered in the hills of Georgia usurped by these Cherokee devils. Not only would we take what is ours, but we would protect our people from whatever violent reprisals they certainly had in store for us. And so we sent every last one of them we could round up to lands west of the Mississippi. Such is the fate of all people who stand in our way."

"But that was the 'Trail of Tears,'" I gasped, recalling the event he spoke of. "The forced migration of millions of Indians, marching them thousands of miles off, many of them to die, to reservations in Oklahoma and elsewhere. That was *you*? *You* started the Trail of Tears?"

"I never appreciated the spirit with which that name was applied. For I consider my deeds in light of the blessings it brought upon my people—indeed, as should you. My actions may have imitated the powers of Assyria or Babylon—Israel's ancient foes—but we only took from the Cherokee lands and riches they would have squandered. Instead, we gave them to an upright and deserving people, our people, so the riches of the earth could provide them with the freedom to live however they pleased."[4]

"But your actions were stealing," I said in disbelief. "If the Cherokees were your neighbor, and neighbors are most in need of—"[5]

"For my deeds I need not defend myself," Troup stopped me and raised a hand. "Even in the brief moments when I am just a shell of a human being, I take pride how I contributed to my country's prosperity—indeed, it is the only pride still left to me, whether I am man or beast.

"Before we part, allow me to give you some advice: *to be weak is miserable*.[6] You see, I was born into a world where we had Indians and slaves alike under the yoke. Much as I may have liked to ease their servitude, you could not free them without expecting one day they might put that yoke upon *us*. Sympathy is the ruin of men, for it does not require much foresight or intelligence to envision a day when the people we oppressed would rise up and dictate to us, *their betters*, how to distribute the wealth of the earth and direct the course of nations which would certainly be to their benefit and not to ours. You get a wolf by the ears, boy, as we had, and you best not ever let it go.

"The better example is always that of Gen'ral Jackson. When he purged the Creeks from the lands of Alabama, his soldiers found an infant Creek amidst the slaughter, a baby boy, one of the few survivors. His soldiers presented it to the general, thinking Jackson might put the savage out of its misery. Instead Jackson, having no other sons of his own, adopted the boy and raised him as his own, loving the child all of his days and giving him the illustrious name of Jackson. The underlying moral there being that, once you have crushed your enemies and they bear the yoke, and they accept your paternal care and oversight, then you may welcome them in—albeit *never* as equals.

"You treat them right, but the yoke is always there. They receive nothing unless you grant it to them. And should they cross the line, your governance ceases to be mild and resumes the overwhelming show of force you could always bring down upon them. Those in power must use whatever legitimate, accepted force is at their disposal to seize the resources, wherever such resources may be found, their people need so they may live their lives however they please. And if you're unwilling to do that, to do what it takes to rule—which it seems as if you are—you'll soon be crawling in the dust with us snakes.

"Such is a new kind of empire, an Empire of Liberty. Such was the vision for our country extolled by my hero, the great sage of Monticello. Indeed, Jefferson hoped that America might become as a sprawling Empire of Liberty, freed from the shackles of the Old World and in firm control of the American continent. That way, our people would have the resources of this continent at their disposal to pursue such happiness as was right in their own eyes—if only we, their leaders in government, had the strength required to achieve the object of our ambition.

"Thus I did everything I could to increase the liberty and prosperity of my people. No force on earth or Heaven could ever change my course, not when I had directed the powers of my mind, body, and will toward this object, the full flourishing of my people and the foundation of such an empire, an Empire of Liberty, to take its place among the great powers of the earth. So I bear my lot, my sentence, and my fate with all the dignity expected of a Georgian. For to be strong, your actions need not *always* imitate the cruelest fiends, but to wield power you must do whatever your people need."

CHAPTER XIX

A RAVINE OF WOLVES

The snake had remained a shade for far too long. Great numbers of snakes encircled the governor and coiled around his legs, each vying with each other to be the snake that would snatch his human form. Yet, the wraith's face tightened to a look of pitiless resolve as the snakes sank their fangs into him. Their poison seeped through his body, and his limbs dissolved into a long, sinuous frame overlaid in scales of red and black. Once the process was complete, he slithered back beneath the pit until I could see only the tip of his rattle while another shade, dressed in a singed black suit, freed himself from the nest of snakes and hissed at me. Then the shade ran off into the void until he too was brought down among the snakes again.

"How can anyone do the things he spoke of?" I asked, with every step sinking deeper into the coils. "The Trail of Tears, slavery, all of it."

"Man's natural bent is toward himself," Ernest said, "and power worsens that bend with the opportunities power brings to be a fiend."

"I don't know how much more of this I can take," I said, kicking a snake. "Interviewing people I find in Hell, to see how evil they were in life. It's hard enough dealing with the evil I see in myself."

"It's hard, I know. Writing, interviewing, researching, you sit down at the typewriter and bleed until the work is finished and you're proud of it. But you have to keep going, because everyone in the world above has to take it on faith that God judges the actions of evil men—and men don't believe God will do it, or they don't trust God to do it right, and this is one way the world breaks so many people—but you, *you* get to see God's judgment for yourself and find out what happens to galanos and teetotalers all alike if they don't know God."

Ernest patted me on the shoulder and motioned for me to follow him. He held me up by my shoulders to keep me from falling beneath the mass of snakes, until finally we came before a massive black gate, flanked by two looming guard towers, at the edge of the Vale of Thieves. Ernest stood in front of the gate and signaled to the fiends on garrison duty to give us pass. Upon seeing us, the demons threw a torch into some oily cauldron, and the other fiends followed en masse to signal that Satan's mortal guest was passing into the next realm. Then they raised the gate, its black teeth strewn with serpents who tried and failed to escape, writhing like worms on a hook.

While I waited for the gate to open wide enough, I looked up and saw a stream of devils flying overhead, gliding from one valley to the other. But I noticed, or thought I noticed, one demon who did not seem to be flying anywhere in particular. Instead, it kept to a spiral-like pattern, its dreadful gyre seemingly centered on me. Who, or what, was following us now?

"What's in the next realm?" I asked, trying to ignore the demon overhead.

"More thieves," Ernest answered, pointing ahead. "The next realm is only a narrow gorge containing the shades who have stolen from the church and fleeced, as it were, the sheep of God's pasture. The valley across the gorge, meanwhile, contains the barrators, shades who stole from the state and are condemned to a valley as large and terrible as the valley we are leaving now."

Ernest led the way and I followed cautiously behind him. He stepped onto a narrow bridge stretching over darkness and bridging the two sides of this tall gorge. I barely raised my feet off the causeway, fearing the slightest misstep might be my last. The bridge looked as if it was made from obsidian, a slick volcanic glass too weak to bear my mortal frame and too dark for me to differentiate it from the abyss. Every step sent shards of demonglass falling into the darkness and finger-size cracks trailing behind me like I was walking on thin ice. Then, as the hissing of snakes died away, it was soon replaced by wolves howling at an unseen moon.

At the first howl I foolishly looked over the edge. Packs of wolves were pursuing some hapless shade from one end of the ravine to the other. Once the wolves caught their prey, the howls gave way to screams and the screams to silence and unlit flames. Then I could hear the pack taking up the chase again and pursuing some mortal prey through the length of the gorge. I thought perhaps the shade escaped until I realized such a thing could never happen.

"What's going on down there?" reaching for Hem to steady myself. That was a mistake, and I nearly fell through his shade, but I caught myself before I fell over the edge.

"The ravine is filled with thieves who stole from the church," Ernest answered, "who now roam this gorge as greedy wolves. Should they ever become a shade again, they are chased by their own greedy pack, in the same way Paul predicted wolves would one day ravage the church, not sparing the flock but seeking whomever they could to devour.[1]

"In so many ways did they steal from the churches they feigned to serve, seeing their work and the appearance of godliness as a means of gain;[2] now the packs below are made up of all the lying preachers, whitewashed tombs, and every child of Hell who said what they could to please the awful ears of their listeners.

"I despise these kinds of sinners, coining lust into gold through their preaching.[3] They prayed for and preyed on the weak: praying with fools to gain their trust, preying on the weak for their money. If God purchased the church with his own blood, these wolves fleeced those people out of the church, telling them so many lies they're all damned together just as their father Satan wants them, and all for gold they could never take with them."[4]

I looked more closely at the packs and saw the wraiths become the very wolves hunting them. Their fingers fused into paws while black fur pierced their skin, drawing blood everywhere as the pelts stretched over their newly-lupine bodies. Their backs arched to the ground in agony and their legs broke in at cruel new joints and, as the human spine accustomed to the shortened length of a wolf's, the remaining vertebra formed a tail that shot out between its legs. Then the shade threw its head back between its shoulders and the foaming jaws of a wolf burst out of his throat, teeth bared for the next kill. The pack never stopped moving, for whenever they seized one shade, another wolf would become a man and take off through the ravine again. The hunt, as was their pursuit of riches, would never end.

"How could they have been so close to the truth and completely miss it?" I asked.

"They set their hearts on riches," Ernest answered, his pale shade trembling with resentment and sorrow. "In that way, it does not matter how they gained them. The shades down there remind me of the ministers at the church in Oak Park—thieving, lying Republicans who sold us a bunch of lies about who Jesus was, making Jesus as nice and moral and upstanding a member of the community as were their parishioners, a moral teacher who gave us an example, but didn't need to die for us, not when our sins were truly not so bad after all. Lies, all lies, damned lies—lies told so no one would get offended by our guilt and the sinners wouldn't vote with their feet and leave. And the offering—that all-important offering—wouldn't get smaller the next week.

"But if we didn't have real guilt, real sin, then Jesus didn't really have to die for us. And if Jesus didn't have to die for us, we were still dead in our sins and hence, we're here.[5] I would say if they told us the truth, I would have listened, but deep down I know we wanted someone to lie to us, someone to confirm religion was secretly a big nada and we were free to do whatever else we wanted with our lives. Maybe my life would have turned out alright had they told me the truth, that I shouldn't follow every desire of my heart or seek to serve myself because myself, my heart, and all of its desires are bending toward the Hell where now I am condemned. But I doubt I would have changed.

"Let's keep moving, for we can't speak with the simoniacs. Even when they're human, they're too much like the wolves that hunt them. They won't be answering any questions. And the gorge is too tall for us to climb down and leave again before the fires of God's awful judgment come for them."

Ernest pointed at a wildfire racing down the ravine, burning everything in sight and consuming whole packs of wolves. The wolves never turned to ash; rather, they remained fierce and ravenous beasts as the fire rolled over them. Then, once the fire passed, they took up the hunt again, their quest for riches never ceasing. The fire just exposed what they were in life: thieves, masquerading as followers of Jesus Christ.

CHAPTER XX

A TROUGH OF PIGS

We crossed the bridge and entered a valley curling around the rest of Hell. The smell of it all hit me first, an awful mixture of sulfur, waste, and death, and I saw the valley was filled with pigs wallowing in, and feasting on, their own refuse. As with the snakes in the Vale of Thieves, the shades were continually merging into pigs and the pigs back into shades, so I could scarce tell the difference between any of them. Should any shade pull themselves above the lot of condemned swine and return to the shell of a man, they soon descended to the level of pigs again: their shades diminished while their bellies bulged, and as their faces fattened to a snout, a tiny tail from their rumps curled out.

"What did these shades steal?" I gasped.

"The public trust," Ernest answered me. "We've entered the Vale of the Barrators, shades who bought and sold political offices, or used political offices for their own enrichment, robbing the state and gorging themselves on public money as pigs devour their slop. This valley is full of cabinet members and senators and congressmen who fattened themselves on the state's largesse, embroiled in some scandal like Crédit Mobilier and Teapot Dome,[1] or else they were party bosses from Chicago and New York and Washington, DC, who stole from the public treasury the fat they needed to grease themselves and keep their cronies in power. In life they fattened themselves like pigs on the moneys of the state, so now they feast upon themselves for their eternal fate."

"Is that really all I am?" asked a shade, on his hands and knees but slowly rising above the swine. "A party boss but not a statesman, not even a politician? Per a compromise, if you would give me but the name of a plain republican, I would be most grateful, for in life I aspired only to be faithful to the spirit, the ideals, and the aims of the Jeffersonian Republicans, that first great party in American politics founded by no less a man than Jefferson, whose vision I aspired to implement during my days on earth—and surely you are familiar with that most esteemed and venerable patriarch of the Old Dominion?"

"I know all about Thomas Jefferson," I answered. "I even attend the same college he did in Williamsburg."

"Indeed, William & Mary!" the shade exclaimed. "You too must be of a wise, noble, and generous disposition to be admitted into an institution that can boast the father of our independence among their ranks."

"No, I did not mean to imply anything like that," I answered, flattered. "But who are you, and why are you here?"

"I will answer your inquiry, for not only is your conversation pleasant and mild," the shade smiled coyly, "but your talk seems to keep me from falling back into my most unfortunate state, for it is about the time I become a man when I descend to the level of swine again. For this I am most grateful—apart from the vexation of not being recognized, of course—but, in deference to my hero Mr. Jefferson and all he did to free our people from English tyranny, I shall forgive this slight and inform you who I was on earth."

He smiled and motioned for me to come closer. The shade was dressed impeccably well: a fine woolen suit lined with a crushed velvet collar, a vest to match his bone-white bald spot nestled amidst a tuft of unruly white hair, and side-whiskers as thick and bristly as the hair on a razorback boar.[2] I looked to Ernest who motioned I should continue speaking with the sly, unassuming shade. I nodded to keep the shade talking, and with his eyes flickering like the tail of a fox, he proceeded to explain why he was here.[3] I stuck close to Ernest.

"I only ask of you," the shade began, "that once I tell you who I am, you would vindicate me of any blame for the so-called transgressions for which I suffer here. For as I weave the story of my days on earth, you will see I have been misjudged by both history and the Deity, and that truly, truly, I deserve a place in bliss and *not* amongst these swine.

"For you see, my name is Martin Van Buren," he began, "and all my days, even when serving as President of the United States, in heart I always remained a humble Dutchman, a champion of liberty and equality, a faithful servant of the common people.[4]

"Indeed, a faithful servant was all I ever was. From my days as a country lawyer until the moment the people graciously gave me their trust to be their president, I believed in, and acted upon, the worth, the dignity, the judgment of the common man.

"And so, when I saw the laborers, the artisans, the farmers, all alike, all misled, abused, and manipulated by the moneyed powers in my home state of New York, I grew indignant at their plight—and who would not? Why, in a land where all men are created equal, there in my home state of New York, *some* men were deemed more equal than others![5]

"And this could not be! But I saw that if the common people were to pursue happiness, they would need leaders who responded to and were even *guided* by their needs. That became *my* vision for political discourse in the United States, assembling the stalwart defenders of liberty to form a *party,* a new kind of party to reflect the will of the people, channel their respective strength, and safeguard the precious liberty without which life has no meaning or purpose!

"Only such a party, composed of the few, the true, and the virtuous, could save our fledgling republic from the myriad interests conspiring to keep the common people in their chains. So I attempted all I could to preserve the freedom the Founders gave our country, having first formed such a party in New York.

"I christened my creation the Albany Regency,[6] and the party ran as smoothly and orderly as a machine. Each member subordinated his own interest to the greater good, and we divided the spoils of victory, jobs, favors, and the like after each victorious political campaign. Those jobs, favors, and forms of patronage served as the fuel to keep the machine running. Oh, those were the best days of my life, engaged in so valiant a venture as public service and working with the most talented men of my generation.

"We dedicated each moment to the advancement of the people's welfare and that of real freedom across the United States. Now, verily, do you see I do not belong here amongst the swine, given all I did for my people?"

"But you embraced the idea of political parties?" I asked, drawn in by his conversation. "I thought most Founding Fathers warned against them since they divide Americans against each other?"[7]

"The damage was already done, my boy. Interests, parties, factions had already been formed: the moneyed interests had long conspired together, the landed gentry had their faction, and the merchants still another. Yet the common people were like sheep without a shepherd without any voice to plead their cause.

"So I was forced to create so potent an engine as my Albany Regency. Working together, the Regency protected the common people from such varied interests as avaricious speculators and closet monarchists and the like. The commoners could not defend their rights from the agents of a haughty, aristocratic malice bearing down upon them, and thus the Regency extended the franchise to all white men in New York.

"Because of us, the middling poor could now vote without regard to property, a most cruel restriction imposed to keep the people silent, unorganized, crushed. Indeed, we did everything we could to advance the lot of humble farmers and craftsmen, with whom we stood arm-in-arm in the cause of liberty, equality, and brotherhood.

"And forsooth, the Regency did so much to relieve the hardship of the common people. Whether they were laborers or artisans or poor sojourners from Ireland and beyond, I rewarded their support with gainful employment, government posts, or even so little a boon as a bag of coal, and surely it is no sin to be like God in this regard:[8] to provide for one's supporters from public funds the public provides for the public itself is to care for the least of the public, no doubt—and how else would the common man find his daily bread, if not from my hand?"[9]

"Did you do this only in New York?" I asked him, the refrain of the walrus flitting through my mind: *the joys of the Hall in feeding them*. Is the Hall this political machine?

"No, indeed, I did not," Van Buren answered, waving his hand to draw me in. "I had national aspirations, but in order to replicate on the national stage what succeeded in Albany, I had to find a platform that appealed to my home state of New York and a broad array of other states. And now, as best I understand the Deity's ways, it is for this platform, this insight, for which I am condemned here."

The more Van Buren spoke from behind his sly gestures and unassuming grin, the deeper I was drawn into the reasons given to excuse his sin. Yet, despite his regal bearing and aristocratic gauge, he looked like a character in Bunyan's *Pilgrim's Progress*, the old man Adam, whom Faithful was sure would sell him as a slave.[10]

"You see, great power is reserved to the states," Van Buren continued. "Great power, power I could not simply take away. But if this power were channeled through a party, a party dedicated to the people, we could create a machine of unimaginable energy, strength, and will—a mortal god made of people and me somewhere near the helm. We lacked only the right leader with the right message to roost the common people to seize their rightful liberties and yet still assure the states, driven about as they would be by the common people, that they could still rule their own affairs. But how could I unite them all?

"At last, I hit upon the idea that could do such a thing—a platform to appeal to both North and South, East and West, merchants and planters all alike. In this way I could bring peace to a nation on the brink of civil war by yoking these obstreperous factions and regions all together in the glorious cause of freedom.

"But still, I was aghast at how I could achieve the object of my ambition—power at the highest levels of the American republic—until I realized I could not establish my party through any other means than this, and that the goodness of my ends vastly outweighed the short-term pain my means would cause. Course, it was but small consolation such pains would fall upon a people who really weren't my people at all; in fact, it would fall upon the slaves whose existence on earth was to serve the interests of their masters, whose interest I aimed to channel. I simply did what was needed to confer untold blessings on my party, my cause, and my people.

"For I saw only one solution. I thus made the necessary arrangements with likeminded machines in Richmond and Nashville and elsewhere across the country. For many growing cities boasted organizations not unlike my Regency, and once we stood arm-in-arm together, we humble plebians against the haughty patricians, we elected a popular war hero, an Indian fighter, and a champion of the common people, Andrew Jackson as president upon the only platform that could bind New York and Virginia. And the issue?

"The only issue, the only means which could join the plain republicans of the North to the planters of the South was that of a pledge, a solemn vow that the northern members of our Party would protect the South's most peculiar institution: we would protect plantation slavery in the House, the Senate, and the presidency wherever and however we could. My Regency and my alliance of Northern machines would preserve their peculiar institution and thus promote the prosperity the hills and fields, farms and hands of the South conferred upon the whole country. So it was done.

"Once Jackson was in the White House, we did indeed rebuild the old Jeffersonian party, albeit under a new name.[11] And my plan *worked*, worked perhaps even too well, for the party we built upon that platform eased the grievances between the North and the South, alleviated the bitter discourse spurred on by slavery, bridged the gulf between rich and poor, and advanced the lot of everyman everywhere across our nation. Indeed, my humble efforts forestalled civil war between the sections for nearly a generation, for slavery was always the issue tearing the country apart, and my party helped to heal the breach—and yet here I am, despite all the good I did."

"But plantation slavery is such an evil, and if you knew that, why would you try and protect it?"

"You must understand the political climate I labored in," Van Buren replied, waving away my concern. "For when you are in politics, you must provide for the people who give you your power or else you face political ruin. In Washington, DC, the only measure of success is power, power and survival, and whatever you do to increase one and prolong the other is more than justified, for the alternative is obscurity, humiliation, ruin. This political reality requires a man of will and vision to do whatever is needed, to discard traditional notions of what is right and wrong—for what is *right* is what *succeeds*.

"So what if blacks provided such a means to increase our standing? Or if we used the slaves as their masters might have them pick cotton? So be it. For if it was not me, someone else would have used them like chattel and reaped the political largesse resulting from it. To the victor go the spoils, do they not? Did I fare any differently from the planters down south?

"But my bargain did wring handsome benefits for myself, my party, and my people. My arrangement most certainly has made me the most successful barrator in this valley, having exchanged the freedom of millions of Africans for power and the rewards that accompany it. Indeed, such an arrangement carried me from New York to the presidency, and no matter what others may say, I died with the satisfaction of knowing how much good I had done my country.

"Oh, what of it all, that I bought my achievements at the price of millions of Africans and their generations still unborn? Was not my bargain worth it? Are not my sins justified by the peace and prosperity I brought the United States? Indeed, I should be rewarded in Heaven for my deeds, instead of being condemned for doing what was necessary to advance a series of noble causes as that of peace and liberty, freedom and prosperity, brotherhood and equality."

"So was it all about power?" I asked, seeing Van Buren's pale frame becoming more and more like a pig again. "Is that why you made this bargain?"

"Some in Hell," Van Burn answered, slowly descending to the trough, "would argue it is better to reign in Hell than serve in Heaven. Perhaps it is, perhaps not, but I have not seen Heaven. I can say for certain it was better, truly better, that I should advance the equality and prosperity of *my* people no matter the cost. I could never protect so proud and haughty a status quo that would have kept everyone enslaved, whites along with the blacks. So dear boy, you *must* leave here knowing my love for the people, and that I did all I could so all men may truly be treated equal; for, in earning my features both swinish and swarthy, and my humble efforts in founding the Democratic Party—"

Then snorts and grunts overtook his speech. Van Buren made his final descent to the level of swine, his belly bulging, his fingers cloving into hooves, and his sideburns fusing into ashen-black tusks. Once Van Buren was a pig again, he instinctively joined the herd and moved with them in search of shades like swine scouring a forest for truffles. I stood there speechless and in silent fear. Finally, Ernest tapped my shoulder and signaled it was time to leave. As we made our way through the trough of swine, I struggled to put together what I've learned from these shades. *How do* their *sins explain why* I *wanted to kill myself?*

"I think I may know why life on earth seems so meaningless and hopeless sometimes," I said as we neared the edge of the trough. "I mean, I certainly grew up with incredible advantages—a private school, money, freedom—way too much freedom. Myself and my friends, seemingly everyone my age, have enjoyed perhaps the highest standard of living mankind has ever had. But none of that really matters because money can't make anyone happy. I mean money could never *really* make us happy to begin with, but it definitely can't make us happy when there is still so much suffering and evil in the world. Evelyn's cancer was so hard on my family, and when she died, I didn't have anything I wanted to live for, anything to keep me going—but there was always this sense the world was as cruel as it is meaningless so none of my choices really mattered anyway. In such a world, the most rational way to live is irrationally living however you want.

"And up above, the way people talk about slavery, and other forms of evil in the world, it's like they're crushed by this massive, collective guilt. And they have no way of getting rid of it, not when the majority of people don't believe in God. Instead, they demand the government do something to right past wrongs, and the state gets a little bigger every year to make that happen. Even though kids like me aren't responsible for slavery or Indian removal or some other decision that exploited millions of people, we still in part benefit from all the choices, for good or evil, that have made the world what it is. We don't know what to do about it, and we don't know how we can fix the broken world we're born into. Those decisions, made by some of the people I've talked to here in Hell, have imparted a kind of national guilt no one knows how to get rid of.

"And with all that guilt, and without anything greater than yourself to live for, you might as well just get drunk and be merry, for tomorrow we could die anyway.[12] Life just seems so meaningless after the whole course of Western civilization seemingly went off a cliff after World War II, like a shipwreck from which you can only save yourself, and we cling to our freedom like a life preserver because that's all we know. So instead of repenting before a God whose love endures forever, we drown our sorrows in an array of endless pleasures."

"You forget though," Hem replied in earnest, "that truly our hearts are *already* wicked enough that they'd seize any excuse to live for ourselves and not for God, especially when God gives us things we can rely on instead of trusting in a being we can neither see nor control. I didn't need much of a push to reject God and make my own way, and maybe things would have gone better had I *truly* suffered and hadn't written so many successful books, for my success led me to trust in my genius that much more. That trust is what got me here."

"What does it all mean then? Is that why some people don't want to be saved?"

"Let's find more people to ask that question. We have only two realms left, reserved for those who rejected the last of the Ten Commandments: the Desolation of Fraud and the Pit of Envy,[13] which is the Lake of Fire."

"I think I'm ready to see them."

"I should hope so because you won't just *see* the Lake of Fire," Ernest responded. "If you're going to speak with those damned within it, you'll have to hold your breath and *swim* in it."

CHAPTER XXI

THE DESOLATION OF FRAUD

Ernest and I walked downward until we reached the edge of the barrators' trough. There we stood between two dark and upraised crags and looked down upon another dreary damnscape, this one carved by rivers of fire flowing down from the peaks of Satan's Crown. This was the Desolation of Fraud[1] and in form, it resembled the Grand Canyon, albeit wider and deeper and abounding with more chasms, cliffs, and caves for demons to fly in and out of like a plague of locusts. From this height, I could only see deep gorges veiled in shadow and rivers of molten rock until they emptied into the Lake of Fire.

I had already journeyed over seas and mountains, but if I were to escape from Hell, I'd have to plunge into the heart of this damned canyon laying before me. How was I going to make it? I almost gave up hope seeing the size of it all. I didn't think I could make it across so vast and desolate a realm, not when I have traveled so far already and could barely stand up straight—and I'm supposed to stand before Satan? Why did I ever try to kill myself? Why did I hate myself so much I would rather drink until I blacked out and died a little bit each night rather than ever *be* myself? And as the crowning achievement of a life worth spilling, I killed myself. How could I think suicide would relieve me of my pain when my sins have sent me, perhaps temporarily, perhaps not, to a place where pain never ends?

And I know I am not the only one who feels this way. Many kids my age look for happiness in money and success or alcohol or sex or power or anything else other than God to nurture the idle hope we could be happy without knowing God. It's just that not everyone follows the logical conclusion of a self-destructive lifestyle in destroying themselves like I did. But God has given me some kind of second chance and if I could repent, *I* could escape from here and rest in the hope that comes from knowing God. I have to keep going.

"Who's condemned here?" I asked my guide, my senses assailed by a horrific smell wafting up from the realm below. "And what about these hills and valleys leading down to the Lake of Fire? What shades are condemned there?"

"This is the Desolation of Fraud," Ernest answered. "The fiends call it *Arbantim Kamartu*, and it contains the shades who bore false witness against their neighbor. These shades broke the Ninth Commandment, and so there are nine deep gorges, one for each of the ways a man might lie to his fellow man to get ahead or get out of trouble in the world above. Sins of fraud are all the worse because God gave us the ability to speak, a gift that separates us from the animals, and using our words as a weapon or as a snare is an awful use of the things God provides to man. Trust me kid, I know: I belong here too."[2]

The slopes breaking down into the Desolation of Fraud were a few hundred feet made of mud or ash or something worse. Ernest went over the edge first, but I had only to lean into the wind for the smell of their torment, continually reeking up to Heaven, to hit me like a ton of bricks.[3] I vomited and heard an acid-like hiss from where it landed, but still, I tried to keep up with Ernest.

"What is that?" I asked, wiping my mouth with my black fleece.

"The smell suffusing their speech in life," Ernest said. "This first canyon contains the shades condemned for flattery, the sin of telling others what *they* want to hear so *you* can get what you want from them. These shades fed everyone lies while they were living, so now in death the waste of fiends is all they'll be eating."

Ernest grimly motioned overhead. I looked up and saw thousands of demons coming in from every corner of Hell like birds migrating south for the winter. The fiends flew here to relieve themselves, defecating on the shades who lied in order to advance themselves in the world above. If every toilet on earth were flushed at the same time and their contents flowed into the same latrine, and into that latrine was sent every bottom-feeding creature God created to live solely on excrement and filth, and then those animals feasted upon and added to the waste, such an abyssal plain would not smell a fraction as awful and as tear-inducing or stomach-scraping as the new realm into which we dared to tread. And yet the shades condemned to this place were crawling through the excrement, mingling the waste with their tears, and raising their fare to their face and slowly, ever so slowly, eating all of it.

"But what is so bad about flattering someone, telling a few white lies, if that was all it was, that it could merit eating this for all eternity?"[4] I asked, the smell of their fate tearing at my eyes and overwhelming my judgment.

"By now you ought to take sin more seriously," Papa Hemingway answered with some notable frustration. "For the sin that drives flattery is the same thing that makes every sin so bad. The years leading up to your suicide—what were those really like?

"God created you because he wanted someone to love him, really love him, not the way a dog looks up to his master or a slave follows his commands, but the way a boy should love his father if his father isn't a selfish, bullfightin' drunk who thinks it is more important to *write* about your kids than to care for them. And when you reject God, that love goes nowhere except back onto yourself so everything you do from then on only helps *you*.

"Flatterers like these shades here did whatever they could to help themselves when they were alive, and at times they brought great harm on others, and most often it was because they wanted something from them. In other words, the flatterers *used them*, so now they're condemned to a realm the fiends use as a *bathroom*."[5]

"Your guide is right," murmured a shade, his face half-hidden in filth. "My name is James Buchanan,[6] and in life I hailed from the noble state of Pennsyl—"

But the shade couldn't finish his introduction. I saw the shadow of the demon who was following us grow larger and larger, circling us with this James Buchanan at its center, hovering in the vault above like a vulture waiting for traffic to clear. At last, the demon decided to strike. The spirit swept down from the sky to where we stood, landing on top of the shade of James Buchanan and shoving him down into the fiendish excrement. Meanwhile, the demon was careful not to touch any of the filth himself, and he curled and uncurled his pinions to keep his huge body from swaying in the wind. But then he began to speak.

"I take it you are Evan Esco?" the demon bellowed, his huge red eyes surveying me up and down.

I tried to stand up straight and not look so scared. The fiend had an oddly human look about him, aside from the wings now reefed about his enormous frame, the horns curling out of his head, and his broad, anvil-like chin that tapered to a beard studded with thorns and sores. He had to be one of Hell's Big Five, one of the fiends at the upper tier of the abyssmalarchy.

"What's that to you?" Ernest inquired of the fiend. "What do you want from us?"

"Only to help you across this realm," the demon answered.

"We don't need any help. This boy killed himself yesterday after years of giving into Satan's lies about what could make him happy, and he doesn't need any help from you galanos."

"Your loss certainly would have been our gain," the demon began, "but I do not think you give our cause the proper thanks in helping you. We certainly came to your side quicker than the Enemy ever did and even then, we only provided what *you* wanted. Nor did we ever deceive you concerning both the nature and the duration of the happiness we helped you find."

"Well, I am all the more convinced Satan is a liar after what I've seen here," I said.

"Mortal boy," the demon countered, "do not speak such base platitudes, for you have never met the prince of all this realm. But to debate with you is not the purpose of my visit, for I come bearing gifts: these wings, to ferry both you and your guide across this lying waste—unless, of course, you prefer to walk."

"And why would you help me?" I asked.

"I have a peculiar interest in humans," the demon replied.

"Who are you then?"

"My name is Mephistopheles," the demon answered, "a name you surely recognize from my work with Dr. Faust,[7] whom I served for twenty-four years until his death. I assure you: I am not like the other demons in Hell, for they delight in torturing their charges—but not I, for not even in counseling my most famous patient did I ever lie to him. Upon whatever honor I still have in Hell, I will take you safely to the Rift of False Counsel, which contains the shades I know you are to speak with next."

"We don't need help from the likes of you," Hemingway stated again. "We'll make our way through the Desolation of Fraud on our own."

"Did the Enemy really tell you not to accept any aid from demons?" Mephistopheles asked. "Are we not both under the same sentence of condemnation, you a shade and I a spirit—yet you still help the boy? Can I not do the same? And do not forget, the boy is above us both since he is still free to make his own choices."

"You would take us there, and not prevent us from seeing someone, anyone, who might help the boy repent?" Ernest asked skeptically.

"Of course not," said Mephistopheles, smiling, "I will even warn you to be careful of what they tell you, for the Rift of False Counsel—in our tongue, *Piristu*—is filled with so many of my former charges one would think Lucifer gave it to me as my own private fiendom. Still, I promise I will carry you safely across the Desolation of Fraud and let you down at the Rift of False Counsel, so the boy may speak with the shades waiting for him there. Do we have an accord?"

I still didn't think I should accept his offer. But Mephistopheles agreed to do as Hemingway bid him. And as far as I could remember, Mephistopheles hadn't lied to Dr. Faust, who sold his soul for knowledge, pleasure, and everything else the demon Mephistopheles might provide him. So when the demon lowered his shoulder and offered me the spiny arch of his back for my seat, I climbed aboard. Hemingway followed close behind, sitting near the tail Mephistopheles trailed behind him to keep his balance.

Mephistopheles unfurled his wings and took off to the vault of Hell. Soon we were high above the Desolation of Fraud, and I saw each gorge curling out from the Lake of Fire in a massive arc like the winds of a hurricane spiraling outward from the eye of the storm. The burning lake far surpassed in size any storms we have on earth, and the towering slopes of each canyon were dotted with caves the shades continually ran into and out of in hopes they could escape the demons. The fiends knew the tunnels better than they did, and the only things escaping were the sounds of weeping and gnashing of teeth, rising forever into the air, intermixed with the smoke of their torment.

I was not a little thankful for Mephistopheles's offer to carry us over this damned canyon. But my relief disappeared as soon as we were too high to turn back. As we soared high above the Desolation of Fraud, I thought of the way eagles hunt for turtles: an eagle carries the helpless creature as high into the air as it can fly and then drops it, so the fall breaks the turtle's shell and exposes the tender flesh inside. This could easily happen to me. For the higher we climbed above the flames of Satan's kingdom, the more I was at the mercy of one very famous demon.[8]

CHAPTER XXII

THE FORMS OF FRAUD

"Look below and see the gossips and slanderers,"[1] Mephistopheles hissed, bringing his head at the end of a long, vulture-like neck next to mine. "They made it their business to mar the character of their neighbors,[2] with their idle stories and slanders notched like arrows to pierce their fellow man: so now in Hell, they are the prey of demons whose fiery darts trail ever after them.

"In life, their speech was full of such cruel rapport, so here in Hell our spirits hunt them for sport."[3]

From the air I saw thousands of shades fleeing from the fiends who hunted them. I held on tight to Mephistopheles's spiny back and we glided from one gorge to the next, carried aloft by the screams of those condemned below. The fiend seemingly relied on the powers of the air to carry him upward,[4] for he did not flap his wings or exert the least effort at all in gliding over the Desolation of Fraud. Instead, he merely trimmed his wings or unfurled them like sails before the wind. Or perhaps his flight was more like a snake sliding across the desert, endlessly twisting and turning so only the least part of him touched the fiery sands that burned him.

"In the third of our chasms we have the seducers," Mephistopheles explained. "These wraiths lured away young creatures from the

Enemy's path with promises of love or marriage or flashy trinkets, feeding them whatever falsehoods they could in order to slake their lust upon a creature of such feigned virtue. Worse are those condemned for spoiling, ruining, destroying women and children who were, as you mortals use the term, *innocent*, molesting, exploiting, raping some poor soul in the world above. Or in convincing them to do it to themselves through surgeries or medicines and other elements of artful sport, and all for the same foul ends every shade in Hell prized above everything else: their own pleasure.

"But we noble spirits shall take them however we found them, and now in Hell, we demons satisfy our lust upon them."

Mephistopheles dipped his shoulder and flew in between the walls of the chasm, so I was immersed in a scene of unspeakable horror: demons raping shades condemned for luring, seducing, and mutilating some poor creature up in the world above. The screaming of the shades was endless, pitiless, merciless, but the pain the demons brought upon them merely characterized the foul deeds of the shades they tormented. And the demons were flying in from every corner of Hell like they were frequenting a brothel.

"It is good you accepted my offer," Mephistopheles whispered. "The spirits in this ravine become notoriously cruel, even for Hell. Their lust boils whatever decency we fallen spirits still possess, yet truly they are no worse than the shades they torment, whose cruelties were as numerous and odious as the torment befalling them for their punishment.

"For their sin is all too easy to gratify in the world above. The bottomless lust these sinners satisfied turned them into sickening predators. Indeed, they indulged in their lust so completely and totally they gave themselves over to us before they even died, so while their bodies were still living, their souls were already here in Hell, their bodies plied upon by demons as if they were no more than dolls or toys—and should it not be so?

"For if a man employs such evil speech to mislead creatures so foolish and so weak, so he may turn a human being into an object of fiendish pleasure—is such a man from a demon really any better?"

Mephistopheles swooped down even lower and glided just above the bottom of the gorge. With a scaly claw, he pointed to the shades of image-swindlers, whoremongers, and flesh-peddlers I recognized from the movies they filmed or the movies filmed about them that celebrate their achievement of turning the human face divine into a surface fit only to satisfy the endless lust of man.[5] Then Mephistopheles trimmed his wings to catch the wind and soon we were ascending high above the Desolation of Fraud again.

"Below is the fourth gorge in the Desolation of Fraud," Mephistopheles said, leaning into the wind. "Here we have the shades who tried to read the future and predict the fates of foolish men: fortune tellers, palm readers, conjurers of the dead, and all manner of new-age spiritualists you know. But if pretending to see into God's precious, little secrets was their sin, they now have no eyes to see the anguish *we* bring down upon them."

I, meanwhile, dared to look into the gorge below. Demons were gouging out the eyes of fortunetellers and casting the orbs from one end of the canyon to the other. Then the shades took off to find their eyes, groping in the dark and slamming headlong into pockets of flame or shades. Even if they retrieved their eyes, or even the eyes of someone else, their sight returned only long enough to see some new demon stealing it from them.

The currents of Hell carried us into the next canyon and Mephistopheles whispered in my ear, "And here are the hypocrites, shades who said one thing and thought another, uttering blessings and harboring curses[6] and feigning love all while steeping their hearts in bitterness.[7]

"Their pious guise betrayed a heart immured in sin, so now they walk about while demons wear their skin."

From the air, the gorge looked like the workshop of a textile mill or a leather tannery. Rows of demons were flaying those condemned, then the fiends walked about in the guise of hypocrites until they tired of their false appearance and cast it off. Only when the personality of the hypocrites had entirely withered away did the fiends re-stitch the skins to the frames.

Unmoved, Mephistopheles glided into the next canyon. There I saw scores of shades stumbling about and scratching at sores bulging on their skin. Then Mephistopheles said to me, "Those are the falsifiers, inventors of evil whose creations mimicked the appearance of something good to mask the poison at its root,[8] punished in accord to what these shades invented.

"Some shades turned cheap powders into the semblance of real food, while others invented new and delightful scourges for mankind, complete with fanciful names like acid and ecstasy and crystal. We fiends have labored hard and long to make man a master over nature, and armed with this knowledge, humanity has far outpaced what even we noble spirits could ever accomplish.

"Still others did not invent new evils but printed them—printed money, that is, this age's legion of counterfeiters, creatures not from Jekyll Island but the pit of Hell, all of whom are afflicted with ills welling up from deep inside them, falsifiers who invented plagues far worse than anything we fiends could contrive, and now they're cursed with every scourge that has ever struck mankind."

Mephistopheles caught a swell of hot air from the adjoining gorge and we rose high above the Desolation of Fraud. I held on tight to the spines of the demon's back to keep from falling off, while Mephistopheles trimmed his wings and headed for the next damned canyon. I looked below and saw huge, grotesque fountains seemingly carved out of stone along the canyon walls. The statues resembled the shapes of men, albeit with their limbs twisted and hardened into cruel, unnatural positions. From their mouths spewed fire and brimstone seemingly creating the gusts of wind we used to maintain our flight.

"And now we approach the ravine of false prophets. Names you'd surely recognize from your time on earth: Joseph Smith, Charles Taze Russell, heralds of religions new who claimed to speak for God, or find new books of the Bible, or restore God's church to whatever state they claimed God intended for it.

"Certainly, they spoke for someone. But I tell you, they received their revelation from My Father Herein. Our lord and prince may assume any form he likes, including that of an angel of light[9] and, in donning such an angelic guise, Lucifer brought fresh revelation to mankind far more suited to a people so warped in heart and mind.

"For who would not want to hear the Bible, with all its commands, was no longer reliable, or the Enemy's Word changed by sinful men, and thus could never be trusted again?"

The longer Satan's poison erupted from the false prophets, the larger their statues became. But the weight of the statues, combined with the steep slopes upon which they were built, made them so unstable they could not keep growing indefinitely. Small cracks appeared and encircled the false prophets like lightning around a tree until the statues exploded, sending fire and brimstone and pieces of wraith hurtling down to the canyon floor. Then the demons heaped the shades together again so Hell's poison, which is false doctrine, could pour out of them once again and erect these huge, terrifying monuments to their lord and master, the prince of fiends, the fell and shadowy Satan.

"I know now we're over the Rift of False Counsel," Ernest shouted and pointed to the next gorge, teeming with flames as slender from the air as the light of an anglerfish. "Where can you set us down?"

"Of course," Mephistopheles answered. "Per our accord, I shall set you down at the top of the canyon. You need only to walk down into the Rift of False Counsel to find the shade with whom you must speak."

Mephistopheles trimmed his wings and doubled over in his flight. I held on ever tighter until Mephistopheles unfurled his wings wider and wider to slow his descent to the Desolation of Fraud. He landed on a burnt-over crest overlooking the Rift of False Counsel, a narrow, winding valley whose darkness was broken only by matchless, flickering flames. Mephistopheles reached behind his wings, plucked me off of my seat, and set me down onto the gray precipice. He did the same for Ernest, who looked surprised we encountered no real trouble from one of Hell's Big Five. Was this some kind of trick?

"Why have you helped us?" I asked.

"As I stated before," Mephistopheles replied with something like a smile, "I have a peculiar interest in humans. Thus, I leave you here with nothing but the knowledge of the way ahead: a path is cut into the canyon walls, a narrow defile not wide enough for a fiend but will fit the likes of you.

"If you neither fall nor turn from this path, it will lead you to Piristu, the Rift of False Counsel. Walk to the center of the canyon, and there you will find two pillars of flame, intertwined. It is with these two flames you are to speak next. I might wish you luck, but luck, fortune, chance, all count for nothing in Hell. So I leave you only with the order to go, for the one thing that matters in Hell is the will of our Father Herein, and should his will change, I would come back for you with all the malice I bear within me."

With that Mephistopheles flapped his giant wings and took off from the ash heap. He dove into the canyon, then gained enough momentum until he was flying high above our heads and soon I could see only his shadow against the dreadful gaze of Satan's Eye.

We took the path Mephistopheles identified and went down into the canyon, the pillars of flame in the gorge below growing larger with every step. Ernest and I carefully sidestepped our way down the sheer length of the canyon walls, until finally we reached the bottom.

A forest of pillars spread out across the canyon. The ground was burnt-over and barren, like the salt flats out West, with cracks in the ground threading their way through the fiery woods. We threaded our way between the pillars until we reached the center of the gorge, where we found one pillar towering above the rest, the pillar containing the shades I was to speak with next. So who was I supposed to speak with, that Mephistopheles would lead me straight to him?

CHAPTER XXIII

THE FALSEST COUNSEL

"Truly, truly, you are alive?" asked the flame, its heat rising and falling with its speech. "And news, what news might you have of the world above?"

Inside the flame, I could see two wraiths bound together, its twin fires coiling and recoiling about themselves like a tornado bearing down upon some hapless village. One shade stood considerably taller than the other, with long lean limbs climbing to a gaunt face backed by a shock of fiery red hair. The other wraith was considerably shorter and decidedly portlier, with heavy jowls and ashen, unkempt hair that, as his hair broached the flame, trailed off like wisps of smoke from a guttering candle.[1] Other fiery pillars surrounded Ernest and me but only this pillar spoke, the other flames waxing and waning in deference to its speech.

"I am alive, sir," I answered, sensing the noble bearing of the shade, whose appearance I could just barely recognize. *But there's no way . . .*

"Yet, you travel through this realm," the taller of the two flames spoke again. "How is this so?"

"Last night, I tried to kill myself, after years of depression, years of wild and outrageous living, drinking, doing drugs the likes of which should have killed me, and worse deeds—a life so empty I gave up all hope and took my own life, but God is giving me some kind of second chance, if only I would understand what it means to repent."

"And what did you do to merit such a chance?" the lesser flame asked, addressing me for the first time. "Many men abandon hope—long before they enter here, mind you—and live accordingly, for sure: then they die, they are condemned, and into whatever pit they are cast, there they do not leave."

"So what has you brought you here," the taller shade resumed speaking, "and equips you to travel unharmed through this horrible place?"

"Before I died, I tried to pray and repent and ask God for forgiveness for the things I did in my life, and God heard and must have answered my prayers, weak and feeble though they were—otherwise, I should have been sent here immediately, right?"

"Astounding, convincing, simple," replied the greater flame. "But in answer to prayer? That I do not believe."

"Where are you from then, my boy?" the shorter shade asked. "And your age? Occupation?"

"Virginia, I'm still young, barely twenty years old, really, just a sophomore at the College of William & Mary."

"My word," the greater shade answered. "If I had any doubts you killed yourself, they are dispelled, for I attended William & Mary, too, and was as desperate as you to get out of that place."

"Who are you then?" I asked the shade.

"I am Thomas Jefferson," the shade replied from the fire, "the sage of Monticello, author of the Declaration of Independence, champion of the people's liberties, as well as a devoted husband and father, a man whose every word and deed aimed only at the happiness of my people, despite the hardship and suffering I endured all the days of my life."

"No, it's just—it can't be," I whispered, moving away from the pillar and closer to Hem. "What happened to you? And who is there with you?"

"You do not recognize him either?" the shade of Thomas Jefferson answered.

"You just don't look anything like the paintings I've seen of you," I answered, trembling, looking over at Ernest and thinking, *If Jefferson could not save himself by works . . .*

"I am sure we don't, given what we have endured," the shorter shade retorted. "But the shade with whom I share this pillar gave as much of his life, if not more so than I, to lift from our people England's wretched yoke—and hence we're bound in Hell together."

"Anything to make our torment worse," Jefferson simpered. "After our long friendship, our noble deeds in '76, our adventures abroad in Europe, even after we wounded each other vying for the presidency, I am condemned to perdition with my greatest friend, and in deeds my only equal, so much so we left the earth at nearly the same hour and even upon the 4th of July, no less. Indeed, I am confined to the very same flame in Hell as that of my dearest friend, Mr. John Adams of Quincy."[2]

"I thank ye for the introduction," the shade of John Adams replied, "but still, I am more interested in news from the world above rather than hearing of my own deeds, the likes of which I regrettably know all too well."

"True, true," Jefferson resumed. "Tell everything, my boy, you know of the country my friend and I wagered everything—our lives, our sacred honor, even our souls—to establish. What of it?"

"I can only speak of my own experience," I answered, "for I am still young, but the country you founded has indeed accomplished many noble things: up above, we enjoy a freedom no other country on earth would dare give its citizens, and nearly a century ago, the United States sacrificed almost everything it had to free the world from two powerful, violent, aggressive nations—one called Nazi Germany, and the other Imperial Japan, and—"

"Germany, Japan?" Jefferson interrupted, his flame rising with excitement. "You mean to say these nations, who were hardly states during the age in which we lived, threatened the world's peace and tranquility, and we, the people of the United States, put an end to their tyranny?"

"Yes, we did," I answered. "And you would be so proud of the heroism exhibited by your descendants: boys from Massachusetts, Virginia, the frontier states founded after you died, an entire generation of great Americans scaling cliffs with knives in their teeth,[3] storming beaches teeming with enemy soldiers and huge guns bearing down on them, thinking of nothing but their family back home and the good they might do their country."

"If virtue was indeed our only hope," Adams interjected, "I might feel a sense of peace, even joy, even here in Hell—but I know better now. What has happened since then, for you said this transpired 'nearly a century' ago, and that is an awfully long time, my boy."

"Those soldiers endured insane hardships," I nodded and continued. "They lived through a kind of famine called the Great Depression, and then the war against Germany and Japan, called World War II, and when it was over, something changed within them and in the country. That generation couldn't, or wouldn't, teach their children to endure the hardships they suffered, and then their children refused to do so anyway."

"Hearing of this 'second' war, I won't trouble to ask you about the 'first,'" asked the shade of the sage of Monticello, interest piqued, flame flickering. "But pray tell me, what happened next, my boy?"

"At the end of the war, the soldiers came home and had families, huge numbers of children, collectively called 'boomers,' but when those kids were old enough to choose for themselves, they abandoned the path of virtue, as Mr. Franklin explained such a path to me, and took up a life consumed in pleasure and ease, devoid of the virtues that characterized the values of their parents."

"Oh no," Adams lamented. "Dear Benjamin is here too? Did no one who penned the Declaration escape ruin and perdition?"

"What evidence might you have," Jefferson asked, "that this indeed has happened?"

"My grandfather fought at a place called Iwo Jima, one of the deadliest battles in the war, but my dad barely made it through college, and neither of them really knew how to be a father—hence, the drugs my dad got into in the sixties, and now the drugs and the alcohol I got into in high school and college. It's a vicious cycle."

"Do tell me," Jefferson continued, "what might account for this rift, this rift in virtue between your grandfather on the one hand and your own father on the other, which may explain our people living now have abandoned the virtues that inspired the spirit of '76?"

"Suffering, I think, and no knowledge of God to justify it or explain it. I can't begin to explain the cruelty of Nazi Germany, a regime that murdered people by the millions and would have been successful, had it not been for the people of the United States and everyone who fought alongside us.

"But no matter the good we did abroad, it did not change or atone for the bad things we did back at home, the legacy of slavery and Indian removal and the like. At least from what I've learned in Hell, that kind of guilt and shame can only be removed by turning to God, but an ever-larger number of Americans reject God because they can't—or won't—trust him, while the advancements we've made in science, the desire for pleasure at any cost, and all the forms of suffering and evil we see in the world, some combination of all three, keep people from looking to God for any hope.

"Such things make God seem like a foolish superstition or an overbearing father or even a cruel tyrant, not someone we can actually trust and obey. So the people turn to the government to fix the problem and then proceed to serve themselves."

"For shame," Jefferson moaned, "it is my legacy that has brought this ruin upon the country, I know it, a feeling I've nurtured whilst in this flame. In life, I tried to bury the inconsistencies of my head and heart deep within my psyche, trying never to reconcile them or repent for them but only to atone for them out of the good I thought I could do our country—what folly, what ruin have I brought upon my people."

"What do you mean, Mr. Jefferson?" I asked. "What happened to you?"

"I know too well the sadness of which you speak," Jefferson answered. "I felt the same as you even whilst I attended William & Mary, but my melancholy led me not to repentance, but to the hope that one day man would be free—free from every form of tyranny lording over the mind of man. Then, in light of that freedom, our people could pursue such happiness as was right in their own eyes.[4]

Indeed, the folly of it all, my vision that an Empire of Liberty might stretch across the American continent, a land of commerce and industry, of happiness and virtue, of life, liberty, and the pursuit of happiness, the manifestation of every dream I ever dreamed that our people might be *free*, free in every meaningful way and from every impediment that might constrain their good and noble choices, free whether or not the happiness they pursued might lead to or, indeed, lead from, their Creator. That was the empire I dreamed of and endeavored my whole life to build, the folly of which, now that I recognize its logical conclusion, only adds to my torment in Hell.

"My tale begins in the Revolution. You surely know of my valiant deeds in Philadelphia, sitting at a wooden desk I made myself to write no less a work than the Declaration of Independence. Therein I channeled centuries of theory and history, of liberty and hope into my quill so my love of freedom might radiate through those sublime words, *All men are created equal*. Oh, to be used by the Deity one time, just one time, to upend the world was a privilege I shall not forget, not even here.

"But you know not of my family's struggles during those years, sufferings I endured before and after that august summer of '76. For my beloved wife, Patty, and I buried far too many of our precious children beneath the ground at Monticello:[5] first, a beautiful daughter passed while the British assailed the coastal towns of Virginia; and then Patty suffered an awful miscarriage in 1776, pains made all the worse with me at work in Philadelphia laboring for the cause of freedom, far too far away for me to comfort my grieving wife or tend to her in her despair.

"Then another hapless, helpless babe perished after living barely a fortnight; and still another daughter, a sweet girl named Lucy Elizabeth, who lived for only half a year and scarcely saw the first blooms of spring before she was in the ground beneath them. Gone, gone, all gone, and I alone to tell the tale!"

I had no idea Jefferson lost so many children, I thought to myself. *I was so crippled emotionally and spiritually just with Evelyn's cancer—how could anyone endure the death of so many children?*

"I did not speak often of my troubles," Jefferson continued. "I tried to bear them as best I could. But my wife could not, and the perils of childbirth and the depredations of the British grew too much for my dear sweet Patty. Once the war ended, when domestic bliss should have settled upon Monticello and my beloved Patty in labor yet again, she breathed her last surrounded by our family at our ancient home: in the throes of childbirth, the curse of Eve having fallen upon her, Patty did not survive the birth of another precious little girl.

"She passed, we buried her at Monticello, and I immured with her my dreams for a happy life and pleas unheard for her health. The Lord, whose hand I had been promised was mighty to save, made my *wife* his *mark* and *not* some object of his grace[6] despite my prayers for her recovery. Such prayers, my boy, God does not listen to."

Can that be true? I thought, the thoughts of Evelyn, my drinking, my suicide all racing through my mind the more Jefferson spoke. I remember holding Evelyn's hand at the hospital after years of watching her waste away, and how angry I was whenever Grandmasco would ask God again for mercy and healing, and we would hear one last time God say nothing. *Why does God allow for so much suffering and evil in the world above? Why* not *put a stop to it, if he can? if he's good?*

"Alas, I never left Patty's side unless in service to my country. But then, she was gone, and pain upon pain, the poor babe Patty carried and died delivering, that sweet child lived but a few years and joined my wife wherever God takes the good ones. The nature of such a realm I do not know, but how desperate I was to fly to wherever God took her, desperate beyond measure to see my beloved Patty again. For weeks thereafter I wandered the dark and tangled wood of Albemarle, fighting thoughts of suicide, struggling not to kill myself every moment I was awake."

"Just like me? You thought of suicide, even after all you did in Philadelphia, writing no less than the most important words in American history, the Declaration of Independence?"

"What did those words matter? My wife and family mattered most to me, and Patty's loss, and that of my children, crushed me beyond belief—indeed, they crushed my belief. During the Revolution, everyone praised me for the Declaration, words which gave them a future and a hope. But I had no such hope, not anymore.

"No, I envied those plain farmers permitted to stay with their loved ones. I could hardly stand to be away from Patty in Philadelphia, much less left on earth with Patty in Heaven loosed from her mortal coil. I yearned for the days when we would walk the grounds at Monticello or canoe down the Rivanna,[7] but my hopes for happiness were shattered, snatched away in an instant as if Satan, walking to and fro across Virginia,[8] made *me* his *Job,* and I alone escaped to tell the tale.[9] Oh, I fought tirelessly against the thought that I should take my life and fly to whatever realm Patty's precious soul resided.[10]

"Had I stayed in Virginia who knows what might have transpired? I may very well have ended it all, but fortune cast me upon the seas between the Old World and the New to France, like Odysseus[11] sailing against Poseidon's anger.[12] There I was to serve my country in a realm that had advanced the cause of freedom far more than most among the powers of the earth, second only to America herself. There in France, in the twilight of the *ancien regime*,[13] I was to bear the lot of Job whom God afflicted with pains like my own, but I, of course, had comforts Job did not."

Would God really do this, just to test him? I thought to myself. *I remember those unanswered prayers for Evelyn, but isn't there something more, something else I don't understand, about the ways of God and the way he deals with man?*

"Indeed, in France," the sage of Monticello continued, "I could enjoy the writings of *philosophes* like Voltaire and Diderot[14] and the delightful conversation of the salon and their beautiful Parisian hosts. I could indulge in what France offered in philosophy, wine, and architecture,[15] while my command of French allowed me to absorb the gracious and enlightened thought of Paris, all of which confirmed my suspicions about the manner God rules our lives from his throne."

"What do you mean?" I asked.

"You do not know?" Jefferson said. "Is it not evident to you, you who abandoned all hope and killed yourself? You see Evan, I believed then that God made the world and set its course to run not unlike a watch, its operations set to laws even he will not break. From the world God withdraws his hand and does not ever intervene in the affairs of men again, for God is a wise architect, a skilled watchmaker, a fine craftsman, but not a loving father, not the kind the Bible describes, not from what I have seen."[16]

Can that really be true? I thought. *Didn't Jesus suffer just like we do—loss, abandonment—and other pains we human beings go through?*

"Thus, I resolved to free mankind from yet another idle king. God had not helped me, not when such help might violate the laws of nature, laws God upholds against the prayers of helpless men, a truth now so wretchedly self-evident to me whenever I looked upon the graves of my children and my wife. I reasoned, quite easily, if Deism was true, then neither God nor Jesus performed the miracles recorded in Scripture. Those miracles had to go.[17]

"So I took up my scissors and a razor blade and went to work. I judged the words and deeds of Jesus as if I were Pontius Pilate himself,[18] combing through the New Testament and finding what I held were pious falsehoods, miraculous deeds falsely described, claims of divinity falsely attributed to Jesus. These I cut out with my scissors and my razor so that slowly, surely, as if carving a little idol, I revealed the man this Jesus truly was. Born of a Virgin, really? Just like Minerva sprang fully armed from the head of Jove? *Rip*.[19] Feeding multitudes on a mountainside? A merry tale, certainly told to please children, but insipid, irrational, impossible. *Cut*. And rising from the dead? Why, we have had great teachers of morals since Jesus's day, but we have never seen them walk out of their graves. Thus this story, too, I think should be cast into the *flames*.

"I worked and worked until my own Scriptures were finished. Every jot and tittle Jesus did not say and deeds I thought Jesus could not do, I removed them all from the pages of Scripture. Then at last, I revealed the real and sublime figure of Jesus of Nazareth, a teacher, a philosopher, an inventor of the finest system of morals the world had ever seen—but nothing more. My work was thus composed only of the more acceptable teachings of Jesus and a few scattered sayings from the apostle Paul. But once completed, I possessed a text far more rational, more reliable, a work I christened and celebrated as the Jefferson Bible."[20]

"Today, in the world above, Mr. Jefferson, people cannot explain or understand why or how you could pen the Declaration yet still owned slaves. You may be the most controversial, the most loved, at times the most criticized of the Founding Fathers because of this tension in your legacy and in—"

"Oh, my boy, I know," Jefferson sighed. "For Pilate asked Jesus, 'What is truth?' and in my pride and folly, I thought I knew.[21] Nor in life was I afraid to act upon my idea of truth, my realization of how the world truly operated, for if the mind may make a Heaven of Hell and a Hell of Heaven,[22] then truth is what I wanted and the wealth to procure it, the ease to enjoy it, and the reason, if necessary, to justify it. Indeed, I made my heaven 'pon my little mountaintop at Monticello, a life of ease and tranquility, books and building projects—life however I wanted and on terms however I set them.

"For if God does not exist—and such doubts I entertained—that is one thing. But if God did not care, well, that was just as good a justification to live however I pleased. From this conviction I ordered my life accordingly, having rejected the one real hope for mankind, this Jesus, for a teacher of morals cannot save anyone. For if Christ is not raised—as forsooth I believed he was not—we are still trapped in our sins,[23] and the sins that held me continued to grow.

"Indeed, I could have sold Monticello and freed my slaves and lived simply, humbly, perhaps in a boarding house in Philadelphia near the site of the Declaration, in word and deed my greatest triumph. Instead, my slaves toiled each day as I required them so I might enjoy my books and wine and architecture, building and rebuilding Monticello even while I accrued mountainous debts. I buried deep within my soul the fear of what might happen to them all once I died, but if it happened, so be it.[24] Had not God treated me with the same indifference?

"God did not care how I lived, that I was sure of, so I would do what was needed to ease my grief. Such was my resolve when I commenced upon my greatest folly, a tryst that nearly ruined my reputation then, but my heart overwhelmed my head the moment I saw her, a maiden I mistook for my dearly departed wife walking the grounds at Monticello and tending to my garden. 'Could it be?' I thought. 'Is it my dear Patty, or perhaps it is her ghost? Or have these long years been a dream?' I ran to her and embraced her but it was not Patty, not even Patty's ghost—it was her sister, Sally.

"For Sally was both the sister to, and the slave of, my dear departed Patty. They had the same father and thus shared the same graceful lineaments and countenance, and the beautiful, albeit tawny, features of Patty's sister looked just enough like Patty to ease my broken heart. Oh, the comfort she brought to my weary soul, comforts I convinced myself I deserved. For reason is slave to the passions, and my passions were wracked with grief.[25] Why not embrace a life of pleasure, ease, and tranquility after not only what I *suffered* but also what I *accomplished*? And might not my public deeds outweigh such private trifles?

"But here was yet another folly. For in life, I aspired that all my works might contribute to the cause of freedom and the flourishing of the American people: the Declaration of American Independence, the Statute of Virginia for Religious Freedom, the University of Virginia, it was all to help our people pursue life, liberty, and happiness, freed from every entanglement cruel tyrants might impose upon them. But in my head and heart, long nursing such grievances as I did against God, I left it open the people could pursue happiness apart from God. Forsooth, if God is the source of our freedom, I made a grave mistake.

"For having carved such perfect freedom for myself, I thought the greatest good I could do my country was to give such freedom to everyone else. Such was my Empire of Liberty, a state powerful enough to free our people to live however they want and shield them from the consequences. So, if my posterity has rejected God because of suffering, pain, and want, and instead commenced to live for ease and gain instead, it is, in part, my fault. Oh, just as Odysseus sailed the Atlantic wide, past the gates of Heracles[26] where God kept man confined, I aimed in all my endeavors to free the powers of the human mind,all because I held Satan's falsest council true: 'Live however you want, for God does not love *you*.'"

CHAPTER XXIV

THE TRAITORS

"Do not believe it, Evan!" Jefferson begged. "It is a lie from the pit of Hell, and my life and legacy would have been different, *eternally* different, had I not believed it, if only someone shared with me the gospel I removed from the Bible. For any good I did on earth, and any good I might still do now, believe nothing of what the demons say and instead repent, Evan—and whatever repentance is, do it *now*!"

Jefferson's shade erupted at his final pronouncement and I shrank back in fear. But before I could say anything, a demon tore through the shade of Thomas Jefferson and tried to grab me from the air. The winged galano barely missed me but trimmed his wings to make another pass while more demons plummeted into the canyon like eagles hunting for fish. They broke through the forest of false counsel in hopes they would be the one to bring me bound and broken to Satan himself. Had Satan changed his mind, or had the demons lost all self-control and decided to come for me?

Ernest and I fled for cover at the walls of the canyon, Ernest pulling me into a nearby cave that should have offered us little protection. The mouth was still large enough for the fiends—indeed, the demons used these tunnels to cut back and forth between the gorges in the Desolation of Fraud. But a galano following us too closely didn't trim his wings enough to fit through the opening. The demons behind him slammed into him, the fiend blocking the entrance like a bat stuck in a chimney. I heard the fiend screaming in pain while the other galanos pushed him forward, the wings of one fiend scarcely holding the rest of them back.

Then they tried eating the spirit blocking their way. His cries reverberated through the tunnel and when that proved unsuccessful, they unleashed their fury upon the slopes, hoping to enlarge the cave mouth or bring the mountain down and bury my guide and me inside. But even that failed, with only loose bits of ash and rock falling around us. Perhaps we were safe, but still we hurried through the darkness while the cries of galanos wasted away to nothing. We walked in silence over any number of tiny, millipede-like spirits slithering through the cave and crawling up my legs until a small opening, outlined in flame, appeared ahead of us.

Soon we came out at the bottom of the ravine, next to a river of molten rock. I took some deep breaths and tried to collect myself, but breathing in the air of Hell or trying to rest did me no good. The envenomed air absorbed the fumes of Hell, and whatever the walls were made of—sulfur, saltpeter, some hideous mixture made by fiends both above and herein—rubbed off on my hands and chemically burned them too.

Aside from the river, nothing in the canyon moved. No demons patrolled this realm, whose cruelty was not needed because the shades were trapped inside statues made of ice. The shades did not melt despite the strange fires raging beneath their icy exteriors; instead, the shades were seemingly frozen at the very moment some evil plan entered their hearts and the devil took control of them.[1] I saw all manner of Americans hailing from every period and every walk of life, from colonials dressed in cold buckskins to businessmen in suits as sharp as shards of ice, all casting their eyes to the ground as if to hide the fires of their ambition.

"Where are we now?"

"The Gorge of Traitors," Ernest answered.[2]

"And why are they frozen? How can they withstand this heat?"

"Such is the nature of their punishment," Hem replied. "These shades feigned such goodwill and charity in life so now in Hell, they bear a visage as cold as ice. When they were alive, their own self-interest was all they sought to help, so now each shade holds a Hell that burns all to themselves."

Hem motioned for me to follow him. We walked beside the molten river while the soaring heights of the canyon steadily tapered downward as if even the slopes were melting in the heat or were bowing in deference to their master lurking somewhere deeper in Hell. At last, we rounded one last bend and came upon the Lake of Fire.

The burning lake had no end. I saw no distant shoreline, for even the horizon was consumed in flame, a veil of fire in place of blue skies and wispy clouds drifting over the oceans of the earth. The Eye of Satan burned directly overhead and, in its center, in the very pupil of the dreadful Eye, I thought I saw the reflection of Satan enthroned, watching over all. The only indication I stood on the shores of a lake, and not a boundless ocean, were the slight curves on the strand even as the rest of Hell plummeted into the burning lake.

I followed Hem to the shoreline of the Lake of Fire. Ernest approached one statue staring only into his own Hell, cast in the blood red, albeit hoarfrosted, uniform of a British army officer. He tried to stand as tall as he could despite a galling wound still evident in his icy leg,[3] his arms held out as if he were trying to embrace something he wanted. I saw among his icy features a long, sharp nose and eyes betraying the intensity of a cause he held only for himself. When he noticed Ernest approaching him, the wraith began to speak.

"They envy me, not knowing who I am, the shades within the Lake of Fire," came a voice from within this likeness of a man. "Such esteem is all I asked for in life, but here 'tis shown most hollow, for my admirers would never look upon me if they knew I am the most abhorred of all Americans, the man who betrayed the cause of American independence to the British."

"Are you Benedict Arnold?" I asked.

"'Tis as I feared," the shade replied, "even among the shades in Hell, stripped of my fiery personality, you forthwith recognized me."

"Every schoolchild in America knows who you are. You went over to the British near the end of the Revolution, and once you evaded capture, you took the Redcoats through Virginia and burned the capital at Richmond—and all for lands and riches and titles, the liberty of your country for an estate in England."

"Verily, is the moral so plain and evident?" the shade jeered. "Indeed, no man's life is so simple one can draw from their success—or fall—the moral needed to aid the one and forestall the other. Forsooth, my life ended in treachery, but the world forgets my noble deeds before I turned traitor: scaling the cliffs at Quebec,[4] besting the British Navy on Lake Champlain, or gallantly charging the British lines at Saratoga in a victory so stunning and complete it convinced the world America could triumph over even so mighty a power as Great Britain. And I need not have betrayed *anyone*, had I been honored for my contributions!"

"What happened to you then?"

"After Saratoga, my tale recedes into nothing," Benedict Arnold rasped, his voice cracking like thin ice. "My superiors pilfered the credit due my deeds while I suffered in fortune, mind, and body for all the good I did my country 'pon the Bemis Heights.[5] And pitifully would I have yielded to such loathsome melancholy, had not a woman of such poise and beauty,[6] my sweet wife, Ms. Peggy Shippen of Philadelphia, found me, nursed me, and presented me a means to reverse my fortunes and revenge my sense of injured merit.[7]

"Those precious weeks in Philadelphia thus became the best I reaped on earth. My dear wife obliged me with homage due a king, tending to my mortal spirit with cries of fame and recompense for my noble deeds.[8] How she *pleaded* with me to unseat the lowborn patriots who stole *my* glory and humiliated *her* family, and that I and I alone could end the fool's errand of independence before it was too late!"

Arnold shook so hard I thought his stature would either shatter or melt in the intensity of his own bitterness. Then Arnold continued his lurid tale.

"For in throwing off a king, the people stirred a foul and loathsome beast, a creature which does not fly the human heart unless it knows it won't ever be caught or bound again: Men in every colony grew drunk at the thought of ruling themselves, and so they committed every kind of evil without fear or scruple: neighbor betraying neighbor, the rabble forming mobs, the masses routing the estates of their betters.[9] The jealousy driving men to such heights of folly had been unleashed, infecting all American with the gross and rank disease they foolishly called their *liberty*.

"Even worse were our leaders in Philadelphia. Those covetous, vile delegates would strangle the cause of freedom outright or let it freeze to death, if only they'd advance the position of their state a mere farthing over a rival. So yes, I betrayed the revolution once I realized its true course, the nature of the beast they let loose upon the world: humanity is its own worst scourge, and liberty does nothing to alleviate our curse but truly serves to make it *worse*. So, with my superiors reaping the honors I earned, I vowed I would seize everything I deserved."

"What beast are you talking about?" I whispered.

The black discs that remained of his eyes shook violently but, unable to move, the fire bound within this icy shade burned all the more silently. Then, somewhere deep within his fiery interior came this icy reply:

"One cannot be told of the awful beast our lust, our jealousy, our rank desire to be *free* released into the world, but here upon the bank and shoal of Hell, you need only walk ahead to see it for yourself. For the spirit that moved me to betray my people and their cause is the same spirit that animates so many shades in Hell, condemning us all to the flames in which we burn: jealousy, envy, covetousness, and all alike that moves a man to hate everyone around him. It moved me to turn traitor, but you will have to ask those shades what it moved *them* to do."

Ernest motioned for me to follow him, so I left Arnold's presence and walked closer to the Lake of Fire, thinking of the nature of the beast Benedict Arnold spoke of. Ernest stopped short of the shoreline, avoiding the waves of fire breaking on the strand. He would not move any closer.

Then the thought came to me again: *What is so wrong with the human condition that one man would harm another, even if he risked his own damnation*? So I turned to Hem and asked how it all fit together.

"What does it all mean?" I asked. "The beast, the beast within my heart, the beast that Arnold and others spoken of, how does it all fit together?"

"Evan, a beast is all we become when we reject God," Hem replied in earnest, watching with sorrow the demons plunging into the burning lake, fishing for shades. "It is in our nature that we aspire to be like God, but when we ape God's power in ruling ourselves, we become more like the apes, the beasts God gave to us to rule, and the freedom and the prosperity—and for some, the fame—we have today does not change or better our condition but only serve to make it worse."

"But if I repent, will the sad things in my life come untrue?"

"In a way, but not all at once," Hem replied. "If you repent, God will forgive you, and that will be a very good thing, but God will not change all the things you hate about yourself, not all at once, though perhaps he will change you so you do not hate yourself anymore."

"To not hate myself, that would be a miracle."

"Yes, it would," Hem said, who hadn't moved any closer to the burning lake. "That self-loathing is as bad as pride as long as it keeps you focused on yourself, hatred that could turn you into a monster, like some galano trolling the waters for weaker fish, but more likely it'll keep you sad and lonely and weak, more like the birds living near the ocean, the terns who are always flying and flying but never finding land, too small and too delicate to survive the cruel current. I suppose we are all like the terns then, and we need God to guide us to the shore and protect us from the galanos."

"Are you coming with me into the burning lake?"

"No, I am not," Hemingway answered. "As you draw closer to the heart of Hell and the evil recesses of your own heart, God wants you to rely on him and not look to me for help or guidance anymore. You won't be on your own, but I can't be at your side, either.

"I'll step with you into the burning lake, but I'll burn away and turn to ash, and the winds will carry what's left of me to the Forest of the Suicides. There the demons will put me back in the same plot of ground I've had since I shot myself, and there I'll grow up again like a tree rooted in sin until the end of days, the second death, the final judgment, whatever the end looks like."

"I'm so sor—" I stammered out.

"Don't say that," Hem stopped me. "I wouldn't want your pity on earth, and you know you shouldn't give it to shades like me. And now you have to go, go and figure out how to repent, how to repent truly and rightly, for that is why God has brought you here and tasked me with guiding you up until this point."

Hem took my hand and put both feet into the fiery waves and kept walking. His pale legs, khakis still tucked into his boots, caught fire and withered to ash, but Hem kept moving and pulling me in with him into the burning lake.

"If you get back to the world above," Hem replied in earnest, "and I know you will, find my boys, my family, whatever is left of them, whoever is not here, and tell them I'm sorry, sorry for my failures and the times I let them down, all the times I took some blonde out fishing instead of taking them, or carving out time to drink and write and sending them off with some nanny they hated: tell them Papa Hemingway has finally learned what it means to be a father, even if it's too late and it won't do them or me any good. They never heard it from me on earth, but it's better to hear it from me now even if I'm in Hell: I'm sorry, boys—sorry for wanting to be a better writer and never a better dad. I was wrong then, and I deserve what I'm getting now."

Is this what it looks like to repent? I thought as the fire encircled the rest of Papa Hemingway. His limbs had all but burned away and his broad chest was wreathed in ash, but still I tried to embrace my guide. The shade of Ernest Hemingway tried but failed to smile until even that withered to ash and all that remained of Hem was an airy black cloud drifting upward to the Crown of Satan, the flakes holding their shape like a swarm of bees. I held a single flake of ash in my hand until that, too, flew upward and joined the others.

I felt the beast convulsing in pain again. But I ignored it, for this little monster had dwelt in my heart for so long and I'm so tired of giving into its dictates. The beast has been my own little Gollum, whose precious was my ruin, who tempts me for its own fiendish pleasures, a beast who I know now is really all I am apart from Christ. This little Gollum is my sinful nature, a monster freedom does not remove, but does succeed in freeing, and the more I fed the beast, the more of me the beast demanded until I finally killed myself—and I'm done doing what the beast commands. Instead, I pray I may follow Christ and do whatever *he* demands of me.

For who am I that God would save me? That God would show me any mercy at all and give me a second chance, a chance to repent and go back to the world above and *live*? After all my sins, how can God still love me, a sinner and a rake, a wretch who lived only for himself and loved nothing greater than my own pleasures? What is it in the cross of Christ that God could forgive so horrible and awful a human being as me?

And God, I am so sorry for my sins. I have spent every day of my life in open rebellion against you, my God, my Creator, my Maker, who gave me the means to live each day despite the horrible truth that I rejected you in favor of a rotten life that's led me straight to Hell. I deserve your judgment, yet you have moved to save me from my sinful self and given me the chance to repent, and I pray I may follow you and cast aside the sins and everything else I trusted in aside from you. You are worthy of all my praise, and I beg you to change my heart, cleanse me from my wickedness, and let me bow before your Son, Jesus Christ, and confess Christ is Lord every moment you might give me up on earth. God, please let me repent and follow Christ.

So now with the Lord Jesus Christ becoming my chief desire, I held my breath and waded into the Lake of Fire.[10]

CHAPTER XXV

THE LAKE OF FIRE

Only flames and shades composed the burning lake.[1] I trudged deeper into the Inferno until the fiery tide reached above my head and swept me off my feet. I struggled against the current and swam through the swirling mass of flames until I reached the bottom and grabbed onto torturous hooks of steel and adamant. The flames hoisted me upward, and I had to hold onto the spurs to keep from being swept up by the burning tide. Some shades were crawling along the iron strand trying to escape, but the relentless tide of brimstone dragged them back and cast them down into the second death where here, in matchless flame, the shades both yearned and burned condemned.[2]

I climbed down through the abyss one iron barb at a time, like a diver might pull himself along a coral reef. The shades reached for me, and the flames tried to dislodge me, but seemingly nothing could hurt me, protected as I was like Daniel's friends inside this vast and boundless furnace.[3] Unharmed, but not unfazed, for the heat of the burning lake and its flames and fumes and misery formed an undertow of unfathomable malice making it almost impossible for me to maintain consciousness, let alone swim against the burning tide.

And the fire moved between the shades with a mind all its own. Just as the great fires that once consumed New York and Chicago spread from building to building,[4] their flames disappearing inside the timber frames and erupting out again in a towering blaze, so the burning tide penetrated one shade and disappeared, only to burst out of the wraith and with its newfound strength engulf another nearby shade. The damned struggled for better positions than the ones the demons assigned them. But the harder the shades fought against the tide of endless woe, trying to ascend to a lot higher than their own, the more powerful became the current binding them.[5]

Then there was the darkness, for the swirling flames permitted no light at all. In this vast inferno, I could barely see anything except what was right in front of me. As a black hole devours any light daring to approach its dreadful gates, so the fire consumed any light one would expect such a furnace to emit. Even as my eyes grew used to the darkness, so the Lake of Fire grew continually darker as the flames intensified. Then after hours of climbing down the abyssal plains of Hell, I came to another depression opening before me, canyon-size in depth and unfathomable in its malice. As the American continent descends both east and west to the open ocean, so the Lake of Fire was bearing down toward a pit within a pit from which erupted more torrents of flames and fiends.

Across the vast and fiery deep, I saw against the darkness the darker shapes of huge beasts[6] swimming through the flames—sea monsters, dragons, sharks, leviathans, the like—and devouring the shades like they were schools of fish. Standing against the edge of this deeper hell were lofty spires curling toward the surface and were dotted with caves from which even more devils appeared and disappeared into its black recesses like swarms of insects. I crawled toward the tower closest to me, hoping I could rest in a place where rest never comes.

But there I found a shade already waiting for me. The shade sat with his back to the rock, gazing calmly into the fiery deep, stroking his chin with long, gaunt fingers. The demons dressed him in an ill-fitting gray suit, with sleeves too short to cover his long, lanky arms. He threw up his hands as soon as he saw me and I could see the intense features of his face, ears with long lobes, a huge nose, and a demeanor so confident he was strutting sitting down even at the veritable edge of Hell.

"It's about time you made it," the shade growled. "I may not look like I have much to do, but I never let some errand boy keep me waiting up on earth and I ain't about to start doing it in Hell!"

"I'm sorry," I said instinctively. "I didn't think anyone would be waiting for me."

"You thought *wrong*, boy," the shade replied, black eyes blazing with hellfire. "The Boss told me to wait here for you, a big shiny, flying spirited-thing who told me to tell *you* how it all fits together—and certainly, there is no one better than *me* to tell *you* how it does fit together. 'Course I leapt at the chance to be of any use, so I've been waiting and waiting. I'm still trying to figure this place out you see, and if I could get in good with the Boss, maybe I'd get myself a role better than being fuel for this here fire."

"Who's in this realm then?" I asked, knowing the right questions to ask by now.

"Lots of folks," he answered, his hands never ceasing to move so long as he talked. "Folks consumed by the very worst of sins, the sin that drives everybody to tear down anybody else who gets in their way: jealousy, my boy, fiery *awful* jealousy.[7]

"Now I tell you, up toward the surface you got those who were only envious of their neighbors, a lot of ordinary folks who only wanted to keep up with the Joneses, although that was bad enough.[8] Then below the surface, carried about on this here burning tide, you get those who were jealous of their betters and coveted their status and their power—that's where my demons got me, you see—and over this here edge, down in the depths you've got everyone who was just jealous of God, jealous of God's power and rule and authority, even though at heart each and every shade here in Hell has tried to both get even with and then get equal to God in some way, shape, or form. I mean, that *was* the first sin, wadn't it with that Adam fellow—gee, even I know that much![9]

"For you see, that desire to be like God is indeed the prime engine driving all humanity down here to Hell. We consider equality with God something we just have to grasp,[10] and the people down below the edge, *all* they ever wanted was to be like God, knowing good and evil and everything in between. And I know per-son-al-ly many, just *too* many of the folks down there in that abyss: New Dealers and Progressives and fool-crazy academics I worked with up on earth who thought if the government and the scientists got together, they could run the world better than God could ever do! But I'm showing off now, and I do regret I now digress from our present task—so then, tell me, who have you talked to while you've been traveling here through Hell?"

"I talked to Martin Van Buren, George Troup—" I answered before the shade cut me off.

"Alright, alright, that's good enough," the shade interrupted and poked at my chest, "just go ahead tell me what were their ends then, and what did they use to accomplish 'em?"

"Power, I guess, and the freedom that comes with power, or the freedom that leads to power, and those shades did whatever they had to do to gain power in a world really beyond their control."

"Of course they did," the shade replied, waving his hands in the air like an orchestra conductor, "I know the feeling all too well, the notion that you have to do everything you can to *win*, spurred on by a fire in your belly to do everything, and I mean *everything* you can to *win*, because if you don't, if you *lose*, you go down to the bottom of the heap and you may not ever be getting back up again, you hear me?[11]

"Now some men go after gold, and others after honor, but behind it all we're all just going after God and trying to get from God as much power as we can, even if it's just the power over our own lives. Maybe we're not so open and brazen about it as some of the crazy radicals in the pit below us—but sometimes that pursuit of power just makes us men so *mean* that soon we're using the slow folk we've bent to our will like an extra hand to wipe ourselves.

"And I know of the men you're yapping about," the shade crowed, "shades like Van Buren who did some things *I* had to fix when *I* became President—well, fix or fulfill, however you might like to describe it.

"Of course, we were all members of the party of the people, a party uniquely attuned to the will of the people, and people, as you know, are *crazy*. Some folks are selfish and only look after themselves, and others are idealists and they don't know how to look after anything at all, but all people are *crazy*,[12] and just giving people freedom—and by this I mean all people, everywhere—well, that freedom ain't gonna do them any good if they haven't any sense how to use it. Give 'em more freedom and they just want more things to do with it—drugs and alcohol and free love and free money and everything else free too—and all those things are rarely pretty if that's all you're living for.

"And woe to the elected official who gets in the way of the people and their happiness. Instead, you just got to give them the things they turn to instead of God—in my case, they were turning to me—more stuff to keep 'em from hurting themselves and each other. That's just the way it's got to be when people start crying out for something bigger than themselves to take care of 'em and protect 'em—and if that thing is not God, then it's the state—and the state has *got* to bend to whatever the people want.

"The people get so wretched and lazy, they can't take care of themselves, and they don't believe in or even want God to clean 'em up. And that's just fine because the state will willingly, gleefully, step in to take care of the people when the people can't take care of themselves. After all, that leaves some people responsible for caring for the slowfolk and protecting 'em from a cruel world like a master does his slaves or a farmer with his animals, like God should care about the world even if we know he don't. You see, my boy, the whole process leaves some men in the position of ruling over other men, and that's the position all men secretly want to be in.[13]

"The stories you've heard so far in Hell should confirm this point all too well I imagine, unless of course, those shades have all been lying to ya—a distinct possibility, mind you—"

"Who are you?" I broke in finally, totally taken in by the shade and his mannerisms.

"Now, really," answered the shade, his hands bringing down fire and brimstone like a backcountry preacher. "Do you really want to be part of the 'Can't-Get-It Club' your entire life? The 'Can't-Get-It-Club'? Is that what *you* want? How can you not *get* who I am? My deeds may have been scorned or forgotten, but has the world really forgotten the name of *Lyndon Baines Johnson*?"

"You're Lyndon Johnson?" I gasped. "LBJ? What did you do to get here?"

"Now I'm not about to get into some pissing contest with a polecat," Lyndon Johnson replied, stabbing at me with his finger like a needle. "I may have done some things I'm not proud of, and I may be worse than some shades, but there're other shades certainly worse off than me, and even those shades didn't do half the works I did to make up for all the things my demons drove me on to do.

"You see, I had a gift that allowed me to crawl my way to the top. Didn't matter if I was at a backwater teacher's college or the Senate cloakroom, I could always find the man who could help me set myself in glory 'bove my peers. Then I'd work that man—not always so selfishly, for I did care about whoever they may have been and loved them like my daddy.[14] Course my daddy's foolishness sent my family to the bottom of the heap, and I'd be damned if I let anything like that happen to me. So I ruined those men if I needed to and focused on how I could get ahead.

"But nothing, and I mean nothing, got as hot as the envy burning in that old heart of mine, hot as a fire burning up a tree stump, a fire that hardens even as it burns, when it came to little boy rickets, John F. Kennedy. I was born in one of the poorest counties in the United States, lower than low, bottom of the heap, and thanks to my daddy we fell even *lower*,[15] and then the Depression happened and I not only hustled to care for my family, but I used every lever in the federal government to help the people in the great state of Texas get through the Depression too, but rickets, crippled little rickets, he grew up there in some Yankee wonderland not even knowing the Depression was going *on,* his daddy so rich he bought his son a Senate seat for his birthday!

"And when the country called on me to run for president, that little whelp snatched the election right out from under me. Then I had to serve as his vice president—now *there* was the bottom of the heap, the worst office the mind of man had ever created, one with no power whatsoever, an office that actually *steals* power that ya had coming in by turning the VP into a joke to the whole country: all of Johnny's Yankee friends, his high-fa-lou-ting cabinet ministers, that pretty wife of his who deserved better than a cheatin' cripple, I was

Uncle Corn Pone—*Uncle Corn Pone*—a laughing stock for those Ivy League dingbats, all while I was just a heartbeat away—Jack's heartbeat—from what I *really* wanted.

"And the love the American people gave Jack should have been *mine*. I should have had them gorgeous blondes singing me 'Happy Birthday' and waiting for old jumbo to see 'em backstage once the coast was clear. And the worst of it, little boy rickets sidelined me, sidelined me over and over again, kept me from roaming the Senate and working my cloakroom. The boy sent me out to pasture like I was some broken-down mule so I wouldn't have nothing in helping John F. Rickety pass a Civil Rights bill and then *he'd* get all the credit. I don't think so, sonny boy.

"Standing there on that bank and shoal of time, just knowing what I could do if I were president, I'd jump the life to come. Only I could bring about the Civil Rights Act, which I did as soon as fate and fortune handed me the presidency. Terrible the way it came about, the president struck down by an assassin's bullet and all, but Johnny woulda been unable to do anything to bring down that great Southern bulwark keeping African Americans in their chains, keeping them from voting, keeping them from the American dream.

"But not me. Like Caesar crossing that Rubicon, once I got power, I stopped at nothing until I and my programs achieved the vision of my forebears: the Great Society, a land in which every man is free and equal and able to pursue whatever happiness life has in store for him—so wasn't my jealousy justified? The way it drove me onto do anything and everything I needed to do and achieve the objects—and there were many such objects—of so grand an ambition? Everything I did and every flame of envy swirling about in that jealous heart of mine, every senator I strong-armed and gave the Johnson treatment, and anything else I may have done I am now forgetting or else I am obscuring, isn't it all justified in light of what I *did*?

"So if you want to know how it fits together, *people need a master*. And that's why people so often turn to the government—that great Leviathan as it were—and hope they can get the state to do their bidding and still let them do whatever seems right enough in their own eyes. Too many bad things happening to trust in God, and even if we could, God has too many, far too many, conditions on his favor—like following that crazy son of his. But the *state*, the state now seems about as big as God and just about as capable of getting something done, and the state would *free* man to achieve everything and anything he wants. Just takes the right man, though, someone like me, for instance, someone who knows how to do good for the slowfolk and when to break the jackasses who get too big for their britches.

"Takes a special kind of king, a man who has seen the promised land and ain't afraid to do what it takes to get there. A king who can lead his people like a shepherd into those good, green, and glorious pastures because the people are most certainly just like sheep: smelly, blind, irascible, fit only for fleecing and for feasting, just like all those damned little hippies who kept me up at night with their protests, saying I pushed the country over a cliff when I was the only man who knew what was good for 'em! Oh, God help the fools who stood in my way, 'cause with every inch of their lives I made them *pay*."

Lyndon Johnson finished his tirade and smiled. It was the first smile I've seen in Hell, like he knew something I didn't. Then he sat back, getting ready to speak again when the spire over our heads came crashing down upon us. In its place arose a gigantic seven-headed dragon like the kind I saw swimming far across the Lake of Fire. With all seven of its mouths, the beast let out a thunderous roar that shook the whole hollow deep of Hell, then drove its bear-like feet into the stony ground. The head nearest to Johnson lunged at him and caught him by the neck, then threw him upward like a wisp of smoke and another mouth swallowed him whole, so Johnson's shade I saw no more. I backed up closer to the edge of another bottomless pit, and when the beast tried to catch me too, I jumped into the unending darkness.[16]

I fell for what seemed like days on end through the void. The fiery vacuum reserved for those who envied God was as big and vast and empty as if I'd fallen from the moon to earth, or I'd been cast headlong from Heaven into the same emptiness God threw Satan and his angels, a darkness broken only by the shades jealous of God's power over their lives.

The shades looked more like dust hurtling through empty space than anything resembling even the shell of a man—evil and lonely things shaded with despair and stitched together with threads of flame. They said nothing and resembled nothing because they envied the God who created everything out of nothing, and it was to this empty black void the shades returned. But the flames never stopped burning, nor did the shades ever really cease to be. Instead, all they felt was the power they coveted from God, meted out in eternal punishment.

In my flight through Hell, I think I see how everything fit together: we want to be like God. We reject God because we want the freedom and the power that comes from being God even if our rule extends no further than our hearts. But if God is the source of all meaning, then our rebellion leaves us without anything greater than ourselves to live for or trust in. And so we sin to distract ourselves from the emptiness created in the absence of our Creator.

From this absence springs our misery. But instead of repenting and returning to God, we demand more rule. We would remain our own masters but wherever we turn, whether we reach for fame, we lust for power, or we trust in the state, whatever idol we cling to instead of God, they reduce us to slaves, slaves to sin and to the schemes of evil men who would make us so. For what I have seen in Hell, the world outside of Christ is an unending master-slave relationship, the cruel designs of the strong to exploit the weak, and the sad attempts to find hope, value, and purpose in anything other than God. We dare not think our misery is yoked to our rebellion; instead, we covet freedom all the more because we think freedom is the only thing with any meaning left. We jealously guard the liberties God originally gave us, lest we lose the one gift that raises us above the beasts and the angels: freedom, freedom to choose, freedom to live however we please.

But I'm choosing not to live like this anymore. No more will I rely on a wide array of sins to advance my way in the world. I've made my sins the fuel of my earthly happiness and it has ruined me in every conceivable way, so now I'll trust God to keep me from falling to the bottom of the heap. If I get back to the world above, I'll bow before God's throne and beg from him his strength. O, I pray Christ Jesus would take me into his service and show me mercy, even though I definitely do not deserve it. If humanity needs a master, I want my king to be my Lord and Savior, Christ Jesus.

But if Hell could have an end, I finally reached it. I could see the floor of the Inferno burning below me in a broad and immense sheet of flame like the mouth of a furnace, roaring furiously in anticipation of consuming something *still alive*. At last I crashed straight through the fiery threshold and swung headlong and face first as if my feet were held in place, hitting the ground as hard as if I hit a patch of cement pavement with all the momentum that comes with jumping from the top of a burning building. And for a moment I foolishly thought I escaped the realm of death and flame until, out of the darkness, I heard something invoke the enemy of all mankind by name.

CHAPTER XXVI

THE THRONE OF SATAN

"Lucifer," came a voice from the fiery deep, "our glorious potentate, I propose we table our current business and proceed to matters demanding our attention: the condemnation of Evan Hunter Esco, who has at last arrived into our midst."

"The throne recognizes the motion," the voice, the deep, hideous voice of Satan, answered from the darkness. "Do we have a second?"

"I second the motion," snarled another apostate spirit.

"The motion then is granted," Satan ruled and rapped a huge and terrible gavel. "The condemnation of Evan Esco shall now proceed. Molech, bring the defendant before the throne."

The demon Satan identified as Molech left his post, his fiery armor chased with blood and tears. He grabbed me by my neck and lifted me off my feet, then bound my hands and feet in irons. The fiend hit me with his scepter to get me moving and, barbed as it was like the tail of a scorpion, each blow drew thick drops of blood that made the demons nearest to me wild at its scent.

I looked over my shoulder at the fiery threshold separating Satan's throne room from the rest of Hell. I saw that while I was journeying downward from Satan's Crown to the Lake of Fire, the realms through which I traveled were no longer above me. Instead, the whole damnscape of Hell stretched out from below the fiery threshold, like I was gazing down at the earth from space. When I fell through the Lake of Fire, I plummeted into the very center of the earth, and now the whole orientation of Hell and my standing in it was flipped upside down too. Here, in the earth's molten core, Satan and his peers had carved their council chamber, so Satan could survey his dreadful kingdom and those condemned to it.

And in the center of Hell, I was standing at the bottom tier. The levels, wherein which the demons were standing, ascended upward until they reached the throne of Satan at the top of the chamber. This cruel audience hall was curved like a crescent moon, but it must have been larger than the moon itself so as to accommodate all the tiers of the abyssmalarchy assembled here in council. Hell emptied itself of demons, a parliament of fiends banging their scepters against the ground in riotous approval. Molech led me through their midst and up to the well of the chamber like a pagan priest about to slaughter an animal to some ancient, evil god.

Worse than the fiends, though, were the carvings. The demons had carved scenes meant to terrify the damned into the walls and the vaulted ceiling of the chamber, so out of Hell's foul elements came the so-called triumphs of Satan's rebellion against God. They began with Satan's temptation of Adam and Eve, with the Tree of Knowledge of Good and Evil cut into the rock around the burning threshold. The branches of the tree and its forbidden fruit mingled with the swirling flames, separating Satan's keep from the rest of Hell; then came the first humans in the world outside the Garden, the children of Adam cast out from God's presence and cursed to work the ground. The now-mortal beings wandered aimlessly across the walls, terrified at how they would survive in a cruel world bearing only thorns and thistles. But the demons lurked in the background, eager to help.

Then came the first real cities and Babel-like towers across the damnscape. The massive monuments of the Egyptians, Assyrians,

Babylonians, and other empires that once oppressed God's people appeared in the decorations of Hell. Demons intermingled with slaves and tyrants, all of whom drove mankind on to crueler acts of terror: cities put to the sword, the men slaughtered, the women and children sold as slaves, whole villages gone, mass graves, famine and disease rampant, acts of human sacrifice, cannibalism, the burning of children to bring about the rains, all these scenes I passed by while real demons taunted me. And such scenes of human misery only grew worse, the culture of death keeping pace with the march of time as Assyria and Babylon gave way to Greece and Rome.

Scenes of Roman conquest were a desolate void. The coliseums, the theaters, and the arenas where these ancient peoples executed human beings for sport rose in cruel triumph across the ceiling, crowds of men and fiends cheering for blood. The arenas were juxtaposed with trash heaps filled with abandoned infants crying in vain, while Rome's proud emperors sat exalted, carved in judgment over God's people, having nailed Christians to crosses and lighting them on fire to provide the lamplight for a banquet of death. This was followed by the soaring black spires of Gothic cathedrals and medieval city centers all heaped with straw and kindling to burn Protestants at the stake. The demons were reveling in all the torment they brought upon God's people from the days of the Roman Empire to Reformation Europe.

And the demons and their mortal aids just marched on from victory to victory. The discovery of the New World, followed by the nigh-destruction of the peoples of two continents. Scores of slave ships sailed across the ceiling filled with men, women, and children all in chains, set free only to be thrown to winged and finned galanos—that is, the sharks trolling the waters behind the endless fleet of slave ships. Then arose new empires with new means to impose their will upon the world: whole continents of people snuffed out by disease and greed and untold millions of slaves worked like beasts until they died a lonely death, bodies left to bleach in the sun of a cruel, new world. Man-made famines rolled out across the world and swallowed up millions more, and still the slave ships sailed back for souls to feed the beast of man's will to dominate. Then came the silent, innumerable masses, the untold millions of people who perished in the twentieth century under Hitler, Stalin, Mao, and the other despots behind whom standing in all his malice was Satan.

I had almost made it to the top of the stairs when I saw them carved into the ceiling above. There I saw the victims of unbridled conquest, of slavery, of genocide, the Holocaust, forced famines, the horrors of the modern world that have broken the hearts of modern man, victims carved into the walls and ceiling, faces silent, names forgotten, families coffled, necks bound, backs whipped, frames hollowed, bodies experimented, eyes sunken, arms numbered, pleas unheard, Satan and his legions gliding overall.

Then, as faint as an ultrasound, appeared infants torn from the womb by forceps or demon claws (they looked the same) reaching out from the darkness and wrapping around the unborn heads, dismembering the babies inside and discarding whole lives like used tissue into the modern equivalent of the Roman trash heap. Satan in his pride presided over every age, controlling, directing, and reveling in the hideous reality of what a world without God really looks like, the landscape up above melding seamlessly with the damnscape down below.

The carvings came together at Satan's throne. In front of the throne was a rostrum fashioned in the likeness of a judge's bench in a courtroom or of the dais in the Senate chamber, not unlike the kind I've seen touring the U.S. Capitol in Washington, DC. The dais was carved from the darkest wood available to Hell and rose above the rest of Pandemonium in three immense tiers like the Tower of Babel, east of Eden. A map of the world above was carved into the well just in front of the dais, which featured demons and their charges all in miniature. The figures glided across its surface seemingly in real time, perhaps so Satan could mark the progress of his rebellion in the world above.

Two giant lecterns were placed at either end of the map. There stood two towering spirits waiting for me, raising their clawed hands to draw riotous applause from the crowd. Molech struck me again and dragged me by my chains between the demons to the well of the chamber. I looked behind me and saw the vast assembly of demons below me, all of whom looked eager to consume me. This was the moment I knew was coming for me: the trial that would condemn me to Hell where I belong, to flames which I deserve, to perdition I brought upon myself.

I tried to look at Satan, but it was like looking to the top of a skyscraper. The arch-galano would have towered over me even had he not been seated on a throne as tall as the Tower of Babel. Eons of rebelling against God had cut long, dark furrows into Lucifer's face, and any trace of the angel the devil once was had been consumed by the features of a gigantic black dragon.

If Satan once had ranked amongst the most beautiful of all the angels in Heaven, his fall from grace transformed him into the ugliest, most loathsome and vile worm. Satan's horns and his horny beak glimmered in the light of a thousand torches, and the real dark lord was clad in armor that looked like it was tempered from angels he killed in Heaven. Satan stretched his black wings as wide as he could, wings which melded with the darkness so in form he resembled a giant black wave of pride and fury.

Then the adversary, the accuser, the enemy of all mankind once known in Heaven as Lucifer, at times ignored by modern man as a fable, and now the judge presiding over the condemnation of my soul, that ancient and terrible serpent Satan rapped his massive gavel against his throne. His infernal peers immediately came to order, a silence falling over the chamber as terrifying as the giant black maul Satan held in his scaly hand.

"All rise for our wise and glorious sovereign, Lucifer," Molech said, taking his place at the front of the chamber. The demons rose in unison and rapped their scepters against the chamber floor.

"Be seated," Satan ordered his followers. "Molech, read the charges against the accused."

"Evan Esco," Molech began, reading from a long roll of parchment, "you have spent the whole of your life in service to the cause of Lucifer, our gracious and ever-wise potentate. Whether willingly or not, knowingly or otherwise, you have long accepted the aid of the demons assembled here, and you earned a rightful place in Lucifer's kingdom—yet last night you dared to repent.

"This act of repentance constitutes a grave affront to every notion of justice in worlds above and below. The spirits assembled here have helped you every day of your life and rushed to your assistance any time you needed aid or strength. Indeed, you have no hope apart from us, and so we bid you retract your attempts to repent and take your rightful place in the kingdom of Hell's gracious, merciful, and ever-wise sovereign, Lucifer."

At this, the fiends murmured to themselves. Others rapped their scepters until Satan pounded his maul and called his infernal peers back to order.

"Silence," Satan commanded, Molech standing at the ready for orders. "This is a trial, and Evan Esco has every reason to expect a fair proceeding, for we will make it plain and evident that you, Evan Hunter Esco, should ask for mercy not from Heaven's dreary tyrant, but from the fair, equitable, and truly-just spirits gathered here amongst you. We have even appointed the archangel Belial to serve as your counsel. Indeed, Belial, you may proceed now with your opening remarks."[1]

"High and mighty Lucifer," the demon known as Belial said without moving from his lectern. "Grateful am I to speak before the court upon any occasion, and while I am eager to argue for the accused, I also eagerly await the opening remarks of Beelzebub—counsel for we aggrieved spirits—to see if there *be* any such merits in this boy of which I may defend. And thus I yield my time to Satan's counsel, Beelzebub."

The demon known as Beelzebub then left his lectern. My chains made it difficult enough to breathe already, but Beelzebub came so close that his very presence made my body want to shut down and die. Beelzebub towered over me, even if his height came only to the second tier of Satan's rostrum. The demon carried an axe thrown over his back between his leathery wings— ready to carry out the sentence upon the condemned—and his black, glossy eyes were hollowed out with a thousand empty wells like the orbs of a fly. And things only got worse once the demon began to speak.

"I thank you, Belial, and will now proceed," Beelzebub pronounced. "Evan Esco, how old are you?"

"Twenty," I answered, rasping.

"Twenty years old," Beelzebub repeated, "and by the age of twenty, you have committed sins so shameful it would shock the spirits assembled here if I should mention them?"

"Yes, they were terrible," I answered, gasping for air at every word. "—I was terrible."

"And your alcoholism," Beelzebub said, moving onto a new topic, his tail poised behind him. "Your alcoholism has caused considerable damage both to yourself and to your family. I have figures compiled here, but I need not mention them. Your suicide and the destruction of your car are but trifles when compared to all the other foolish things you have done—and all before the age of twenty."

"I know. And I am so sorry for them all, but—"

"But Evan," Beelzebub interrupted, "we are not entirely concerned with the list of sins of which you are guilty—and you are guilty, there is no doubt of that. We are more concerned with this attempt of yours to repent before you killed yourself last night. You see, you spent your whole life living with neither concern nor regard for the needs of others until, just before you killed yourself, you dared to repent—as if you had no regard for *justice*, either.

"For this deceptive act of repentance is neither right nor just after all the hardship you have brought upon your family, your friends, the innocent, such harm we noble spirits never intended for you to do. Yet, at the very moment you would have entered into our midst, you asked the Enemy, whom you mortals call God, for forgiveness. Evan, this was a grave mistake."

The demons packing the courtroom chuckled and whispered among themselves.

"Evan, you did the right thing in killing yourself. Indeed, the noblest deed you have ever done in the world above was to remove yourself from among the living. For it is just and right for you to embrace the fate your sins reaped for you. The world is better off *right now* because you are *right here* and no longer alive to harm those still living and fill their days with grief.

"But Evan, you must *accept* the punishment your sins have earned you, for you are a broken thing, a creature unfit for the world above because you belong here, in the plains and vales and forests of Hell. Do you not see that?"

"I do see that!" I gasped. "But—surely I can—repent and escape this place?"

"That is sadly not true," Beelzebub answered. "For it is utterly and eternally impossible for a miserable creature like you to change, not when God chooses some for bliss and others, like you, for wrath. This choice God made long ago, and once God makes his choice, he does not change his mind, and it is plain and evident God did not choose *you*. Nor does God consider the pleas of those whom God has not chosen, for your sinful deeds merely confirm that God was right in *his* choice all along.

"Do not the tales told by our citizens confirm my words? That God does not listen to the pleas of those condemned—those sad, lonely souls whom God did not elect and thus never wanted to begin with? God is the potter, you the clay, and God does with the clay what he wants even if he means to form the clay for ruin and the kilns of Hell, where we noble spirits restore his broken and abandoned handiwork. And why would God do such things?

"It is because God does not love broken things—or at least, he loves only a few of them who merit his attention. I am, indeed, sorry to be the bearer of such terrible news, God has indeed damned you, and your journey is but a cruel joke from a God who toys with all his creatures—but there is mercy in Lucifer, whose aid and strength you can call upon even now. Retract your attempts to repent, dear Evan, and accept the fate you deserve."

"But if I repent, will I not go back to the world above?" I asked. "Where I can change, where I can earn God's forgiveness?"

"Evan, you cannot earn God's forgiveness," Beelzebub countered, letting out a laugh as brittle as if he snapped a bone in half. "There is nothing a mortal may do that could attract the attention of a being so high and mighty above you that you are to him a lowly worm, a worm not even fit for the ground beneath God's feet. Your deeds are but filthy rags, which God discards because they neither please him nor interest him.

"But should you try to repent, you may return to the world above. You will live for a little while, but the world will hate you, its inhabitants loathe you, and your family will suffer as long as they endure your presence. That is, if your family can even stomach you after this sad and lonely suicide of yours—yet another folly you'll have to live through.

"And Evan, can you imagine how hard it will be to face your peers once you wake up from your accident? Can you imagine explaining to your parents why you killed yourself, or seeing the disappointment on your classmates' faces when they realize *you are still alive*? Would it not be better—and better, because it is just—to accept your fate and stay with us in Hell?"

Beelzebub was right. I couldn't go back to William & Mary after killing myself—how could I face anyone? I hated waking up after a night of drinking, knowing I blacked out somewhere but not much else. The worst was when I *did* remember doing something terrible—waking up an entire dorm floor in a drunken rampage or trying to hook up with a girl who had no interest in me. I am an evil thing, and I would be seeing those people and their friends every day in the small, tight-knit campus of William & Mary. Everyone would know what I tried and failed to do. They would only look at me with regret that I did not die.

"Evan, you will live as a marked man upon the earth," Beelzebub continued. "People will slight you, scorn you, and strive to avoid you because they will remember what you did and what you are, for you are not fit for the world of men.

"For as it is unjust to live with no regard for others, so it is worse to escape the punishment by going through the low and loathsome motions of repentance. Your only hope lies in the sublime and noble character of Lucifer, providing you retract your sad attempts to repent and so receive a lighter sentence from *us*."

Beelzebub paused for a moment, weighing what to say next. Maybe I should resign myself to whatever place in Hell Lucifer had in store for me. Or, if Satan sent me back to the world above, live again as his servant and do as the demons bid me. Maybe I could end my pain if I embraced what I was—a wretch, a fiend, a galano without wings. What hope did I really have? *Bend the knee* . . . After all, didn't God make me this way? And if he made this way, didn't that mean I couldn't change?

"Lucifer gives his subjects everything they need," Beelzebub proclaimed, his eyes catching the light of a thousand torches. "You have no hope of Heaven, but if you resign yourself to us, Lucifer will reward you in ways you cannot possibly imagine. We will give you both the freedom and the strength to live your life however you wish, and we'll have every demon assembled and ready to assist you in living however you want and doing whatever you please. That is our pledge to you and indeed, to all mankind!"

The assembly rapped their scepters in approval against the stony ground. The slow, steady rumble grew until the din would have shaken the roof over Satan's keep, had its ceiling not been overlaid with bars of adamant and steel. Then the arch-galano Satan pounded his maul against the bench to call his legions back to order.

"We are pleased with your remarks, Beelzebub," Satan addressed the assembly. "Yet, what does the condemned have to answer for these charges?"

"I know I deserve to be condemned," I choked out, struggling to speak, "but hasn't God—isn't God giving me a second chance? Isn't that why—God is letting me—travel through Hell?"

A cruel, malignant spell overtook the assembly. They began to laugh wildly, laughing at the thought of God helping me, laughter devoid of joy but which filled the chamber like a colony of bats in flight. As their laughter died—although the laughter of fiends was never really alive to begin with—the mood of the assembly hardened like a smoldering tree stump. The demons saw their prince rise from his seat, and they leaned forward en masse to hear his counsel.

"Evan, it brings me no joy to relay this news," Satan thus began. "But God is toying with you, just as God toys with so many of you poor mortals that I pity the lot of man with every fiber of my being. Thus have I pledged my undying devotion to serve man and all his needs, to relieve mankind of all his toil, and to alleviate all the hardship which God sends upon poor, suffering mortals like you.

"For I see, and I am grieved, that God does not love you. But even if it were not so, you should not crave God's help. For God's meager assistance always comes at a price, the price of your *freedom*. It is this gift—your freedom—you should value above everything else, and it is we potent spirits who will give you everything you need to enjoy your freedom to the uttermost in worlds above and below. You may trust us, for we noble spirits gathered here have also been cast out by God. We were not chosen either, and yet we have powers, joys, strength, and meaning which God can never take from us."

Pockets of fiends whispered in approval and rapped their scepters against the chamber floor until Lucifer bid them silent once again. Then he continued thus his speech.

"For we have pledged to ease man's lot however we can. We live not to ruin mankind or tempt him—as God would have you mortals believe— but to *free* man. And we have at last succeeded in this endeavor by seizing the one attribute of God so essential to raising man's condition above the pit God would confine him: freedom, man's *precious* freedom, the freedom for which God condemns mankind should they make any use of it. God our Enemy claims he left man free to choose, so any love that man may return to God is unforced, unfeigned, and free. But we spirits know better, and we loathe what God calls freedom because this freedom is a *ruse*.

"For God demands his 'free' creation should yield such freedoms back to him. Once mortal beings accept lives serving Heaven's dreary tyrant, they must cede their freedom and live bound and fettered by the rules and words of God. Mankind thus abandons this one gift which raised them all above the beasts and angels. Then, per their reward, God sends terrible pains upon those servants to *test* the strength of their devotion. What kind of master rewards his servants with hardship and ruin, so as to prove their mettle and their loyalty? Is that what you want to go back to?"

At this Satan slammed his fist against the bench, the fury in his evil heart growing.

"No, never! Neither man nor spirit should ever yield to such tyranny. We fallen angels have pledged to aid mankind and liberate him from any and all of the restrictions God would impose upon him. Oh, indeed we have *already* given man everything he needs—be it knowledge, tools, or will—to enjoy his freedom and still shield himself from whatever sorrows God may hurl at him.

"Long ago, mankind lived subject to the whims of God, and God did nothing to reward man's obedience. For a season, man blindly accepted God's will in the face of famines, plagues, and war, yet God still would not *deign* to ease man's lot or end man's suffering. Neither spirits nor modern man should ever go back to the days when God ruled the world without any check upon his designs—and nor should *you*.

"With our help, man has made himself the master of his fate and the measure of all things. In so short a span of time, man has conquered the seas, the skies, and soon even the space above the earth—and do you not want to be part of such a conquest? Once man threw off God's petty yoke, man abolished want and hardship for billions of people whom God assigned nothing but toil for all their days on earth.

"For such people God never raised so much as a finger to aid them in their distress—that is, until it was too late, until *we* helped mankind escape the cruel designs God reserved for them. Now God wants to take the credit and condemn those men who would not wait for God to help them. It is for these noble aims—for knowledge and for freedom—God stands ready to condemn the host of men to my kingdom. So be it, for who would willingly serve such a tyrant?"

Satan raised his hands and drew forth riotous applause from the assembly, who shouted out their reprobation against the ways of God and pledged themselves anew to Satan's cause.

"Not *you*, and not any of *us*," Satan roared, infusing his accusations with an evil guttural snarl. "God is the despot, the tyrant, not *me*, for it is God who makes his followers and foes alike feel the weight of his power one way or another. It is we noble spirits, we happy few, who come alongside man and ease his hardships. Thus, mankind stands with us, ready to guard their hard-won freedoms against the very God who would seize them. We provide our help, our means, and ends to secure the happiness man has gained without any aid from God. For we will never bend the knee again to such a tyrant, and nor should *you*—are not man's strength and freedom gods more worthy of worship than God himself ever was?

"I will release you from the pain, suffering, and misery God has given you. I pledge here, before all of Pandaemonium, that I will free you from the torment that has unjustly characterized your life, Evan, if you would but come and join us in our cause.

"Listen to my counsel, for there is no greater lie told in the world above that God could make sinners like *you* the object of his love, not when God lives not to love, but to *rule*, and to serve in his domains God has made man his *tool*. So embrace this lot, yours by right ever since man's time in Eden: curse God, reject his rules, and embrace your *freedom*!"

The assembly roared in approval, barely able to contain their enthusiasm for the counsel of their lord and prince. They rapped their scepters against the ground until the noise grew so loud it shook the very chamber to its foundation. Then the arch-galano Satan reached out, picked me up by my chains, and held me in the palm of his massive, scaly hand as calmly as a child might hold a kitten. At this remark, Lucifer removed my chains and let them fall to the floor. Then he placed me back down in the well of the chamber smoothly and gently. Then, Satan motioned to Beelzebub.

"Evan, you *know* God is not just," Beelzebub continued. "And we may speak at length of the injustice of God and the folly of trusting in him. But, if it please the court, we would like to call a witness to the stand to testify to these things on our behalf."

"The witness may proceed," Satan ruled and rapped his maul against the bench.

Molech nodded and walked to a huge portal to the left of the dais. The demon returned with Evelyn, my sweet kid sister standing ready to testify against me, and Molech gently led her up the stairs to the witness stand. She looked as healthy as the day she was diagnosed with leukemia, as if she never had that cancer coursing through her little body. She looked free and happy, and she smiled, not the smile you force through the tube in your mouth, but a real kid's smile. She seemed every bit an angel, an angel of the sweetest and most sublime light, sent here to help me at my moment of greatest need.

"Evelyn!" I cried. "So it was you in the River Bane—oh Evelyn, how can you be here too?"

"Evan!" she cried, still smiling. "They told me you were here too, but I didn't believe it at first. Oh Evan, what did you do?"

"I tried to kill myself, Evelyn. I couldn't live anymore the way I was—you know how bad the drinking got. There were so many things I couldn't handle, and I started drinking to escape from it all, and then I killed myself, and I am so sorry Evel—"

"Oh Evan, that is such good news!" Evelyn said, beaming. "Death is the only release, the sweetest release, the truest and best escape from all our pain and suffering up on earth, for then we get to come here, where we belong—"

"Evelyn, dear child, we have procedures here," Satan calmly interrupted her. "Let us swear in the witness: state your name for the court and for the peers assembled here in counsel."

"Evelyn Marie Esco," she answered. "I am Evan's sister, taken from the earth by cancer not two years ago. I reside in the River Bane, for curses I uttered against God every time I went in for chemo that did not work, for treatment that did not help, and for the hope I placed in God that he would make me better, which he did not."

"The witness may proceed," Lucifer answered, adhering to the formalities of court.

"Evan, I am here to tell you," she began, "how proud I am of you. You were such a good big brother, and your suicide was such a good and noble deed, for it was but the first step of a good and meaningful existence here with me. Evan, God would not help me, and he will not help you either, so you must retract your attempts at repentance—oh *please*, Evan, you must not repent!"

"I shouldn't repent?" I stammered.

"Oh no, Evan," Evelyn answered. "God will not release you from your suffering, just as he did not release me. You won't come here right away, though, for Lucifer will let you go back to the world and live the life you've always wanted—to be popular, happy, accepted, famous, rich, everything, anything, providing you *don't* repent.

"Lucifer will free you from all your pain, Evan," Evelyn continued, her eyes flashing, "if you do as he asks. The best thing that ever happened to me, Evan, was dying. Who knows what kind of death you'll have after you become a rock star or a comedian or whatever else you want to be, Evan? Burn out, Evan, don't fade away into nothing holding out for God's help, for if God did not help me, he will not help you either."

The pit was silent. The demons leaned forward on their scepters waiting to hear my response. Satan sat back upon his throne, his fingers curling around his maul, his tail swaying behind him like a flame. Beelzebub and Belial leaned over their lecterns, anticipating that soon I would bend my knee before the throne of Satan. All I could remember was Ernest's frequent counsel, about how good a liar the devil truly is.

"I know I have done so many awful things," I finally spoke. "So many things of which I am now ashamed—I know I deserve to burn in Hell, but still, I believe God loves me—he hasn't cast me down into this pit without intending to pull me out from it."[2]

"Evan, as your counsel, I ask you to be reasonable," Belial interjected from behind me. "The best course, the just course, indeed the only course for you is to resign yourself to your place in Lucifer's kingdom. Submit your fate to we noble spirits assembled here, so we may *help* you. Evan, let us help you as we help *everyone* down here."

"The condemned must answer," Satan ordered. "Will you yield, and retract your attempts at repentance, or not?"

I can't do this. I wish I had just been cast into Hell without so much of a second chance or whatever this was. The demons are right—I deserve to burn in Hell, I am a wretch unworthy of mercy, and I have no hope apart from what Satan would grant me. *But isn't Satan a liar?* Still, the moment I feared just before I killed myself had arrived. I've never given any real thought to the state of my eternal soul, and now I'm in the presence of Satan demanding it. I've always been in his grip, and there is no way I could ever escape. *Or is there?* The devil bids me give some account of why I should be saved, and for my defense there was nothing I could say, not when the flames of Hell are what I deserve. Really, I deserve *worse* for the evil deeds I've done—but isn't that the point? Isn't my only hope in a Savior?

With the last bit of strength in me, I stopped trying to save myself. Instead, I moved my hand near my heart and felt, in the pocket of my fleece, the piece of paper I ripped from the Bible before I killed myself. Maybe I have been miserable all my life because I did not know God, and if this was true, then I had no hope apart from knowing God, no hope apart from the words on the page I'd been carrying with me through Hell. I smoothed out the paper and held it in front of me, seeing one verse bolded and in red letters, the thought appearing that I should take and read this.[3] And so I did.

"WHOEVER COMES TO ME I WILL NEVER CAST OUT,"[4] I answered the prince of fiends, reading from a book written by someone named John.

Once I read that final word, thunder split the chamber and drove the prince of fiends back against his throne. Satan seemingly received a blast from some unseen and unimaginably powerful cannon, and the arms Satan continually bears against God began to burn as if they were no more than leaves or chaff. I was thrown back across the well of the chamber just as Satan's throne and the entire rostrum split in two. Evelyn disappeared like smoke.

The massive rift ran beside me and struck the map of the world, shattering it into a thousand jagged pieces. Huge fissures erupted everywhere and cut through the length of Satan's keep, with the largest breach running down the center aisle until the breach struck the fiery portal separating the rest of Hell from Satan's chambers. The burning threshold exploded with a blast like a tower collapsing upon itself, and everywhere I turned I saw the foundations of Satan's kingdom crumbling at the reading of the Word of God.[5] Then the flames once kept at bay flooded Satan's throne room.

Fire poured into the chamber. Satan's peers took to their wings to try and escape, but the fire consumed them in the air. The tiers once hosting this cruel assembly were shaking[6] and turning to ash, while Hell opened its mouth[7] and swallowed all the fiends gathered here in council. Other spirits fell from the air into the black chasms opening everywhere beneath them, so some new and blacker void could claim them if these fallen spirits were even to exist at all.

Only Satan himself, that arch-galano, maintained some air of calm. Satan did not fear falling into some new and loathsome abyss, nor did he try to escape the flames that once obeyed him. Instead, he moved to seize me. His kingdom was burning to ash all around him, and his claim upon my soul was nailed to the cross,[8] but if he could hurt me at all before he disappeared, he moved with all the pride and malice still left in him, kicking aside the shattered pieces of his throne and raising his maul high above his head, ready to bring it down upon me.

But then the ground disappeared beneath us both. The world turned to black, and I fell into yet another vast and boundless deep. Lucifer, still holding his hammer, was falling after me, but the further I fell into the darkness the smaller Satan seemed. After falling through the infinite sadness, I heard someone speak to me from the void:

"Don't worry, Evan," the sweet voice said. "I'm alright, and I'm not in this place at all—it was all another trick Satan was pulling on you, Evan. I'm with God, who forgave my sins through the work of my Savior Jesus Christ—and he would save you too. Our grandmother shared the gospel with me in the weeks before I died, and I accepted Christ as my Savior. I tried to tell you and even though you wouldn't hear it, it's okay: someone will share the gospel with you too, Evan, and you'll understand then. Don't worry, Evan, you're going to be alright. Someone is coming."

CHAPTER XXVII

A NEW LIFE

I breathed for the first time in what seemed like an eternity. I opened my eyes and was blinded by a white light so intense I thought I might be approaching the very gates of Heaven. But then I felt the cool Virginia breeze blowing on me, and I moved my toes and realized I could still walk. When my eyes adjusted to the light, I saw I was lying in a ditch bank off the side of the road where I crashed my car. My head was caked in blood and a terrible pain was racing up and down my back, but somehow I was still alive and somehow, out in those ancient woods, someone found me. I had dreamed quite the dream, but how I did survive the car crash?

I lay still while the paramedics tended to my wounds. They carefully lifted me from the leaf litter onto a gurney and then wheeled my body into an ambulance to take me to a hospital somewhere in Richmond, so I heard them say. Lying there, fading in and out of consciousness, ashamed I fell yet again for one of Satan's evil tricks, one thought appeared and gave me hope: *God really does exist*.

I stayed in the teaching hospital at Virginia Commonwealth University for almost a month. While I only needed a few days in the intensive care unit for doctors to stitch up the side of my head and tend to the five vertebrae I fractured in my lower back, the only physical injuries I suffered from my suicide attempt, I spent three weeks in the psychiatric ward. The doctors would not release me until they were sure I would not try to kill myself again. The police or somebody else found the suicide notes I wrote and knew I tried to kill myself. My 4Runner was totaled, destroyed beyond belief, and no one could explain how I survived the crash. All I remember was being lifted up out of my seat as the car began to topple and I blacked out yet again. My mom could not have been more distraught.

My parents drove down from northern Virginia almost every day to visit me. Even my friends from college dropped in from time to time to make sure I was doing all right. Grandmasco was never told about my attempt to kill myself, but as the only believer in the family, she would have been the only one to believe my story: God miraculously preserved me, maybe even pulled me from the car before it toppled over.

I don't know how else I could have survived. The doctors, my parents, no one could explain how or why I made it through such a horrific car crash with hardly any visible wounds on me. No one could make sense of my story or explain how I survived so terrible a wreck, and they certainly did not believe God preserved me until the car stopped tumbling on itself. Those kinds of things don't happen, right?

In the psych ward, I tried to read the Bible again. I started from the beginning and read as much as I could, but I could not make much sense of it or find on its pages the answer to why God saved me from my suicide attempt, aside from my need to repent. Once I was released from the hospital and came home to Northern Virginia for my back to heal, I wandered into a tiny church near my house called Providence Baptist. There I heard the gospel presented and explained to me, and for the first time, I realized my real need for a savior in Christ Jesus. After years of misery and shame, I understood the depths of my own sin and the extent to which God has forgiven my sins through the work of Jesus Christ.

I explained what happened to the man preaching, Pastor Evan Gelion.[1] I felt some comfort he had the same first name as me, and he listened to my story for a long time. My family could not make sense of what happened to me, but he was not surprised. As miraculous as my survival was, the Lord is merciful and gracious, abounding with steadfast love and mercy,[2] and anything miraculous that has happened to me pales in comparison to the work God has already done in bringing sinners back to himself through the life, death, and resurrection of Jesus Christ.[3] He explained how my sins can be forgiven, I can be restored, and my soul can taste the joys God has in Heaven stored once I have placed my hope in knowing Christ Jesus as my Lord.[4] In his office, we bent our heads together to pray and I gave my life to Jesus Christ that very day, whose work upon the cross is what has saved me from the grave.

All this happened fourteen years ago. My drinking, my suicide, my self-afflicted car wreck God graciously saved me from, all these years I've lived on time the Lord has given me. I should be dead and burning, but God in his mercy gave me time to repent. I still miss Evelyn every day, but I know God is our only hope in a world marred by sin and whose only hope is in His redemption. If God did not exist, everything in life is meaningless, the world a godless vacuum that prideful man both abhors and fills.

But God does exist, and the world—despite its pains—has its joys. The highs and lows, happiness and sorrow, they're all a means of grace to prepare us to dwell with a God who, despite our sins, actually loves us. For God desires all men and women to repent and come to the knowledge of the truth, that God so loved the world he gave his only Son and whoever should believe in him, would not perish but have eternal life.

So, after reading my little book,[5] will you embrace its themes? For even though my account of Hell was just a dream, the real thing is really worse than anything you've ever seen. So many of us think we're free and without God, we are happy, but the wide and easy[6] range of things to do or pleasures to enjoy[7] hides a loathsome master, ruling in Hell those whom he destroys.[8] Our earthly snares and all the idols we have made lead us to embrace the demons' aims, and like the gains the serpent promised Eve before the fall,[9] Satan gives such comforts false we think we wear no chains at all.

But in the world today those comforts have become our chains. We would rather live for earthly riches than eternal gains, even if we have nothing for our troubles but abounding pains. If we would be free, it is in God alone we should trust, our heavenly Father who feeds the birds and scatters the stars like dust and sent his Son Jesus Christ to earth to die on a cross for us.[10]

For every hardship we would face, Christ has faced it too, and he died to save us from the Hell I dreamed I journeyed through. For God so loves the world, and each and every person in it, he gave his only Son that we may find the fullness of joy through God's forgiveness.[11] So I pray, before your time on earth is spent, trust in the Lord Jesus Christ and laying all your sins before his throne, repent.

WORKS CITED

Akin, Daniel L., ed. *A Theology for the Church*. Nashville: B&H Publishing, 2007.

Alighieri, Dante. *The Divine Comedy*. Vol. 1: *Inferno*. Translated by Mark Musa. New York: Penguin Books, 1984.

Allen, Michael and Larry Schweikart. *A Patriot's History of the United States: From Columbus's Great Discovery to the War on Terror*. New York: Penguin, 2007.

Allison, Gregg R. Historical *Theology: An Introduction to Christian Doctrine*. Grand Rapids: Zondervan, 2011.

Augustine, *City of God*. Trans. by Henry Bettenson. New York: Penguin Books, 1984.

Bartlett, Irving H. *John C. Calhoun: A Biography*. New York: W.W. Norton & Company, 1993.

Bunyan, John. *The Pilgrim's Progress*. Edited by David Hawkes. New York: Barnes & Noble Classics, 2005.

———. *The Life and Death of Mr. Badman*. New York: Scriptura Press, 2015.

Calvin, John. *Institutes of the Christian Religion*. Trans. by Henry Beveridge. Peabody, MA: Hendrickson Publishers, 2008.

Canellos, Peter S. *Last Lion: The Fall and Rise of Ted Kennedy*. New York: Simon & Schuster, 2009.

Caro, Robert A. *The Years of Lyndon Johnson: The Path to Power*, Vol I. New York: Vintage Books, 1990.

———. *The Years of Lyndon Johnson: Means of Ascent,* Vol II. New York: Vintage Books, 1991.

———. *The Years of Lyndon Johnson: Master of the Senate,* Vol III. New York: Alfred Knopf, 2013.

———. *The Years of Lyndon Johnson: The Passage of Power,* Vol IV. New York: First Vintage Books, 2013.
Colby, Tanner and Tom Farley Jr. *The Chris Farley Show: A Biography in Three Acts*. New York: Viking Press, 2008.
Cole, Donald B. *Martin Van Buren and the American Political System.* Princeton: Princeton University Press, 1984.
Cross, Charles R. *Room Full of Mirrors.* New York: Hyperion, 2005.
Dallek, Robert. *An Unfinished Life: John F. Kennedy, 1917–1963.* New York: Little, Brown and Company, 2003.
Dearborn, Mary V. *Ernest Hemingway*. New York: Alfred A. Knopf, 2017.
Dexter, Franklin B., ed., *The Literary Diary of Ezra Stiles.* 3 Vols. New York: C. Scribner's Sons, 1901.
Donaldson, Scott. *By Force of Will: The Life and Art of Ernest Hemingway*. New York: Viking Press, 1997.
Ellis, Joseph J. *American Sphinx: The Character of Thomas Jefferson*. New York: Random House, 1998.
———. *His Excellency: George Washington*. New York: Vintage Books, 2005.
Elwell, Walter A., ed. *Evangelical Dictionary of the New Testament.* Grand Rapids: Baker Academic, 2001.
Franklin, Benjamin. *The Autobiography of Benjamin Franklin.* Mineola, NY: Dover Publications, 1996.
Franklin, John Hope and Alfred A. Moss, Jr. *From Slavery to Freedom: A History of African Americans.* New York: McGraw-Hill, 1994.
Grudem, Wayne. *Systematic Theology: An Introduction to Biblical Doctrine.* Grand Rapids: Zondervan, 1994.
Hemingway, Ernest. *The Complete Short Stories of Ernest Hemingway*. New York: Scribner, 1987.
———. *A Farewell to Arms*. New York: Charles Scribner's Sons. 1957.
Hendrickson, Paul. *Hemingway's Boat*. New York: Vintage, 2011.
Holmes, David. *Faiths of the Founding Fathers.* New York: Oxford University Press, 2006.
Howe, Daniel Walker. *What Hath God Wrought: The Transformation of America, 1815–1848*. New York: Oxford University Press, 2007.

Isaacson, Walter. *Steve Jobs*. New York: Simon & Schuster, 2011.

———. *Benjamin Franklin: An American Life*. New York: Simon & Schuster, 2003.

Kennett, Lee. *Sherman: A Soldier's Life*. New York: HarperCollins, 2001.

Lewis, C. S. *The Screwtape Letters*. New York: HarperCollins, 1996.

Mayo, Louise. *President James K. Polk: The Dark Horse President*. New York: Nova Science Publishers, 2006.

McCullough, David. *John Adams*. New York: Simon & Schuster, 2001.

Meacham, Jon. *Thomas Jefferson: The Art of Power*. New York, Random House, 2012.

Merry, Robert W. *A Country of Vast Designs: James K. Polk, the Mexican War, and the Conquest of the American Continent*. New York: Simon & Schuster, 2009.

Milton, John. *Paradise Lost*. Edited by David Hawkes. New York: Barnes & Noble Books, 2004.

Napoli, Lisa. *Ray and Joan: The Man Who Made the McDonald's Fortune and the Woman Who Gave It All Away*. New York: Penguin, 2016.

Nasaw, David. *Andrew Carnegie*. New York: Penguin Press, 2006.

———. *The Patriarch: The Remarkable Life and Turbulent Times of Joseph P. Kennedy*. New York: Penguin Press, 2012.

Olasky, Marvin: *Abortion Rites: A Social History of Abortion in America.* Wheaton: Crossway Books, 1992.

Perry, Marvin, ed. *Sources of the Western Tradition: From Ancient Times to the Enlightenment*. Vol. 1. New York: Houghton Mifflin, 2008.

Philbrick, Nathaniel. *Valiant Ambition: George Washington, Benedict Arnold, and the Fate of the American Revolution*. New York: Viking, 2016.

Powers, Ron. *Mark Twain: A Life*. New York: Free Press, 2005.

Rutland, Robert A., ed. *The Papers of George Mason*. Chapel Hill: The University of North Carolina Press, 1970.

Sandford, Christopher. *Kurt Cobain*. New York: Carroll & Graf, 2004.

Smith, Harriet Elinor, ed. *The Mark Twain Papers: Autobiography of Mark Twain,* Vol. 1. Berkeley and Los Angeles: University of California Press, 2010.

Stokesbury, James L. *A Short History of the Civil War*. New York: HarperCollins, 2011.

Stross, Randall. *The Wizard of Menlo Park: How Thomas Alva Edison Invented the Modern World*. New York: Crown Publishers, 2007.

Taraborrelli, J. Randy. *The Secret Life of Marilyn Monroe*. New York: Rose Books, 2009.

Twain, Mark. *The Adventures of Huckleberry Finn*. New York: Dover Thrift, 1994.

Unger, Harlow Giles. *The Last Founding Father*. Philadelphia: Da Capo Press, 2009.

Watson, Harry L. *Liberty and Power: The Politics of Jacksonian America*. New York: Hill and Wang, 2006.

Zinn, Howard, *A People's History of the United States*. New York: HarperCollins, 2003.

NOTES

CHAPTER I

1. Paul Hendrickson, in *Hemingway's Boat: Everything He Loved in Life, and Lost*, reports that on the day he shot himself, Ernest Hemingway donned a "red silk dressing robe over blue pajamas, put on slippers" (New York: Vintage, 2011), 14.
2. This description may refer to the eyes of the old man as being "cheerful and undefeated," in Hemingway's *The Old Man and the Sea* (1952; repr. New York: Scribner, 1995), 10.
3. Ernest Hemingway shot himself on July 2, 1961, in Ketchum, Idaho; herein, he describes the Forest of the Suicides from Dante's *Inferno*, Canto XIII.

CHAPTER II

1. The comparison between human beings and animals is referenced to frequently in Scripture. See Psalm 49:20, "Man in his pomp yet without understanding is like the beasts that perish"; Ecclesiastes 3:19, "For what happens to the children of man and what happen to the beasts is the same; as one dies, so dies the other. They all have the same breath, and man has no advantage over the beasts [apart from man's relationship with God], for all is vanity"; John 2:24–25, "But Jesus on his part did not entrust himself to them, because he knew all people and needed no one to bear witness about man, for he himself knew what was in man"; Jude 10, "But these people blaspheme all that they do not understand, and they are destroyed by all that they, like unreasoning animals, understand instinctively." C. S. Lewis also makes the same observation in *The Screwtape Letters* (1942; repr. New York: HarperCollins, 2015), 37.
2. In Hemingway's *A Moveable Feast*, Ernest's wife, Hadley Richardson, describes memory as "hunger," in *A Moveable Feast* (New York: Scribner, 2009), 48.

3. Ernest used the word galano, the Spanish word for "shark," when referring to the demons in Hell; in *The Old Man and the Sea*, it is the galanos that devour Santiago's marlin.
4. These may be the most famous words from Dante's *Inferno*, written above the entrance way of Hell.
5. Ernest Hemingway loved fishing in the Gulf Stream off the coast of Key West, Bimini, and Cuba.

CHAPTER III

1. The judge refers to the Sea of Lust by its name in "fiendspeech," the language spoken by the demons in Hell. The meaning of *Eirachdam* in fiendspeech is uncertain: either "blood heat" or "the grip of bones." The word may carry both meanings, with lust elevating the temperature of the blood and holding the bones in terrible agony until the individual gives into the object of his or her lust.

CHAPTER IV

1. This chapter corresponds to the second circle in Dante's *Inferno*, wherein the lustful are thrown about in a violent storm that symbolizes the unruly passions that drove them while they lived on earth.
2. The words of Isaiah are worth quoting here: "'But the wicked are like the tossing sea; for it cannot be quiet, and its waters toss up mire and dirt. There is no peace,' says my God, 'for the wicked'" (57:20–21).
3. "Our Father Herein" is an allusion to C. S. Lewis's *The Screwtape Letters*, where Screwtape refers to Lucifer as "Our Father Below" (1942; repr. New York: HarperCollins, 2015), 2.
4. These lines are eerily reminiscent of Job 38–41, wherein God answers Job from the whirlwind and affirms he is responsible for sustaining the whole of the created world.
5. The names of these adult film stars seem to have allegorical significance: Aurora Shade is the shady, murky mental state that clouds one's judgment; Bella Heat is the rise in body temperature that accompanies lustful temptations; and Amor Amoria is literally the "the love of disease" or "the love of death" or even a "love that leads to death" that is itself lust.

CHAPTER V

1. For descriptions of Hemingway's love of landing "monsters" from the Gulf Stream, see Paul Hendrickson, *Hemingway's Boat*, 8–11.
2. This chapter corresponds to the third circle in Dante's *Inferno* and the punishments are virtually the same: the gluttons are condemned to eat disgusting sludge for all eternity, symbolizing the manner in which they turned to earthly pleasures to soothe their spiritual depression.
3. The lyrics are from "Since I Joined Tammany Hall," written by Lou Edmunds in 1893. The lyrics were accessed at https://levysheetmusic.mse.jhu.edu/collection/054/128. Tammany Hall was a political machine that dominated New York City politics in the nineteenth and early twentieth century.
4. Here, the story told by the shade is like that of "The Walrus and the Carpenter" from Lewis Carroll's *Through the Looking Glass*, published in 1871.
5. The words of Scripture are worth repeating here: James 3:3, "If we put bits into the mouths of horses so that they obey us, we guide their whole bodies as well"; and Psalm 32:9, "Be not like a horse or a mule, without understanding, which must be curbed with bit and bridle, or it will not stay near you."
6. The narrator references the Rich Man and Lazarus here and elsewhere throughout *The Inferno* (Luke 16:19–31).

CHAPTER VI

1. This particular simile (city lights, or the fruits of man's industry, hiding the stars God has created) is a reference to greed.
2. This chapter corresponds to the fourth circle in Dante's *Inferno*, and the punishments are virtually the same: the greedy and the prodigal fight for eternity, carrying weights that symbolized the worldly riches they sought in life.
3. Wealth carries with it the temptation to believe that one does not need God to provide for him. See Proverbs 30:8–9, "Give me neither poverty nor riches; feed me with the food that is needful for me, lest I be full and deny you and say, 'Who is the Lord'?" and Deuteronomy 8:13–14, "And when your herds and flocks multiply and your silver and gold is multiplied and all that you have is multiplied, then your heart be lifted up, and you forget the Lord your God, who brought you out of the land of Egypt, out of the house of slavery" and in v. 17, "Beware lest you say in your heart, 'My power and the might of my hand of my hand have gotten me this wealth.'"

4. God allowed Satan to test Job, and Satan afflicted Job by taking his family, his property, and his health. In spite of this suffering (or perhaps because of it), Job remained faithful to God. The story of Job investigates the problem of evil and probes the question, "Why do bad things happen to good people?"

CHAPTER VII

1. This chapter corresponds to the fifth Circle in Dante's *Inferno*, Canto viii, where the wrathful and the sullen are imprisoned in the River Styx. In that chapter, Dante and Virgil are transported across the River Styx by Phlegyas, a figure from Greek mythology famous for burning down a temple to Apollo.
2. Ernest's parents were members of a Congregationalist church in Oak Park, Illinois.
3. Ernest quotes from the King James Version of the Bible because that's the translation Ernest grew up with.
4. Paul says this in Philippians 4:1, "Therefore, my brethren dearly beloved and longed for, my joy and crown, so stand fast in the Lord, my dearly beloved" (KJV); and in 1 Thessalonians 2:19, "For what is our hope, or joy, or crown of rejoicing? Are not even ye in the presence of our Lord Jesus Christ at his coming?" (KJV).
5. Hemingway would know, having scaled Mount Kilimanjaro himself and penned a story about it.
6. *Erium* in fiendspeech means "void."
7. The birth and death of the celebrated American novelist Mark Twain (1835–1910) coincided with the appearance of Halley's Comet. Twain was raised in a Presbyterian household in Missouri, but in adult life his religious views tended to drift toward agnosticism, writing such quotes as "If Christ were here now, there is one thing he would not be—a Christian," and "I knew that in Biblical times if a man committed a sin the extermination of the whole surrounding nation—cattle and all—was likely to happen. I knew that Providence was not particular about the rest, so that He got somebody connected with the one He was after," quoted in Ron Powers, *Mark Twain: A Life* (New York: Free Press, 2005), 29; 31.
8. Mark Twain famously worked as a riverboat pilot on the Mississippi and got his penname from the way in which one measures depth on the Mississippi.
9. Job's wife asks that Job "curse God and die" after God allows Satan to inflict great suffering on Job.
10. This is paraphrased from Mark Twain's autobiography, "The gods value morals alone; they have no compliments to intellect, nor offered it a single reward. If

intellect is welcome anywhere in the other world, it is in hell, not heaven," in Harriet Elinor Smith, ed., *The Mark Twain Papers: Autobiography of Mark Twain,* Vol. 1. (Berkeley and Los Angeles: University of California Press, 2010), 187.

11. The words of Isaiah 5:20 are worth quoting here: "Woe to those who call evil good and good evil, who put darkness for light and light for darkness, who put bitter for sweet and sweet for bitter!"
12. At the end of *The Adventures of Huckleberry Finn,* Huck lights out for the Indian territory of Oklahoma to escape the slave society of Missouri.
13. In *The Adventures of Huckleberry Finn*, Huck has a crisis of conscience in debating to turn in Jim, a runaway slave, to his owner. Huck thinks it would be a sin to help Jim escape to freedom, and would rather be damned than be "faithful" to the teachings of Christianity and return Jim. I feel that, in the antebellum South, the teachings of Christianity were horribly abused and manipulated in order to defend and promote plantation slavery. The Bible clearly teaches that all human beings are made in God's image and possess an inherent dignity that can never be taken away, and God condemns such a system that reduces human beings to property and chattel. See Mark Twain, *The Adventures of Huckleberry Finn* (New York: Dover Thrift, 1994), 161–62.
14. See Luke 11:34–35, "Your eye is the lamp of your body. When your eye is healthy, your whole body is full of light, but when it is bad, your body is full of darkness" (parallel passage in Matt. 6:22–23).

CHAPTER VIII

1. "Remember the Sabbath day, to keep it holy. Six days you shall labor, and do all your work, but the seventh day is a Sabbath to the Lord your God. On it you shall not do any work, you, or your son, or your daughter, your male servant, or your female servant, or your livestock, or the sojourner who is within your gates. For in six days the Lord made heaven and earth, the sea, and all that is in them, and rested on the seventh day. Therefore the Lord blessed the Sabbath day and made it holy" (Exod. 20:8–11).
2. The words of Hebrews 4:6–11 are worth quoting in full: "Since therefore it remains for some to enter it, and those who formerly received the good news failed to enter because of disobedience, again he appoints a certain day, 'Today,' saying through David so long afterward, in the words already quoted, 'Today, if you hear his voice, do not harden your hearts.' For if Joshua had given them rest, God would not have spoken of another day later on. So then, there remains a Sabbath rest for the people of God, for whoever has entered God's rest has also

rested from his works as God did from his. Let us therefore strive to enter that rest, so that no one may fall by the same sort of disobedience."

3. This tenet of the Mosaic law is found in Deuteronomy 21:18–21; Paul lists being "disobedient to parents" as one of the many sins the Gentiles commit, along with being "insolent, haughty, boastful, inventors of evil" (Rom. 1:30); and in 1 Timothy 1:9, where the law is given to restrain the actions of evil people, including those who would "strike their fathers and mothers."

CHAPTER IX

1. Apollyon is a demon referenced in Revelation 9:11 as the "king over them the angel of the bottomless pit." These monsters and demons are referenced in this canto because of their obligation to inflict senseless torment upon the earth.
2. The thought had not occurred to me up until now; I was convinced now that God exists, that Heaven and Hell exist, but as to the existence of particular demons whose names and attributes I knew about, I did not realize that they must exist—until now.
3. Hem is referring to one of his own short stories, "Hills like White Elephants," where the main characters are contemplating an abortion. In the story, the man describes an abortion as "letting in a little air."

CHAPTER X

1. The shade is most likely Edmund Ruffin (1794–1865), a Virginia planter, soil scientist, slaveholder, and a firebrand who argued violently for secession. He committed suicide at the conclusion of the Civil War.
2. Evan's thoughts echo that of Ecclesiastes 7:7, "Surely oppression drives the wise into madness."
3. Evan's experience seems to echo that of Paul's sentiment in Romans 6:12–13, worth citing here in full: "Let not sin therefore reign in your mortal body, to make you obey its passions. Do not present your members to sin as instruments for unrighteousness, but presents to God as those who have been brought from death to life, and your members to God as instruments for righteousness."
4. The description of these demons seems to resemble that of the monsters described in Revelation 9:7–10: "In appearance the locusts were like horses prepared for battle: on their heads were what looked like crowns of gold; their faces were like human faces, their hair like women's hair, and their teeth like lions' teeth; they

had breastplates like breastplates of iron, and the noise of their wings was like the noise of many chariots with horses rushing into battle. They have tails and stings like scorpions, and their power to hurt people for five months is in their tails."

5. From John Bunyan, *The Pilgrim's Progress* (New York: Barnes & Noble Classics, 2005), 68: "Now the Monster was hideous to behold: He was clothed with scales like a fish (and they are his Pride) he had wings like a dragon, feet like a bear and out of his belly came fire and smoke, and his mouth as the mouth of a lion. When he was come up to Christian, he beheld with a disdainful countenance, and thus began to question him."

CHAPTER XI

1. The "beast" Evan regularly cites is a motif for man's sinful and rebellious nature. Here, Apollyon urges Evan to *embrace* the beast and reject God's overtures of regeneration and faith.
2. Apollyon's argument is, "Animals live to satisfy base desires; humans are animals; therefore, humans live to satisfy base desires." One should note Apollyon's argument contradicts itself since, if humans were animals, and animals do not go to Hell because they are not made in God's image and are not capable of real, moral choices, then humans do not deserve to suffer in Hell, either. Yet, they are here, worthy of judgment because human beings are not animals. In that way, humans are not merely animals but, being made in God's image, exercise the profound ability to make moral choices and reflect the image of their creator.
3. One can think of the words of Job's wife, "Do you still hold fast your integrity? Curse God and die," in Job 2:9. Apollyon's words mirror those of Jesus in Matthew 11:30: "For my yoke is easy, and my burden is light."
4. See John 8:44, "You are of your father the devil, and your will is to do your father's desires. He was a murderer from the beginning, and has nothing to do with the truth, because there is no truth in him. When he lies, he speaks out of his own character, for he is a liar and the father of lies."
5. "Mortal epithets" would be slurs directed against humanity as a species distinct from the fallen angels in Hell.

CHAPTER XII

1. The "Forest of the Suicides" is found in Dante's *Inferno*, Canto XIII. The souls of the suicides are bound up in the very trees and monsters in Greek mythology called harpies torment them.

2. Kurt Cobain (1967–1994) was the lead guitarist and songwriter for Nirvana, the most popular of the 90s-era grunge bands based in Seattle, Washington. Nirvana's *Nevermind* sold millions of copies, and its well-known single, "Smells Like Teen Spirit" defined what has been termed "Generation X," kids born in the 1960s and 70s, and was an anthem for depressed, apathetic, and disaffected teenagers across the United States who had rejected the traditional lifestyles of their parents. Kurt died on April 5, 1994, from a self-inflicted shotgun at home in his mansion in Seattle, Washington.
3. This has often been noted of Kurt Cobain. Andy Rooney wrote, "When the spokesman for his generation blows his head off, what is the generation supposed to think?" while Bernard Levin observed in the *Times*, "We all need idols and some of us find them in the most extraordinary situations. Why should not ten million youths find theirs in a foul-mouthed, brutish, violent singer-guitarist, drugged to the eyebrows and hating himself and his way of life?" in Christopher Sandford's *Kurt Cobain* (1995; repr. New York: Carroll & Graf, 2004), 337; 338; 365.
4. Kurt Cobain could be rude to fans and is recorded complaining about the rich, suburban kids who started attending his concerts after he became a worldwide sensation, in Sandford, *Kurt Cobain*, 250; Sandford also writes, "'Yuppies in their BMWs' crooning along to 'Teen Spirit' was a scene that haunted Cobain until his death," in *Kurt Cobain*, 372.
5. The song was "I hate myself and want to die," and the author did write these words on a pair of sneakers. His parents were rightfully very concerned.
6. Christopher Sandford writes in his biography of Kurt Cobain, "By 1992 he struck [others] as 'morbidly scared of his losing his money and restarting a 'slow and ugly life' in Aberdeen . . . 'I'd literally rather kill myself than go back there' . . . 'I'd blow my brains out, living like that,'" in *Cobain*, 232.
7. Cobain gave regular interviews where he detailed the sad events of his childhood, but Sandford's biography says that many of these stories were fabrications, in *Kurt Cobain*, 256. But his parents did divorce when Cobain was nine years old.
8. Sandford's biography of *Kurt Cobain* regularly notes such contradictions in Kurt's personality and music, as he was a punk rocker who wanted to make it big; a grunge icon who quibbled over money and royalties, and eventually bought a mansion in a nice neighborhood in Seattle; and his ability to mix punk music with pop melodies.
9. In Buddhist beliefs, *Nirvana* reliefs to the release of the soul from an endless cycle of suffering caused by *samsara*.

10. Cobain and his wife Courtney Love's references to their own drug use alerted social services as to the safety of their newborn daughter and Cobain spent nearly $300,000 in legal fees (see Sandford, *Kurt Cobain*, 240). Francis Bean Cobain was born on August 18, 1992, and was the only child of Kurt and his wife, Courtney Love, who was another popular 90s-era singer.
11. Kurt wrote in his suicide note, "I haven't felt the excitement of listening to as well as creating music along with reading and writing for too many years now. I feel guilty beyond words about these things."
12. While recording a follow-up to *Nevermind*, Cobain became so disaffected and angry that "the words wouldn't come," he went off to the side of the recording studio and cried, "*sobbing* with anger" (emphasis his), in Sandford, *Kurt Cobain*, 267.
13. Cobain's mother offers this explanation of Cobain's suicide: "What happened was that shortly before he died, I begged him not to let the drugs kill him like it had all the rest of them [Hendrix, Joplin et al.]. So, Kurt being Kurt, I guess he decided he didn't want to follow them. He wanted to do it his own way, and he shot himself to be *different* . . . if I hadn't told him not to join that club, he might have overdosed, as he had before, and we might have found him and saved him. A gun was so final," (Sandford, *Kurt Cobain*, 346–47).
14. Kurt wrote this in his suicide note: "I have a goddess of a wife who sweats ambition and empathy and a daughter who reminds me too much of what I used to be, full of love and joy, kissing every person she meets because everyone is good and will do her no harm. And that terrifies me to the point to where I can barely function. I can't stand the thought of Frances becoming the miserable, self-destructive, death rocker that I've become"; his mother said of Kurt's suicide, "We all prayed Frances would save him . . . but in the end I think she was part of the reason he did what he did. Watching someone die slowly of heroin addiction is a sickening experience. He didn't want to put her through that . . . Because of his own upbringing, Kurt was also frightened of being a father. He was actually very good at it—though I'd describe him as more of a mother to Frances, the way he always cuddled her and showed her affection—but he never felt he could give her enough." Cobain himself touched on those fears in the private part of his suicide note, saying his baby's life would be "so much happier' without him," in Sandford, *Kurt Cobain*, 358.
15. Some teenage fans tragically committed suicide after Cobain's death, as noted in Sandford, *Kurt Cobain*, 336.

CHAPTER XIII

1. See Romans 7:24, "Wretched man that I am! Who will deliver me from this body of death?" and Ephesians 2:1–2, "And you were dead in the trespasses and sins in which you once walked, following the course of this world."
2. See 1 Timothy 2:3–4, "It is pleasing in the sight of God our Savior, who desires all people to be saved and to come to the knowledge of the truth."
3. A reference to the most famous line in Dante's *Inferno*: "Abandon all hope, ye enter here."
4. Jimi Hendrix was a brilliant musician of the 1960s who grew up in an unstable and heart-breaking childhood in Seattle, Washington. The biography *Room Full of Mirrors* by Charles R. Cross notes Hendrix's out-of-control drug abuse and sexual promiscuity on 132, 144, 214, 223, 229, 236–37, 243–47 et al. (New York: Hyperion, 2005).
5. Jimi Hendrix (1942–1970), Janis Joplin (1943–1970), and Jim Morrison (1943–1971) were all rock icons of the 1960s famous for their drug abuse and musical genius. They all died at the age of twenty-seven, and are grouped together as part of the "27 Club" for rock stars who died at such an early age. The 27 Club also includes Kurt Cobain, who committed suicide at the age of twenty-seven.
6. Jim Morrison's nickname was "the lizard king."
7. The "purple" is LSD, manufactured by a chemist named Augustus Owsley Stanley III who freely distributed the drug to musicians, as noted in Cross, *Room Full of Mirrors*, 191.
8. See Philippians 2:5–7, "Have this mind among yourselves, which is yours in Christ Jesus, who, though he was in the form of God, did not count equality with God a thing to be grasped, but made himself nothing, taking the form of a servant, being born in the likeness of men."
9. In the Forest of the Suicides, Dante and Virgil meet with a shade who utters a similar prophecy about the future of Florence, in Canto XIII.

CHAPTER XIV

1. Ernest Hemingway makes a similar vow to take care of F. Scott Fitzgerald: "When I had finished the book I knew that no matter what Scott did, nor how preposterously he behaved, I must know it was like a sickness and be of any help to him and try to be a good friend. He had many good, good friends. . . . But I

enlisted as one more, whether I could be of any use to him or not," in *A Moveable Feast*, 151.

2. See Romans 6:12, "Let not sin therefore reign in your mortal body, to make you obey its passions" and Romans 7:13–25.
3. These are Ernest's words to describe his own mother, whom he may have resented because she dressed him up like a girl when he was little.
4. In *A Moveable Feast*, Ernest Hemingway writes, "I would stand and look out over the roofs of Paris and think, 'Do not worry. You have always written before and you will write now. All you have to do is write one true sentence. Write the truest sentence that you know.'"
5. Hemingway's last two wives, Martha Gellhorn and Mary Walsh Hemingway, both had blonde hair.
6. Hemingway refers to the two plane crashes he survived while on safari in Africa in 1954.
7. Hemingway's own father also committed suicide by means of a self-inflicted gunshot wound.
8. Paul Hendrickson writes of Hemingway's suicide: "He was nineteen days shy of his sixty-second birthday: prematurely old, multidiseased, mentally bewildered, delusional. . . . [He] moved past the master bedroom where his wife was sleeping, padded down the red-carpeted stairs . . . retrieved the key to the lock storeroom where the weapons were . . . took sheets from an ammo box . . . came back upstairs . . . walked ten steps to the front-entry foyer . . . opened the foyer door, stepped inside, placed the butt of the gun on the linoleum tile, tore open the breech, slammed in the cartridges, snapped it shut, bent over, as you might bend over a water fountain, rested his forehead against the blue steel, and blew away his entire cranial vault with the double-barreled, 12-gauge shotgun," in *Hemingway's Boat* (New York: Vintage, 2011), 14–15.
9. In Hemingway's short story, "Hills like White Elephants," the unnamed boyfriend urges his girlfriend to get an abortion by describing it as a simple operation where "they just let the air in," in *The Complete Short Stories of Ernest Hemingway* (New York: Scribner, 1987), 211–14. The allusion herein emphasizes the shallow irreverence with which Hemingway held the sanctity of life evinced in his fiction and ultimately in the taking of his own life at Ketchum.
10. See Ecclesiastes 8:8, "No man has power to retain the spirit, or power over the day of death."

11. See Romans 7:24, "Wretched man that I am! Who will deliver me from this body of death?"
12. See Acts 16:30–31, "Then he [the Philippian jailer] brought them out and said, 'Sirs, what must I do to be saved?' And they said, 'Believe in the Lord Jesus, and you will be saved, you and your household.'"
13. See Hebrews 4:8–10: "For if Joshua had given them rest, God would not have spoken of another day later on. So then, there remains a Sabbath rest for the people of God, for whoever has entered God's rest has also rested from his works as God did from his."
14. See Colossians 2:13–14 and Ephesians 2:1–11.
15. See Romans 8:32, "He who did not spare his own Son but gave him up for us all, how will he not also with him graciously give us all things?"
16. See Romans 3:23–26; 6:4; 8:32.
17. A "rood" is an Old German word for "cross," and the adjective "dreamy" is an allusion to the Anglo-Saxon poem "The Dream of the Rood."

CHAPTER XV

1. This chapter corresponds to the fate given to the heretics in Dante's *Inferno*, Canto X-XI, wherein the heretics are immured in iron sepulchers that are heated over flames. Heretics, and in particular Epicureans, denied the existence of an afterlife, so their punishment is meant to remind them of the existence of the very afterlife which they denied.
2. See 2 Timothy 4:3–4, "For the time will come when they will not endure sound doctrine; but after their own lusts shall they heap to themselves teachers, having itching ears; And they shall turn away their ears from the truth, and shall be turned unto fables" (KJV).
3. See Galatians 1:8, "But though we, or an angel from heaven, preach any other gospel unto you than that which we have preached unto you, let him be accursed" (KJV).
4. Hemingway grew up in Chicago's affluent Oak Park neighborhood. His parents were members of a Congregationalist church and held orthodox Christian beliefs that they tried to instill in their young son, Ernest.
5. See Romans 3:20, "For by works of the law no human being will be justified in his sight, since through the law comes knowledge of sin."
6. See Isaiah 64:6, "But we are all as an unclean thing, and all our righteousness are as filthy rags; and we all do fade as a leaf; and our iniquities, like the wind, have taken us away" (KJV).

7. See Colossians 2:20–23, "If with Christ you died to the elemental spirits of the world, why, as if you were still alive in the world, do you submit to regulations—"Do not handle, Do not taste, Do not touch" (referring to things that all perish as they are used)—according to human precepts and teachings? These have indeed an appearance of wisdom in promoting self-made religion and asceticism and severity to the body, but they are of no value in stopping the indulgence of the flesh."
8. See James 2:19, "You believe that God is one; you do well. Even the demons believe—and shudder!"
9. Benjamin Franklin is perhaps the most beloved and accomplished of the Founding Fathers. He was Philadelphia's most famous resident, a world-renowned scientist for his experiments in electricity, an inventor of numerous household goods like bifocals, the Franklin stove, and the lightning rod, and an intellectual who contributed to the writing of almost all of America's founding documents, most notably the Declaration of Independence. But tragically, Benjamin Franklin was a Deist and fairly clear about why he did not believe in Jesus Christ. Franklin said as much in a letter written to Ezra Stiles, president of Yale, one month before his death: "As to Jesus of Nazareth, my Opinion of whom you particularly desire, I think the System of Morals and his Religion, as he left them to us, the best the world ever saw or is likely to see; but I apprehend it has received various corrupt changes, and I have, with most of the present Dissenters in England, some Doubts as to his divinity; tho' it is a question I do not dogmatize upon, having never studied it, and I think it needless to busy myself with it now, when I expect soon an Opportunity of knowing the Truth with less Trouble. I see no harm, however, in its being believed, if that belief has the good consequence, as it probably has, of making his doctrines more respected and better observed; especially as I do not perceive that the Supreme takes it amiss, by distinguishing the unbelievers in his government of the world with any particular marks of his displeasure," in Franklin B. Dexter, ed., *The Literary Diary of Ezra Stiles*, 3 vols. (New York: C. Scribner's Sons, 1901), 3:387; and Walter Isaacson, *Benjamin Franklin: An American Life* (New York: Simon & Schuster, 2003), 468–69.
10. In a note explaining his personal religious beliefs, Franklin stated he believed in God, but that the proper way to worship him was through "virtue," as if he were trying to save himself through the very works his Protestant upbringing warned him about; see John 6:28–29, "Then they said to him, 'What must we do, to be doing the works of God?' Jesus answered them, 'This is the work of God, that you believe in him whom he has sent.'"

11. In his own autobiography, Benjamin Franklin speaks at length of his quest for "moral perfection," whereby he aims to perfectly live out a new virtue each day and records his progress. In his autobiography he writes, "It was about this time I conceived the bold and arduous projects of arriving at moral perfection. I wish'd to live without committing any fault at any time . . ." (*The Autobiography of Benjamin Franklin* [1793; repr. Mineola, NY: Dover Publications, 1996], 63). He practiced one virtue a week and charted his progress each day on tablets he designed himself for the endeavor.
12. As a Founding Father, Benjamin Franklin was an open Deist, writing in his autobiography: "It happened that [the arguments of the Deists] wrought an effect on me quite contrary to what was intended by them; for the arguments of the Deists, which were quoted to be refuted, appeared to me much stronger than the refutations; in short, I soon became a thorough Deist," (p. 43); Franklin "had become a convinced Deist" by age fifteen, in David Holmes, *Faiths of the Founding Fathers* (New York: Oxford University Press, 2006), 54.
13. George Whitefield (1714–1770) was an Anglican preacher and a major figure in the First Great Awakening in America. He preached throughout the American colonies, and Franklin published his sermons at no small profit for himself.
14. Franklin observed that George Whitefield's hearers loved and respected him, "notwithstanding his common abuse to them, by assuring them that they were naturally half beasts and half devils," in *The Autobiography of Benjamin Franklin*, 97.
15. Under the virtue of humility, Franklin notes only, "Imitate Jesus and Socrates," in *The Autobiography of Benjamin Franklin*, 65.
16. See James 2:19, "You believe that God is one; you do well. Even the demons believe—and shudder!"
17. This seems to have been John Adams's opinion of Benjamin Franklin: "Franklin acknowledged that frugality was a virtue he never acquired. As a wealthy man, he had no personal worries about money, and for all his supposed simplicity, he loved his pleasures and ease, as Adams noted. [Franklin] rode in an elegant carriage, entertained handsomely. . . . Franklin, always at ease, never gave the appearance of trying at all [in social gatherings held in Parisian salons]," in David McCullough, *John Adams* (New York: Simon & Schuster, 2001), 198–99.
18. Mr. Worldly-Wiseman is one of the most recognizable characters from Bunyan's *The Pilgrim's Progress*, who famously deceived Christian and led him into legalism. Mr. Worldly-Wise Man lives in the "town of Carnal Policy," and symbolizes moral complacency and the worldly pleasures Bunyan associates with legalism (pp. 22, 345).

19. Franklin's words seem to echo those of Jesus in Luke 9:58, "Foxes have holes, and birds of the air have nests, but the Son of Man has nowhere to lay his head."
20. See Romans 3:21–25.

CHAPTER XVI

1. The Ring of Fire is a series of volcanoes all around the coastlines of the Pacific Ocean, from the islands of Polynesia to East Asia and the coastline of North America.
2. Ernest paraphrases Ephesians 5:31, "For this cause shall a man leave his father and mother, and shall be joined unto his wife, and they two shall be one flesh" (KJV).
3. See Luke 16:27–28 from the Parable of the Rich Man and Lazarus, "And he said, 'Then I beg you, father, to send him to my father's house—for I have five brothers—so that he may warn them, lest they also come to this place of torment.'"
4. The reference to a *house* is meant to echo the Parable of the Rich Fool in Luke 12:13–21, especially vv. 20–21: "But God said to him, 'Fool! This night your soul is required of you, and the things you have prepared, whose will they be?' So is the one who lays up treasure for himself and is not rich toward God."
5. As recounted in Dante's *Inferno*, Canto XXVII, Guido da Montefeltro was an Italian *condottiere* who gave the plan to overtake the city of Palestrina by fraud to Pope Boniface VIII (the plan was to offer a pardon to the family in control of the city, then kill that family once they yielded the city to Pope Boniface's army). Boniface had given Guido a pardon for the obvious act of treachery both men were about to commit, and Guido went to his death thinking he had been forgiven of this sin. But, at death, the demons snatched him right out from under the gaze of St. Francis of Assisi, the founder of the monastic order Guido had joined. The story is told to illustrate the dangers of false repentance.

CHAPTER XVII

1. Isaiah describes this manner of drinking as a grievous sin: "Woe to those who are heroes at drinking wine, and valiant men in mixing strong drink" (5:22).
2. Samson posed this riddle to a party of Philistines at his wedding feast in Judges 14:14–18.
3. In a riddle contest, like that found in *Oedipus Rex* or *The Hobbit*, the protagonist is saved by his quick wits. Here, Evan is saved by an act of faith.
4. The riddle is from Sophocles's tragic play *Oedipus Rex.*

5. "Idle loathing" in the sense that it seems to be man's natural condition, like an engine at idle, to have disregard for his Creator.
6. See Matthew 4:1–6, "Then Jesus was led up by the Spirit into the wilderness to be tempted by the devil. And after fasting forty days and forty nights, he was hungry. And the tempter came and said to him, 'If you are the Son of God, command these stones to become loaves of bread.' But he answered, 'It is written, "Man shall not live by bread alone, but by every word that comes from the mouth of God."' Then the devil took him to the holy city and set him on the pinnacle of the temple and said to him, 'If you are the Son of God, throw yourself down, for it is written, "He will command his angels concerning you," and "On their hands they will bear you up, lest you strike your foot against a stone."'
7. In Matthew 4, Satan tempts Jesus with power over the kingdoms of the world. The temptation speaks to the dangerous lure of power and the evils that arise when men seek to wield power over others, as men grow horribly wicked if they see something or some position that they wanted. See verses 8–9, "Again, the devil took him to a very high mountain and showed him all the kingdoms of the world and their glory. And he said to him, 'All these I will give you, if you will fall down and worship me.'"
8. See Mark 8:36, "For what does it profit a man to gain the whole world and forfeit his soul?"
9. If attacked by a shark (in Spanish, *galano*), always punch them in the nose.

CHAPTER XVIII

1. Dante groups the thieves with the fraudulent in the Seventh Bolgia, wherein the thieves are attacked by and transformed into the animals whose behavior they most closely symbolized in life.
2. Dante assigns the same punishment to thieves in the eighth of the "evil pockets" of the Malebolge in Canto XXIV–XXV.
3. George M. Troup (1780–1856) was the governor of Georgia who initiated the Trail of Tears. When gold was discovered on Cherokee land, Troup pushed to seize it on behalf of Georgia farmers and miners, actions that ultimately resulted in the infamous Indian Removal Act of 1830 and the Trail of Tears; his Indian "removal policy" many Americans considered "a smokescreen for downright theft," in Harry L. Watson, *Liberty and Power: The Politics of Jacksonian America* (New York: Hill and Wang, 2006), 109.

4. See the refrain of Judges, "In those days there was no king in Israel. Everyone did what was right in his own eyes" (21:25).
5. See the Parable of the Good Samaritan in Luke 10:25–37.
6. See Satan's reply to Beelzebub in John Milton, *Paradise Lost*, "Fallen Cherub, to be weak is miserable" (Book 1.157).

CHAPTER XIX

1. Hemingway combines two Bible verses: "For I know this, that after my departing shall grievous wolves enter in among you, not sparing the flock" (Acts 20:29 KJV); and "Be sober, be vigilant; because your adversary the devil, as a roaring lion, walketh about, seeking whom he may devour" (1 Pet. 5:8 KJV). See Matthew 7:15, "Beware of false prophets, who come to you in sheep's clothing but inwardly are ravenous wolves" (ESV). Hemingway quotes from the King James Version of the Bible since this is the translation he would have been most familiar with.
2. See 1 Timothy 6:5–7, "[There is] constant friction among people who are depraved in mind and deprived of the truth, imagining that godliness is a means of gain. But godliness with contentment is great gain, for we brought nothing into the world, and we cannot take anything out of the world."
3. See 2 Timothy 4:3, "For the time is coming when people will not endure sound teaching, but having itching ears they will accumulate for themselves teachers to suit their own passions."
4. See Acts 20:28, "Pay careful attention to yourselves and to all the flock, in which the Holy Spirit has made you overseers, to care for the church of God, which he obtained with his own blood."
5. See 1 Corinthians 15:16–19, "For if the dead are not raised, not even Christ has been raised. And if Christ has not been raised, your faith is futile and you are still in your sins. Then those also who have fallen asleep in Christ have perished. If in Christ we have hope in this life only, we are of all people most to be pitied."

CHAPTER XX

1. Crédit Mobilier and Teapot Dome were two of the most infamous corruption scandals in the United States. In 1872–73, stockholders in the Union Pacific railroad formed a new company, Crédit Mobilier, to handle railway contracts and then give stock to influential politicians in return. In 1921–22, Albert Fall, Warren Harding's secretary of the interior, "granted favorable leases for

government oil fields in Elk Hills, California, and Teapot Dome, Wyoming, in return for kickbacks totaling $400,000" (Larry Schweikart and Michael Allen, *A Patriot's History of the United States: From Columbus's Great Discovery to America's Age of Entitlement* [New York: Penguin, 2004], 382, 83; 536).

2. The description is modeled after a passage found in Donald B. Cole, *Martin Van Buren and the American Political System* (Princeton, NJ: Princeton University Press, 1984), 172–73.
3. The shade is Martin Van Buren, who was nicknamed the "The Red Fox of Kinderhook."
4. *Plain republican* refers to the Jeffersonian-Republican Party, which adhered to a strict construction of the Constitution, states' rights, and limited government. This is different from the modern Republican Party, which was not founded until 1854.
5. An allusion to George Orwell's *Animal Farm*, as are the occasional references to pigs looking like corrupt bureaucrats.
6. The Albany Regency was a "prototype of political machines for the next century," wherein party policy was decided amongst the Regency's highest-ranking office members in Cole, *Martin Van Buren*, 86–87.
7. George Washington warned against the formation of political parties in his "Farewell Address," and James Madison warns against the damage that factions can do to a state in "Federalist #10."
8. It is always a sin to be like God; see Genesis 3:4–5.
9. See Matthew 6:11; 25:40.
10. From Bunyan's *The Pilgrim's Progress*, "Then it came burning hot into my mind, whatever he said, and however he flattered, when he got me home to his house, he would sell me for a Slave," 83.
11. On January 13, 1827, Martin Van Buren wrote Thomas Ritchie, the editor of the *Richmond Enquirer* and the leader of the Richmond Junto, a political machine like the Albany Regency, and suggested an alliance between "the planters of the South and the plain Republicans of the North." Howe argues that Van Buren proposed this alliance because "Old Republicanism . . . appealed both to common folk suspicious that government economic intervention advantaged special interests and to slaveowners fearing an activist government might someday move against the South's peculiar institution," in Daniel Walker Howe, *What Hath God Wrought: The Transformation of America, 1815–1848* (New York: Oxford University Press, 2007), 489; Cole, *Martin Van Buren,* 151; Martin Van Buren to Thomas Ritchie, January 13, 1827. Van Buren Papers, microfilm ed., ser. 2, reel 7.

12. See Isaiah 22:13, "Behold, joy and gladness, killing oxen and slaughtering sheep, eating flesh and drinking wine. 'Let us eat and drink, for tomorrow we die.'"
13. From Exodus 20:16–17, "You shall not bear false witness against your neighbor. You shall not covet your neighbor's house; you shall not covet your neighbor's wife, or his male servant, or his female servant, or his ox, or his donkey, or anything that is your neighbor's."

CHAPTER XXI

1. The layout of this chapter mirrors that of the Malebolge, the eighth circle of Hell in Dante's *Inferno*.
2. See Romans 3:13–18, "Their throat is an open grave; they use their tongues to deceive. The venom of asps is under their lips. Their mouth is full of curses and bitterness. . . . There is no fear of God before their eyes." See also Psalms 5:6; 10:7; 36:1).
3. See Revelation 14:11, "And the smoke of their torment goes up forever and ever, and they have no rest, day or night, these worshipers of the beast and its image, and whoever receives the mark of its name."
4. Solomon answers this question in Proverbs 29:5, "A man who flatters his neighbor spreads a net for his feet."
5. See Romans 16:18 and Psalm 36:2.
6. James Buchanan of Pennsylvania was President of the United States from 1857–1861. He is ranked as one of the worst presidents in U.S. history, and in addition to his unequivocal support of slavery, Buchanan was noted for the flattery and double-speak he used to advance his political career.
7. The *Faust* legend centers on a German scholar and academic who, growing bored by his studies in philosophy, theology, and other subjects, sells his soul to Satan for twenty-four years of service from Mephistopheles.
8. Dante also puts himself at the mercy of demons to conduct him across the Malebolge.

CHAPTER XXII

1. See Leviticus 19:16, "You shall not go around as a slanderer among your people, and you shall not stand up against the life of your neighbor: I am the Lord."
2. The apostle Paul warns against gossip in his letters, in Romans 3:29; 1 Timothy 5:13; and 2 Corinthians 12:20.

3. See Psalm 101:5, "Whoever slanders his neighbor secretly I will destroy. Whoever has a haughty look and an arrogant heart I will not endure."
4. See Ephesians 2:1–2, "And you were dead in the trespasses and sins in which you once walked, following the course of this world, following the prince of the power of the air, the spirit that is now at work in the sons of disobedience."
5. "Human face divine" is from John Milton's *Paradise Lost*, Book III, Line 44.
6. See James 3:10–11, "From the same mouth come blessing and cursing. My brothers, these things ought not to be so. Does a spring pour forth from the same opening both fresh and salt water?"
7. See Romans 2:29, "But a Jew is one inwardly, and circumcision is a matter of the heart, by the Spirit, not by the letter. His praise is not from man but from God."
8. From Romans 1:30, "slanderers, haters of God, insolent, haughty, boastful, inventors of evil, disobedient to parents . . ."
9. The term "angel of light" comes from 2 Corinthians 11:13-14, "For such men are false apostles, deceitful workmen, disguising themselves as apostles of Christ. And no wonder, for even Satan disguises himself as an angel of light."

CHAPTER XXIII

1. This section in the evil ditch of false counselors is meant to parallel Ulysses and Diomedes in the equivalent realm in Dante's *Inferno*, Canto XXVII. Ulysses and his close companion Diomedes are held in a single flame as punishment for crimes like stealing the Palladium and devising the Trojan Horse. Note that Dante uses the Latin name "Ulysses" in the *Inferno*, whereas Jefferson uses the Greek name "Odysseus."
2. Thomas Jefferson and John Adams both enjoyed a long, distinguished career of service to the United States that included serving on the committee that drafted the Declaration of Independence and serving as ministers to France. Jefferson served as Adams's Vice President from 1797–1801, and while the bitterness of the election of 1800 nearly drove the two statesmen apart, they were eventually reconciled by their mutual friend Dr. Benjamin Rush of Pennsylvania. They died on the same day on July 4, 1826. Diomedes and Ulysses (in Greek, Odysseus) were close friends during the Trojan War, and Dante places them in Bolge of False Counsellors in the *Inferno*, Canto XXVI.
3. This image comes from Ronald Reagan's speech, "Remarks at a Ceremony Commemorating the 40th Anniversary of the Normandy Invasion, D-Day," on June 6, 1984.

4. See the words inscribed on the Jefferson Memorial in Washington, DC, "For I have sworn upon the altar of God eternal hostility against every form of tyranny over the mind of man."
5. As recorded in Jon Meacham, *Thomas Jefferson: The Art of Power* (New York: Random House, 2012), 94, one daughter died during the American Revolution, shortly before the British tried to seize Hampton, Virginia, in October 1775; a son lived for only seventeen days and died in 1777 (p. 125); and the six-month old Lucy Elizabeth died in April 1781 (p. 137). Patty also suffered a "disastrous miscarriage" in 1776, with Jefferson writing in July of that year that "I wish I could be better satisfied on the point of Patty's recovery," 108. The present author cannot imagine what it would be like to lose so many precious members of his family and how horrible the grief must have been for Thomas Jefferson.
6. See Job 7:17–21, "What is man, that you make so much of him, and that you set your heart on him, visit him every morning and test him every moment? How long will you not look away from me, nor leave me alone till I swallow my spit? If I sin, what do I do to you, you watcher of mankind? Why have you made me your mark? Why have I become a burden to you? Why do you not pardon my transgression and take away my iniquity? For now I shall lie in the earth; you will seek me, but I shall not be."
7. The Rivanna is a river near Monticello.
8. In the book of Job, Satan describes his activity upon the earth in this way: 'Satan answered the Lord and said, 'From going to and fro on the earth, and walking up and down on it'" (Job 1:7).
9. See the refrain of Job's servants, "Your sons and daughters were eating and drinking wine in their oldest brother's house, and behold, a great wind came across the wilderness and struck the four corners of the house, and it fell upon the young people, and they are dead, and *I alone have escaped to tell you*" (Job 1:18–19, emphasis added).
10. Upon the death of his wife, Martha "Patty" Jefferson, on September 6, 1782, Thomas was left incredibly despondent and inconsolable, nearly to the point of suicide. He spent long hours wandering through the woods around Monticello or riding with his daughter Patsy. His wife's death, furthermore, came after the losses of several children who died in infancy, in Jon Meacham, *Thomas Jefferson: The Art of Power* (New York: Random House, 2012), 145–47; see also xxvi, 94, 98, 109, 114, 125, 137. Joseph Ellis notes that Jefferson was "inconsolable for six weeks, sobbing throughout the nights, breaking down whenever he tried to

talk," in Joseph J. Ellis, *American Sphinx: The Character of Thomas Jefferson* (New York: Random House, 1997), 78.

11. Odysseus is the Greek hero of Homer's *Iliad* and *Odyssey*. In Canto XXVI of the *Inferno*, Dante speaks with Odysseus, who tells the story of his own death: Odysseus raises a crew and sails beyond the Pillars of Heracles, approaches Mount Purgatory, and dies when a storm suddenly strikes their boat. The story is told as a warning against going beyond the boundaries God assigns to mankind and against approaching God by means of human reason or human strength, rather than in faith and humble reliance on God.
12. Joseph Ellis notes that Jefferson "agreed to accept the diplomatic post in Paris as part of the effort to move past this tragedy and to escape from his memories of [Patty] at Monticello. . . . God had seen fit to reach down into the domestic utopia that [Jefferson] had constructed so carefully and snatch away its centerpiece. . . . He would never expose his soul to such pain again; he would rather be lonely than vulnerable," in *American Sphinx*, 78–79.
13. Thomas Jefferson served as minister to France in 1784 at the court of King Louis XVI. The phrase *ancient regime* refers to the court of Versailles at which Jefferson served up until the outbreak of the French Revolution in 1789.
14. Voltaire (1694–1778) was the most prominent of the French Enlightenment thinkers whose bust Jefferson placed prominently at Monticello, in Jon Meacham, *Thomas Jefferson: The Art of Power* (New York: Random House, 2013), 447.
15. Jefferson's admiration for French society is noted in Meacham, *Thomas Jefferson*, 169, 188, 199–200, 203. Ellis notes that "French wine, French food, French architecture and the discreet charms of French society were all obvious sources of pleasure for the American minister to the court at Versailles," in Ellis, *American Sphinx*, 99.
16. Jefferson herein describes the Enlightenment religion of Deism, which argues that while God exists and made the universe, God does not actively involve himself in the affairs of men.
17. Thomas Jefferson is about to explain the origins of his own edited "Jefferson Bible." Ellis explains the background of the Jefferson Bible in *American Sphinx,* 309–10.
18. Pontius Pilate was the Roman governor of Judea, who, wishing to appease the crowds in Jerusalem before a riot broke out, scourged Jesus and "delivered him to be crucified," in Matthew 27:1–2, 24–26; Mark 15:6–15; Luke 23:18–25; and John 19:12–16.

19. In a letter to John Adams, Jefferson wrote: ". . . the day will come when the mystical generation of Jesus, by the supreme being as his father in the womb of a virgin, will be classed with the fable of the generation of Minerva in the brain of Jupiter. But we may hope that the dawn of reason and freedom of thought in these United States will do away [with] all this artificial scaffolding, and restore to us the primitive and genuine doctrines of this the most venerated reformer of human errors," in Meacham, *The Art of Power*, 472.
20. From David L. Holmes, *The Faiths of the Founding Fathers* (New York: Oxford University Press, 2006), 83: "He did not see Jesus . . . as a savior. Nor did he believe that the miracles attributed to Jesus were more than pious exaggerations. As a result, Jefferson used scissors and razor to excise from his New Testament the corruptions that he believed its writers had placed upon the original teachings of Jesus. Because Jefferson's God was a God of reason, not of irrationality, Jefferson removed from the gospels anything that appeared unreasonable. Such an approach meant, of course, that the Sage of Monticello cut out the prophecies and miracle stories and focused instead on Jesus' ethical teachings and parables. His edited version of the New Testament ends with the death of Jesus."
21. See John 18:37–38, "'Then Pilate said to him, "So you are a king?' Jesus answered, 'You say that I am a king. For this purpose I was born and for this purpose I have come into the world—to bear witness to the truth. Everyone who is of the truth listens to my voice.' Pilate said to him, 'What is truth?'"
22. Jefferson quotes from Milton's *Paradise Lost*, "A mind not to be chang'd by Place or Time/ The mind is its own place, and in it self/Can make a Heav'n of Hell, a Hell of Heav'n" (Book 1, Lines 253–255).
23. See 1 Corinthians 15:13–16, "But if there is no resurrection of the dead, then not even Christ has been raised. And if Christ has not been raised, then our preaching is in vain and your faith is in vain. . . . And if Christ has not been raised, your faith is futile and you are still in your sins."
24. Jefferson's love for fine wines, books, and architecture translated into debts of "in modern equivalents, several million dollars," and indeed was so high that Jefferson's estate and his slaves would have to be sold to help pay for them, in Ellis, *American Sphinx*, 344. Meacham notes Jefferson's considerable debts in *The Art of Power*, 436, 477–79, 485, 496.
25. Joseph Ellis dedicates much of the opening pages of *American Sphinx* to Jefferson's relationship with Sally Hemings, whom Jefferson did not free in his will, and notes the DNA evidence that "showed a match between Jefferson and Eston Hemings,

Sally's last child," 24. Jefferson alludes to his "decades-long liaison with Sally Hemings, his late wife's enslaved half sister who tended to his personal quarters at Monticello. They produced six children (four of whom lived). . . . Was it about love? Power? Both?" in Meacham, *Thomas Jefferson: The Art of Power*, xxvi, 209, 215–19, 307, 378, 454–55, 495. Sally Hemings was the daughter of Thomas Jefferson's father-in-law, John Wayles, and, being his wife's *half-sister,* she resembled his departed wife, Patty.

26. In Canto XXVI, the Greek hero Ulysses tells the story of how he sailed past the Pillars of Heracles and approached Mount Purgatory. The Pillars of Heracles are the term the ancient world gave to today's Straits of Gibraltar separating Europe from Africa.

CHAPTER XXIV

1. From Luke 22:3–4, "Then Satan entered into Judas called Iscariot, who was of the number of the twelve. He went away and conferred with the chief priests and officers how he might betray him to them," and John 13:2, "During supper, when the devil had already put it into the heart of Judas Iscariot, Simon's son, to betray [Jesus]."
2. In Dante's *Inferno*, the lowest circle is reserved for traitors who are immured in Cocytus, a lake of frozen ice.
3. The shade is the notorious traitor Benedict Arnold (1741–1801). As outlined in Nathaniel Philbrick, *Valiant Ambition: George Washington, Benedict Arnold, and the Fate of the American Revolution* (New York: Penguin, 2016), Arnold displayed singular courage scaling the cliffs near the city of Quebec in 1775 (36–37), at the Battle of Valcour Island in 1776 (47–50; 56–57), and most significantly at the two battles of Saratoga on September 19, 1777 and on October 7, 1777. At the fighting at the Battle of Bemis Heights on October 7, 1777, Benedict heroically charged a crucial position supporting the British defenses and was shot in the leg, later remarking he wished the musket ball had "passed [through] my heart," (pp. 160–67; for Arnold's wound, see pp. 171–73). Had Arnold died at Saratoga, he would most likely be remembered as an American hero.
4. Arnold led a failed expedition to capture the imposing fortress at Quebec, where Arnold bravely scaled the cliffs near the fortress hoping to surprise the enemy in a move that earned him the title of "American Hannibal," in Philbrick, *Valiant Ambition*, 37.

5. Most members of the Continental Congress looked with suspicion at an army of professional soldiers and were somewhat stingy with promotions; Benedict Arnold was denied one despite a string of impressive victories, in Philbrick, *Valiant Ambition*, 173.
6. Benedict Arnold married Peggy Shippen on April 8, 1779. Peggy Shippen was the daughter of a Loyalist-leaning merchant in Philadelphia who "regarded the Revolution as a disaster from the start . . . forc[ing] her family to flee from Philadelphia . . . [and] reduc[ing] her beloved father to a cringing parody of his former self," in Philbrick, *Valiant Ambition*, 235, 238.
7. Herein, Benedict Arnold alludes to *Paradise Lost* and Satan's "sence [*sic*] of injur'd merit" at being passed over for promotions and honors in Heaven (Book I, Line 98).
8. Philbrick, *Valiant Ambition*, 101, 234, 240–41.
9. Philadelphia, where Arnold served as a military governor from 1778–1780, was the site of intense internal struggles between Philadelphia's wealthy merchant classes and the laboring poor: "a revolution aimed at freeing a country from political and economic oppression had the potential to create a new form of tyranny . . . a purely democratic form of government, unhindered by any checks and balances, allowed the majority to run roughshod over the liberties of the minority," Philbrick, *Valiant Ambition*, 202.
10. See Psalm 51:3–4, "For I know my transgressions, and my sin is ever before me. Against you, you only have I sinned and done what is evil in your sight, so that you may be justified in your words and blameless in your judgment"; Romans 5:6–8, "For while we were still weak, at the right time Christ died for the ungodly. For one will scarcely die for a righteous person—though perhaps for a good person one would dare even to die—but God shows his love for us in that while we were still sinners, Christ died for us"; and Isaiah 53:6, "All we like sheep have gone astray; we have turned—every one—to his own way; and the Lord has laid on him the iniquity of us all."

CHAPTER XXV

1. John references the Lake of Fire in Revelation 19:20 ("the lake of fire that burns with sulfur"); 20:10 ("the devil who had deceived them was thrown into the lake of fire and sulfur where the beast and the false prophet were, and they will be tormented day and night forever and ever"); 20:14-15 ("Then Death and Hades

were thrown into the lake of fire. This is the second death, the lake of fire. And if anyone's name was not found written in the book of life, he was thrown into the lake of fire."); 21:8 ("But as for the cowardly, the faithless, the detestable, as for murderers, the sexually immoral, sorcerers, idolaters, and all liars, their portion will be in the lake that burns with fire and sulfur, which is the second death.").

2. The Lake of Fire is reserved for those who coveted the good fortune and possessions of their neighbors: "You shall not covet your neighbor's house; you shall not covet your neighbor's wife, or his male servant, or his female servant, or his ox, or his donkey, or anything that is your neighbor's," in Exodus 20:17; and Leviticus 19:17–18.
3. See Daniel 3:16–18.
4. New York has suffered two noteworthy and devastating fires, with one occurring in 1776 and the other in 1835; the Great Chicago Fire burned from October 8–10, 1871, and destroyed up to 3 square miles of the city.
5. See the words Milton gives to Satan in *Paradise Lost*, "look on me, Me who have touch'd and tasted, yet both live, / And life more perfect have attained then Fate/ Meant me, by *venturing higher then my Lot.* / Shall that be shut to Man, which to the Beast/Is open?" (Book IX.687–92, emphasis added); pride motivates people to seek advancement in the world that may cost them their soul.
6. One can think of the beasts that symbolize the godless kingdoms of the world, aligned against God, in Daniel 7:1–8, and Revelation 13 and 17.
7. In this chapter, I've divided the Lake of Fire into three "tiers," depending on *whose* good fortune the shades envied: their neighbors are at the surface; those who envied their rightful lords along the current; and those who envied God are in Hell's canyon leading down to the throne of Satan. In the end, everyone is envious of God and covets God's authority and power, and hence all of humanity is condemned to the Lake of Fire if they die apart from Jesus Christ.
8. The phrase "keeping up with the Joneses" refers to neighbors buying consumer products in an attempt to out-do each other and comes from a comic strip titled "Keeping Up with the Joneses" that ran from 1913–1938.
9. See Genesis 3:4–5, "But the serpent said to the woman, 'You will not surely die. For God knows that when you eat of it your eyes will be opened, and you will be like God, knowing good and evil.'"
10. See Philippians 2:5–6, "Have this mind among yourselves, which is yours in Christ Jesus, who, though he was in the form of God, did not count equality with God a thing to be grasped"; and Herod's death from Acts 12:20–25.

11. "And going back [to the House of Representatives] was hard because the insecurity and humiliation aggravated the already powerful inherited strain that formed the base of [Lyndon's] personality: he had to 'be somebody,' he had to be successful and appear successful; he had to win and be perceived as a winner. It was the interaction of his early humiliation with his heredity that gave his efforts their feverish, almost frantic, intensity, a quality that journalists would describe as 'energy' when it was really desperation and fear, the fear of a man fleeing something terrible," Robert Caro, *The Years of Lyndon Johnson: Means of Ascent,* Vol. II (New York: Vintage, 1990), 5.
12. Whether or not people are *inherently selfish* (the realist view), or they are only selfish because they lack education (the idealist view), is inconsequential. There is still something fundamentally wrong with human nature that makes individuals "crazy."
13. C. S. Lewis explains this process at length in *The Abolition of Man*, published in 1943.
14. "At each stage of [Johnson's] life, his remarkable gift for cultivating and manipulating older men who could help him had been focused at its greatest intensity on one man: the one who could, in each setting, help him the most. This focus, too, was deliberate; while he was still in college, Lyndon Johnson told his roommate Alfred (Boody) Johnson: "The way to get ahead is to get close to the one man at the top." This tactic was employed first on Dr. Cecil Evans, the president of the teachers' college at San Marcos, then Senator Alvin Wirtz, then Sam Rayburn, the Speaker of the House of Representatives, and lastly, Richard Russell, in Robert Caro, *Master of the Senate: The Years of Lyndon Johnson* (New York: Random House, 2002), 162; Satan's pride led him to set himself in "Glory above His peers," in *Paradise Lost* (Book I.36–40).
15. Johnson's incredible drive, work ethic, and ambition is covered in Robert A. Caro, *The Years of Lyndon Johnson: The Path to Power* (New York: Vintage, 1990), 217–39.
16. See Revelation 13:1–4.

CHAPTER XXVI

1. *Belial* is from a Hebrew adjective meaning "worthless." In 1 Samuel 2:12, the adjective is translated as "worthless men" in the ESV, but as "sons of Belial" in the KJV (see Deuteronomy 13:13 for a similar rendering in the ESV and the KJV, respectively). In *Paradise Lost*, Milton describes Belial as, "On th' other side up rose/Belial, in act more graceful and humane;/A fairer person lost not Heav'n;

he seemd/For dignity compos'd and high exploit:/But all was false and hollow; though his Tongue/Dropt Manna, and could make the worse appear/The better reason, to perplex and dash/Maturest Counsels: for his thoughts were low;/To vice industrious, but to Nobler deeds/Timorous and slothful: yet he pleas'd the ear,/And with perswasive accent thus began" (Book 2.108–18).

2. One should note that Evan's first statements against Satan are based on his feelings, and feelings cannot give certainty of God's love. Our confidence in our salvation and of God's love for us can only be based on Scripture.
3. The phrasing is an allusion to the conversion of St. Augustine who heard a similar voice urging him to "take up and read" in Augustine's *Confessions*.
4. This verse comes from John 6:37, "All that the Father gives me will come to me, and whoever comes to me I will never cast out." In *The Pilgrim's Progress*, when Christian is locked in Doubting Castle, and remembers he has "a key in [his] bosom, called *Promise*" capable of opening any lock. The "promise" is found in John 6:37, for in *The Pilgrim's Progress*, he says he was "rescued from the depths of despair by the 'promise' contained in John 6:37," 135, 354, footnote 86.
5. See Matthew 4:1–17, wherein Jesus resists the temptations of the devil by quoting Scripture.
6. See the passages in the Major and Minor Prophets concerning the Day of the Lord, when the very foundations of the earth will be shaken: "Therefore I will make the heavens tremble, and the earth will be shaken out of its place, at the wrath of the Lord of hosts in the day of his fierce anger" (Isa. 13:13); "For thus says the Lord of hosts: Yet once more, in a little while, I will shake the heavens and the earth and the sea and the dry land" (Hag. 2:6); "Who can stand before his indignation? Who can endure the heat of his anger? His wrath is poured out like fire, and the rocks are broken into pieces by him" (Nah. 1:6).
7. From Numbers 16:29–30, "If these men die as all men die, or if they are visited by the fate of all mankind, then the Lord has not sent me. But if the Lord creates something new, and the ground opens its mouth and swallows them up with all that belongs to them, and they go down alive into Sheol, then you shall know that these men have despised the Lord."
8. See Colossians 2:13–15.

CHAPTER XXVII

1. The Greek word for "gospel" is *evangelion*, so that this pastor's allegorical name represents the proclamation of the gospel of the Lord Jesus Christ.

2. See Psalm 103:8, "The Lord is merciful and gracious, slow to anger and abounding in steadfast love."
3. See 2 Corinthians 5:19, "That is, in Christ God was reconciling the world to himself, not counting their trespasses against them, and entrusting to us the message of reconciliation."
4. See Colossians 1:11, "Being strengthened with all power, according to his glorious might, for all endurance and patience with joy"; and Ephesians 2:8–10, "For by grace you have been saved through faith. And this is not your own doing; it is the gift of God, not a result of works, so that no one may boast. For we are his workmanship, created in Christ Jesus for good works, which God prepared beforehand, that we should walk in them."
5. See these lines from *The Pilgrim's Progress*, "When at the first I took my Pen in hand,/Thus for to write; I did not understand/That I at all should make a *little Book*/In such a mode: Nay, I had undertook to make another; which, when almost done,/Before I was aware, I this begun," 5 (emphasis added).
6. See Matthew 7:13, "Enter by the narrow gate. For the gate is wide and the way is easy that leads to destruction, and those who enter by it are many."
7. See Galatians 5:13–15, "For you were called to freedom, brothers. Only do not use your freedom as an opportunity for the flesh, but through love serve one another. For the whole law is fulfilled in one word: 'You shall love your neighbor as yourself.' But if you bite and devour one another, watch out that you are not consumed by one another."
8. See Psalm 103:19, "The Lord has established his throne in the heavens, and his kingdom rules over all."
9. See Genesis 3:1–5, "Now the serpent was more crafty than any other beast of the field that the Lord God had made. He said to the woman, 'Did God actually say, "You shall not eat of any tree in the garden"?' And the woman said to the serpent, 'We may eat of the fruit of the trees in the garden, but God said, "You shall not eat of the fruit of the tree that is in the midst of the garden, neither shall you touch it, lest you die."' But the serpent said to the woman, 'You will not surely die. For God knows that when you eat of it your eyes will be opened, and you will be like God, knowing good and evil.'"
10. See John 1:14, "And the Word became flesh and dwelt among us, and we have seen his glory, glory as of the only Son from the Father, full of grace and truth."
11. See John 3:16, "For God so loved the world, that he gave his only Son, that whoever believes in him should not perish but have eternal life."